MW01135639

Caine's Time
Published by William L. Bowman Jr.

ACKNOWLEDGEMENTS

First, and foremost, my harshest critic, most stalwart supporter, and the person without whom this book and essentially all of the best things in my life would not exist, my wonderful wife, Sally. Elaine Orr, a true friend, fellow writer, and mentor, and, finally, my father who taught me how to play with words.

PROLOGUE
Alisha's Journal,
April 30, 2010

He's back. I haven't seen him in months, but the Bad Man has returned. I haven't slept well for a couple of nights and last night I saw him. He was riding along in the woods on a beautiful horse, wearing a cloak the color of dried blood and a horrible helmet with horns on it. He had the battle axe from hell which glistened in the moonlight and severed heads hanging from his saddle, one of which wept tears of blood. He turned to look at me but, as usual, I couldn't see his face. Then he pointed at me and I screamed. I screamed myself awake, but I could still feel him for a few moments. In that brief time, he was real and I knew he had been here in my bedroom. I don't care what Dr. Morrissey says, I know he's real...and now he's back. What did I do to deserve this?

CHAPTER ONE

"Hiya, Al. Got a weird one for ya' this time." This was the greeting Alisha received from Sergeant Frank McDonnell. He had been on the force with her father and had more years of field experience than Lieutenant Alisha, "Al", Ferdinand had years on earth, but, like a true professional, deferred to her rank rather than bitching about her age.

"What is it, Frank?" she asked, taking in the scene outside the south side bar as she spoke to him.

"Inside, bar fight. Real gory one, too," Frank chuckled, knowing Al would no more be squeamish than he would. He liked and respected Al, apart from his long acquaintance with her father who had been his partner for seven years before moving up to a gold shield. Al had practically grown up in the fourteenth after her mother had died. All of the old guard at the precinct felt a certain paternalism toward the young detective and followed her career and rapid series of promotions with an almost fatherly pride. All of them agreed that it was too bad her dad wasn't around to see her now. He'd have been the proudest poppa in the world, without a doubt.

Noting that the perimeter was properly secured and the uniforms were doing their job of keeping it intact, Alisha moved into the bar. It was typical of the area, seedy, blue-collar, burned-out neon tubes in the windows. One window, she noticed had recently been replaced with plywood. As she entered, her sensitive nose picked up a sweet odor which seemed out of place in the seedy bar. The bartender looked like he would rather be anywhere else at the moment, though he did brighten at the approach of Detective Ferdinand. Al was not very big, five three, 130 pounds, long dark brown hair, kept up when she was on duty and large, luminous green eyes, and curves in all the right places. She was fully aware of her effect on the caveman parts of certain brains and had used it more than once to elicit information from an unwitting male, and occasional female, suspect. No, Detective Alisha Ferdinand was definitely not squeamish, it didn't pay to be squeamish working homicide in this cesspool of a city. No wonder I have nightmares, she thought, moving toward the shabby, tired looking bartender. She almost laughed at his attempts to tidy himself up at the approach of the attractive detective. He looked, to her, like the birds on the nature specials she sometimes watched late at night when the dreams woke her and wouldn't let her go back to sleep, preening in hopes of attracting a mate. Fat chance, she thought, but turned on her sultriest of smiles.

A sudden motion at the other end of the bar caught her attention and she saw the paramedics raising up their cot. On it was a figure with the left side of his face swaddled in white bandages with just the smallest trace of red soaking through the center over his eye. The image conjured up a vague memory of a dream and, though she showed nothing, Alisha shuddered inside. As the medics wheeled the man out he murmured in a morphine induced torpor, "Stole my fuckin' eye...". Al looked around the bar.

"All right, Frank," she asked turning on the burly sergeant, "where's the body?"

All innocence, Frank replied, "What body?"

Al was tired. She loved Frank like an uncle, he had been there for her more than anyone else since her father's death, but she wasn't really in the mood to play his games tonight. "C'mon, Frank, I don't have it in me. Why'd you call homicide for a bar fight. You know the rule, somebody goes to the hospital and somebody goes to jail. Unless there's a body, I'm going home."

"Oh, there's a body," Frank said. "Bunch of 'em, in fact. Just not here." He reached over and picked up an evidence bag off the bar top and held it up so that Alisha could see it in the dim light of the dive. Inside was a bill. Squinting, she could tell it was a twenty, covered in what looked like blood.

"Dead presidents don't count," she grumbled, waiting for the punch line.

"How about dead bank robbers?" Frank asked. "You recall that case over on forty-third last month?" She remembered it all right. Five punks had robbed the North Central Bank on fifth, getting away clean. The cops had no leads, no clues. None of the cash had surfaced, no ID's on the gang, but someone had found them. Al had been called to a lot of crime scenes in her time on the force, but nothing like what she saw in that little rat trap of a house.

One of the victims had his head nearly twisted off, another two looked like someone had picked one up and beaten the other to death with him. She remembered the look of surprise on the face of the one they found impaled on the handle of the plunger in the bathroom. It had taken a couple of hours to find the fifth victim. He was a big SOB, the coroner said he weighed in at 255, but the killer had broken both of his arms and stuffed him into the chest freezer in the garage. Then, for good measure, flipped the huge, heavy thing over upside down, trapping him. COD was listed as asphyxiation. He had suffocated. There had been a few bills scattered around, all of which traced back to the bank robbery, but none of the rest of the cash had turned up yet. "You ran the serial number?" she asked. Frank nodded, smiling somewhat smugly. "It came back to the bank job." This last was a statement, not a question. At least now she knew why she was here.

She turned her attention back to the barkeep. He was about six two, a flabby paunch spilling over his jeans, three days' worth of patchy beard, and smelled like he was allergic to soap and water. As she approached him, he was actually tucking in his grimy tee shirt and patting down what was left of his hair. She just shook her head in amusement and barely concealed disgust. "Okay," she said, skewering him with her gaze. "What happened?"

"Can I get ya' anything? Cup of coffee?" the simpering booze jockey asked, much more hopefully than he had any right to. Al could see it was time to get serious.

Turning the temperature of her stare down to its most frigid setting and moving her jacket aside to expose her badge and weapon, a Glock nine millimeter in brushed steel with black polycarbonate grips, she said, "What you can get me, Romeo, is the story of what happened here," she told him icily. "And if I smell anything the least bit off, this place will be closed down so tightly it will take a ton of explosives to reopen it and you will be serving something other than drinks to your cellmate in Central Holding. And I have a very sensitive nose." It was all she could do to keep from laughing as she watched the slimy creep deflate, reality finally dawning on him.

"I never saw the guy before," he started, sitting down on a stool behind the bar.

"Which guy, the victim or the perp?"

"No, I know the victim, he's one of my regulars. Or he was at least. Hey, you think he's gonna be okay? He's got a pretty good tab run up." Al sighed and stared at the witness, it was enough to get him back on track. "I never saw the other guy before, big sonofabitch, though. Come to think of it, I can't say as I saw him tonight, for that matter."

"What do you mean, you didn't see him?" she demanded, getting really fed up with the guy and just about ready to hop over the bar and slap him a few times.

"He had a long coat, the kind you see in them old westerns, with the collar turned up and a hat pulled down over his face. He just sat there, smokin' those fancy European cigarettes, the ones that smell like spices and sipping a large whiskey, neat." Clove cigarettes, that had been the unusual odor Alisha had noticed. "Jimmy comes in and orders his usual and tries to start up a conversation with the guy. Jimmy's a real friendly drunk and I could tell this wasn't his first stop of the night. Well the guy just ignores Jimmy, kinda' turns his back. Then Jimmy reaches for the bowl of nuts and accidentally brushes the big guy's arm. The freaky bastard turns toward Jimmy and mutters something like 'You lookin' at me?' Next thing I know,

Jimmy is screamin' bloody murder, and the stranger is wipin' his finger off on that twenty. I never saw a big guy move so fast in my life. Then, he just drops the bill on the bar and walks out like nothin' happened. Damnedest thing..." Frank slid something across the bar to Al. Looking down she saw that it was a highball glass, still mostly full of amber whiskey, the mouth covered in cling wrap secured with evidence tape. She could see that something was floating in the liquid. Peering more closely, she saw that it was a human eye.

"Jimmy's, I take it," she asked.

"He just dropped it in the glass like it was an ice cube," the shaken bartender murmured. Al walked around behind the bar. "Hey, whatta' you doin'?" the filthy gin-slinger protested, weakly. "This is my bar!"

"No," Al corrected him, "this is my crime scene." Then, she reached behind the counter and picked up a rusty old .45 automatic, Popping out the clip and jacking the slide, she saw that it wasn't loaded. "Permit?" she asked cocking an eyebrow at the now nervously shaking rummy. "And how about this?" she asked, extracting a baggie full of pre-rolled joints from an old cigar box. "Medical, I suppose? Glaucoma?" When the barkeep didn't answer, she looked at Frank, who could barely keep from laughing at the man's discomfiture. "Run the serial number on that .45, if it's stolen, lover-boy here gets a free trip downtown. If not, he's just closed, with the added bonus of a bench summons for the pot."

"Gun was my dad's. Brought it back from Korea," she heard the bartender, whose name she realized she didn't know and didn't care to, explaining to Frank as she walked back out into the comparatively fresh air of the parking lot. The night was damp and heavy. The storm which had passed through earlier in the evening had only served to add steam to the heat and clamp a lid on the city, keeping in the moisture and the smells. She had been telling the truth earlier, she was unnaturally sensitive to odors, so the scent of the underlying rot of the city was always in her nose. Sometimes she wondered why she stayed, but she knew. She had grown up watching her dad protect and serve the city that he loved and had inherited his desire to do the same. No matter how much it stank, it was her city now. Al hated the drunks even more than the smell of the city. Every time she had to deal with one, all she could see was her mother, wasted away to practically nothing, beckoning to her. Al had known she was dying, there was no way not to see it. She had crossed over to the bed, expecting some last words of wisdom or an expression of love or regret. Instead the emaciated lush on the bed had said, "Be a dear and get mommy a drink." These had been the last words Mary O'Connell-Ferdinand had spoken to her daughter. Al had never forgiven her.

She heard Frank's heavy footsteps coming up behind her and turned to see him shaking his head with a little smile on his face. "The piece was his dad's but he didn't have a permit," Frank said.

"One more off the street," She commented. "Not that it was doing him much good empty. He'd probably bring a knife to a gunfight. Get anything else useful?"

Frank shook his shaggy head, "No."

"Looks like we're back to The Case of the Battered Bank Robbers," She said.

"Yeah," Frank replied, "and now we have The Mystery of the One-Eyed Rummy, too."

Al shook her head, frowning. "More like The Floating Eyeball Mystery." This was a game they had played since she had been a girl, giving names to cases that sounded like the Nancy Drew books she had loved reading. She still read them, in fact, her guilty pleasure and escape. Nancy always wrapped everything up so nicely, all in under 200 pages! Of course she was surrounded by her loyal friends who did whatever she asked. But, Al did have Frank. No one had ever had a more loyal sidekick. They joked about that often, but she knew she would be lost without him.

"Uniforms are tearing the place apart," Frank told her, interrupting her reverie. "Probably won't find anything else. Lab boys are all finished processing, nothing to report there, either."

"Any other witnesses?" Al asked, knowing full well that, even if there had been anyone else in the bar this late on a Wednesday night, no one would have seen anything. Conveniently blind, her dad had called the phenomenon. Frank shook his head. "Think it's the same guy?" she asked.

"No doubt," Frank replied. "But, with all that cash, what's he doin' in this dive?"

"And why haven't more of the bills surfaced before now. Obviously, he's not smart enough to launder the money, so why isn't he spending it?" As often happened at the beginning of an investigation, there were too many questions and too few answers. Al caught herself wondering what Nancy would do? Probably send one of her chums into some ridiculously dangerous situation to find out more. As she often did, Al mentally admonished herself to find some more age-appropriate reading material. Suddenly, a thought occurred to her, "How'd he get here?" she asked.

"Already have someone running down the cab companies. No results so far," Frank responded, pleased with himself to be ahead of the diminutive detective for once. "Aren't you supposed to be off the clock?" he asked Al, consulting his watch. It was an old self-winder that had belonged to his dad and it still kept perfect time. "Go home and get some rest, I'll call you if anything turns up."

"Prints?" she asked, ignoring his advice.

"Don't know about the bill or the glass. About ten million in the bar, I'd guess," he answered. "It'll take about six months to run them all down. I'm serious, Al. Go home and get some rest. Uncle Frank's got it covered." He only used her childhood name for him when he wanted to exert his semi-paternal authority over her. Sometimes, it actually worked. This was not one of those times.

"I think I'll go downtown and see if anything has turned up. Then I'll go home, I promise," she vowed insincerely.

Frank just shook his head as she headed back to her car and waved to him as she turned around and headed toward the precinct. Looking down, he noticed the reflection of the sickly yellow streetlight in a puddle. It reminded him of the eyeball floating in the glass of whiskey. "This fucking city just gets weirder and weirder," he mumbled as he headed back into the bar to see if the uniforms had turned anything else up.

Inside the car, Al's thoughts also turned to the weirdness of the whole affair, but not as a general observation on the condition of the city. For her, the surreal quality of the evening was personal, very personal. She drove toward the precinct on autopilot, completely unaware of the traffic, the night, even herself. Over and again, she relived the dream. It had tried to come back full force when she had seen Jimmy, the drunk bandaged up, the white gauze over his left eye weeping tears and she had managed to shut it out. Now, alone in the darkness of the car, she could not keep it...him...away. It was almost as though the Bad Man was taunting her, or calling her out, or, maybe, drawing her into some sick twisted game of his own design.

This had happened before. Dr. Morrissey had told her she was imagining it. He claimed that her mind had mixed up reality and the dreams, causing her to remember details later that were not actually in the dreams when she had dreamed them. He insisted that she had not seen events before they happened, but she knew better. That was when she had started keeping the journal. But she had been afraid to show it to him, afraid he would declare her unfit for duty. So, she had agreed that he was right, that the dreams were just a result of the trauma of losing her mother.

She remembered the first one. It had actually been months before her mother's death from cirrhosis. In it, the Bad Man had been standing behind a bar in a saloon like one in a western movie. His ten gallon hat obscuring his face. There had been a woman sitting at the bar with her back to Alisha. It was obviously her mother, dressed as a saloon girl, she recognized her hair, dark and curly, with a few strands of silver.

She had called to her mother, but she didn't turn around. Instead, the Bad Man had picked up a bottle and started pouring the contents into a glass. The label on the old fashioned bottle was black with a cartoon skull and crossbones on it. He kept pouring until the liquid overfilled the glass and flowed out on the top of the bar. The fluid just kept coming and coming, and she saw that it was not the amber whiskey her mother preferred, but dark, red blood. She could smell the coppery scent as the Bad Man had continued to pour, laughing a laugh devoid of humor, or any decent human emotion. As the liquid began spilling over the edge of the bar and running across the floor toward Alisha, her mother put her head down and began lapping it up while the Bad Man laughed. She tried to back away from the river of blood, but she found herself against the wall and the red flow covered her feet and soaked the hem of her nightgown. Alisha screamed.

She had awakened terrified, still screaming, with her nightgown and sheets soaked from the blood of her first menstrual period. The doctors told her parents that nightmares often accompanied the arrival of menses and that they shouldn't worry. Four months later, her mother was dead, a trickle of blood from the internal hemorrhages running out of her mouth and Alisha knew that the Bad Man was real.

Somehow she arrived safely at the precinct, pulling into her parking spot and sitting in the car for several long minutes while she collected herself, pushing the thoughts of dreams and him out of her mind. As a child, Al had read a book set in Japan. In the book, the author explained that because Japan was so densely populated, the Japanese people had learned to compartmentalize their minds. They could shut off the distractions of the teeming populace, or shut off parts of their own minds so as not to give anything away to the thousands of people they saw daily. Since reading this, she had striven to achieve that same sense of walling of her mind. She had gotten quite good at it over the years. It even worked quite well on the very western Dr. Morrissey.

Thinking of Dr. Morrissey reminded her she needed to renew her prescription for sleeping pills. She only rarely took them, not at all as often as prescribed, but refilled the prescription as though she was taking them regularly. She had taken them at first, but not for long. Even now, when she took one, she hated the results. She slept, but it was the sleep of escape. No dreams, no memories, no sensations and, in an odd way...no rest. It was a sleep more akin to death than respite and she awoke more exhausted than when she lay down. But if she failed to refill the prescription, Dr. Morrissey knew. She hated playing the games she had to play to get around Dr. Morrissey, but after what had happened, seeing the department shrink and at least appearing to follow his plan of treatment was the only way she could keep her badge. Lieutenant Detective Alisha Ferdinand would die before surrendering her shield. In fact, that was what had nearly happened, initiating her long-term relationship with the good doctor. She had come home late to find a drugged-out punk with a Saturday night special (a single action .22 revolver with a fixed firing pin) waiting in the bushes near the parking lot of her apartment building. The wiry addict had managed to surprise her and had gotten ahold of her sidearm. Realizing he had a cop's gun, the little pervert had asked to see her badge. She pulled aside her jacket and showed him the gold shield, which he then demanded. "Come and get it, if you think you're man enough," Al had snarled at him.

"Lady," he had whined, " I got two guns and you got nothin'."

"But I have what you want," she had teased, turning on the full force of her seductive powers. The strung out freak had fallen for it, of course. Tucking her pistol in his waistband, he had approached her, his eyes fixed on her badge. Her front snap kick caught him a glancing blow on the left hip. Somehow, he had seen it coming. He fired one shot, catching Al in the muscle on the outside of her left shoulder.

When she staggered back, clutching the wound, he had advanced quickly, grabbing her shield. Al grasped his wrist with her left hand, her right being temporarily useless, and, looking right into the bloodshot eyes of the kid, said, "You'll have to kill me". Then she heard the unmistakable sound of the little pistol's hammer being cocked. Before her attacker could raise and fire the cheap piece, Alisha brought her head down hard, squarely on the bridge of his nose. As the punk staggered back, clutching the bloody fountain of his broken nose, she got ahold of her pistol, pulled it from the waist of his filthy, black jeans and fired three times into, and through, his chest.

Of course, there had been an IA investigation, as there was with all officer involved shootings and the mandatory meeting with the brand new department shrink, the one and only Doctor Kevin Morrissey. Soft-spoken, with the first tell-tale signs of middle age in his thinning hair and slight paunch, Dr. Morrissey was alarmingly easy to talk to. He, of course, knew all about Al before she ever arrived at his airless, windowless little office on the fifth floor of the downtown city office building. He had her file on his desk, open to her personal history. He knew her father had been a decorated member of the force, killed in the line of duty, that her mother had drunk herself to death when she was only twelve years old, and even that she had punched another cadet in the nose when he grabbed her ass during a party her first year at the academy. But he didn't ask about any of that the first day. Instead, he looked her right in the eyes and said, "So, Sergeant Ferdinand, tell me about your dreams".

For the first time in years, Al had been caught off guard after thoroughly preparing herself for a situation, and had told the unassuming psychiatrist about the Bad Man. Dr. Morrissey had listened quietly, making no comments or notes as she recounted the history of the evil character from her dreams, even slipping and relating the prophetic nature of some of the nightmares, beginning with the foretelling of her mother's death.

She found herself unloading to him like she had never done in her life. She had spoken to many psychologists and psychiatrists in her life and had developed a knack for telling them just what they wanted to hear. She had, as a rebellious teenager, even found that she could manipulate the psychological tests to get whatever diagnosis she wanted. That had led to a bit of trouble and seventy two hours on the city hospital psych ward. She did not care to ever repeat that experience and had reined in her manipulations of the psychological professionals from that point on. But Dr. Morrissey was different. Sure, he said many of the same things that the others had regarding the dreams, the Bad Man, and the precognitive nature of many of the nightmares, but still, he was different. Not different enough to just sign off and let her get back out on the streets, however. Al had spent the next three frustrating months flying a desk. Three times a week, she sat in that little stuffy office and talked to Dr. Morrissey. He had managed to slip past some of her defenses early on, in the first days after the shooting, and Al knew from her experiences in the past that she would have to close them back off carefully, slowly, and in such a manner that he was not aware that she was doing so. This was not as easy as it had been with the others. Now, five years, one promotion, and countless nightmares later, she was till seeing him once a month, and the Bad Man had returned. She told Dr. Morrissey about most of her dreams and nightmares, but after the first few visits had avoided recounting those starring the Bad Man. This was not as difficult a task as it might have been in the past, as he had stopped visiting her for a while. She would have to be on her guard Wednesday when she had her monthly session. He would know something was up, so she started concocting her story as she entered the building.

"Evening Lieutenant," Sergeant Porter greeted her from the desk. He was a tall, thin, wiry man with very short, thinning grey hair. In his capacity as graveyard desk sergeant, he ran the desk officiously. He never called her Al, though she had given him tacit permission to do so many times. He was "old school". The rank and file did not cozy up to the higher ups and everything was done by the book. Even his uniform was strictly up to standard. He seemed to be one of those people who could weather anything without falling into disarray. Her mother had said of people like Sergeant Porter that, "You couldn't ruffle his feathers if you hit him with a brick". Even the hot summer night four years ago when there had been a riot right outside the precinct, he had remained calm, nonplused, without a bead of sweat or a wrinkle to show for it. At the end of his shift, he had filled out the logs, made his reports, and headed to the diner down the street for breakfast as though nothing had happened. Probably the oddest thing about that morning was the fact that the all night diner was not only not at least damaged in the riot, but that it had remained open for business throughout. Sergeant Porter, apparently a devout Catholic, had given all the credit to St. Michael.

Captain McElroy gave the sergeant a great deal of freedom in handling the precinct. Al suspected it was not just because he was in charge of the night shift. Sergeant Porter was rock solid. He was definitely someone you wanted covering your back in a crisis. The only things about him which hinted that there was, or had been something which haunted him were his eyes. The were kind, but with a faraway, almost haunted look. It was the look of someone who had seen way too much and remembered it all.

Remembering all of this as she walked down the hall toward the Homicide bull pen, Al found herself unconsciously fingering the St. Michael's medal in her pocket. It had belonged to her father, a gift from his mother upon his graduation from the academy. No one in the family was Catholic, but Al's grandmother had been a theological pragmatist, always covering her bases any way she could. On her night stand, she remembered, had been statues of Jesus, Buddha, Ganesh, and a Lady of Guadeloupe candle. Grams had been an interesting character.

Her desk, as always, was covered with piles of reports, notes, crime scene photos, and various files. A quick glance told her that nothing had been added in her absence. Her colleagues marveled at the fact that she could find anything in the mountainous mess on her desk, but that she also knew where everything was and if anything had been added, subtracted, or moved. Dr. Morrissey had once told her she had a mind like a garbage can. At first she had taken offense, but then he went on to explain that he meant that every piece of information she took in stayed there, and if one had the patience to rummage through it all, each piece could be located. She had decided she liked that analogy and often used it to describe her mental processes to people.

Al shuffled a few papers, logged into her computer and checked her email, and made a vain attempt to complete some reports. She liked the relative quiet of the bull pen at this time of morning, and could usually get some work done, but tonight was an exception. She could tell she would only get frustrated with herself if she continued sitting at the desk, so she shut everything down and headed back out into the few remaining hours of night. Frank was right, she needed to get home and try to get some rest.

It had rained again while Al had been inside the station. As she passed under the tree next to her parking spot, something, a bird, squirrel, or a breeze high up in the branches, dislodged a shower of raindrops onto her. Getting into her car, she wiped the moisture from her face, pushed a few sodden strands of hair off of her forehead and lay her head back on the headrest. She took a great shuddering breath, backed her car out and negotiated the familiar maze of streets home. As her dad had taught her, she varied her route daily, never getting into a routine. Even as a child, she had various routes home from school and varied which one she took. Between her father and herself, they had put a significant number of very bad people where they belonged. Unfortunately, they didn't always stay there, and might come looking for the person who put them away. Varying routes was one way to protect herself. No one could lie in wait on your route home if they did not know what it would be.

Tonight, the streets were empty. Even along the route she was taking this time which led mainly through residential areas, this was unusual. There had been a number of changes since the last time she had come this way. She expected to see the occasional burned out husk of a building and tenements being demolished, but there was more. The most startling change was the huge church which had grown up on the corner of one of the most dilapidated neighborhoods. The sign out front identified it as the basilica of St. Jude. Alisha found this ironically appropriate in this neighborhood, the patron saint of lost causes. There was a light on inside and she was struck by the stained glass, she had never seen such a large piece with so much red. It almost looked as though the building was on fire.

She arrived at her apartment building and parked near the concrete slab which had once been the bed of bushes behind which her attacker had hidden. She was torn about the bushes. Each time she looked where they had been, she felt a surge of relief and safety, but also a sense of loss. She felt the city needed all the clean, healthy life it could have. Her dad had said life was all about trade-offs. You could be safe or have bushes, she reminded herself. "They can plant bushes on my grave," she muttered, chuckling at the gallows humor. Passing by the former flower bed, she thought she heard the sound of something moving in the bushes. She turned quickly toward them and reached for her weapon. As she spun, she caught the familiar outline of the bushes out of the corner of her eye, then...nothing. No assailant, nothing hiding or moving and, she reminded herself, no bushes.

The climb up the back stairs to her fourth floor apartment seemed much longer than usual and Alisha chided herself that Frank really was right, she must be even more exhausted than she realized. Normally, she all but sprinted up the stairs. She thought that maybe she would take a sleeping pill, it had been a while. Arriving at the door into the fourth floor hallway, she found a notice taped to it advertising a spaghetti supper and Bingo at St. Jude's. "Wow," she muttered, "they're really reaching out." Not really knowing why she did it, she took the notice down as she opened the door.

Stepping into the hallway, her sensitive nose was greeted with the scent of incense. No doubt, Mrs. Reynolds, the seventy year old pot head down the hall trying to cover up the smell of her weed. Al just shook her head and smiled as she headed toward her door. When she opened the door to her apartment, it was as if the world tilted slightly and did not quite manage to right itself.

Instead of her familiar surroundings, she found herself in a large hall. There were rows of banquet tables set out and occupied by aged, twisted, desperate looking figures, hunched over Bingo cards. Not knowing why she did so, Al walked dazedly over to the only empty chair and sat down. The elderly woman next to her had about her the slightly sweet and sickening smell of decay. Up at the front of the room, a priest in an old fashioned cassock and broad-brimmed hat was turning a wire basket full of wooden balls which rattled like dried old bones. One of the spheres fell out into a little cup and the priest stopped turning the basket. Alisha was glad for the cessation of that annoying sound. Plucking the ball from the cup, he held it up as he turned toward the rows of eager players and she saw that the priest was him, the Bad Man.

"G-forty eight. G-four eight," he announced. Alisha just sat, immobilized and stared. Then she felt a slimy loathsome touch on her right hand and the woman next to her spoke. Her breath smelled like a corpse which had been lying in a dumpster in the summer heat. Alisha recoiled from the touch.

"Mark your card," the woman rasped, fetidly. Looking down, Alisha saw that she did indeed have the number which had been called. In fact, it was the only number on her card. Across the top was only the letter G and down the card the number forty eight was repeated in every square. Again, the creature to her right patted her hand. Alisha looked down and saw with revulsion that the woman's arm and hand were rotting away. Maggots squirmed and wriggled through her flesh in an orgy of putrid gluttony. "Father doesn't like to be kept waiting," the corpse whispered with decay-laden breath.

"Mark your card, Alisha," an all too familiar voice said to her left. Tearing her eyes away from the sight of the rotted flesh she turned to see him standing next to her holding a ruler. Raising his hand high, he brought the ruler down in an arc toward her right hand which was now pinned in place by the decaying woman on her right.

Al closed her eyes and screamed. Then, she heard an unexpected sound. Instead of the ruler crashing down with a loud smack, it was a gentle tapping. Opening her eyes, she started to see that she was sitting in her car in the parking lot of the station and Sergeant Porter was tapping on the widow of her car. "You okay, Lieutenant?" he asked, his voice muffled through the glass.

"Yes," she mumbled, rolling down the window. "I guess I was more tired than I thought last night."

"Probably a good thing you didn't try to drive home," the lanky Porter replied. "You might have been in an accident. Well, have a good day," he concluded, heading down the street to the Koffee Kup Kafe as was his routine. Al often wondered why he always trekked all the way over to the KKK. It was twelve blocks from the precinct, and had the worst coffee she had ever tasted. Worse, even, than the swill in the precinct break room, and she had always said that you could remove varnish with that stuff. The thought of routines made her remember her dream and she shuddered, rolling up her window. As she turned her gaze forward, she noticed a sheet of paper had been stuck under her windshield wiper blade. The lot was secured and the transients who earned a little drug or whiskey money passing out fliers weren't supposed to be able to get in, but they did. Rolling the window back down, Alisha reached out to pluck the flier from under the wiper blade.

When she looked at it, she nearly screamed again. It was the announcement about the spaghetti supper and Bingo game at St. Jude's. At the top was the piece of tape which had held it to the door in her dream with a chip of green paint still stuck to it, and at the bottom was a picture of a Bingo card, unlike in her dream, there were two numbers circled in red, "G-forty eight *and* G-forty four?" she read aloud.

Alisha's Journal
May 4, 2010

I slept with the pills for two nights in a row, but last night I couldn't stand to take them again. I feel so awful the next morning. I have to admit, I don't feel too much better right now. He crossed a line last night. Or perhaps I should say he crossed another line. I was back in uniform on a drug house raid. The night was wet as if it had just rained, but hot and steamy. I could feel the sweat running in rivers underneath my body armor. I could smell the meth lab a mile away. There's no mistaking that odor, cat piss with an undercurrent of ether. The captain leading the raid raised his hand to signal us to stop. Then he turned, his face shadowed under the brim of his hat, and started firing on the cops in line behind him. The concussions were deafening. the rounds tore through their body armor like paper, exploding out their backs. When everyone was dead, he turned to me, laughing, and raised his impossibly huge pistol and pointed it right at my face. I couldn't do anything, not even scream. The street light reflected on his name tag, and I could read it. Now I know his name. The Bad Man is called...Caine.

CHAPTER TWO

Rob Paulpry sat at his desk at The Times Republican and stared at the Ghostbusters lunch box. He had been getting little gifts like that ever since doing the story on Madame Blageur, the "Mystic of Twelfth Avenue". He hadn't chosen the story, it had been assigned by his editor after she heard him talking about his mother. His mom had been able to see the future. Her gift was sporadic, at best, and indecipherably obtuse at worst, but real. Unfortunately, he let his experience and bias cloud his objectivity. He had taken a lot of heat for his piece declaring her to be the real thing, but nothing like it had been since she was arrested for defrauding an elderly widow out of two and a half million dollars. The cops had torn her little storefront shop apart and his nemesis at the Sun, Mark Ribley, had gotten the exclusive. A detailed account of how the Madame (whose real name was Rose Smith) had conned the "gullible and naive of this city". Rob couldn't help but notice the obvious jibe. Neither could his co-workers and colleagues.

So Rob had been put on the crime beat. The Times Republican had two crime beats. There was the major crime beat which dealt with murders, bank robberies, kidnappings, in short, the interesting cases. Then there was the metro crime beat. The metro crime beat dealt with DUI's, muggings, and hookers. Rob was on the metro crime beat. He sat at his desk going over the arrest and incident reports from the previous night. Computers had made reporting, in many ways, a lot easier, but in others, more boring. Reporters didn't have to schlep down to the precinct and badger the desk sergeant for the reports, like in the old days. Rob sat at his desk, logged onto the city's server with his password, issued by the City Attorney's office and scrolled through the reports. Efficient, but mind-numbing and limiting as the city had complete control over what information he saw. Rob was a people person. Which was not to say that he got along well with others, necessarily, or that people liked him, neither was especially true. Quite the opposite, in fact, he liked interrogating people, needling them, and making them uncomfortable. He hated computers. Mostly because they eliminated so much of that aspect of the job, you couldn't make a computer sweat, or slip up and give out something it shouldn't. You couldn't look a computer in the eyes and tell when it was hiding something, or lying to you.

He scrolled down the list, but nothing was jumping off the screen at him. Mugging, solicitation, drunk and disorderly, bar fight... He was just about to move on, when he saw the name of the lead officer on the bar fight, Lt. Alisha Ferdinand, a young, female homicide detective of some renown in the city. What was a homicide detective with Ferdinand's reputation doing working a bar fight in a seedy, junkie-infested neighborhood on the city's infamous south side? Suddenly, Rob was interested. Clicking on the listing, he read the report. It said that the victim, one James Crooker, was taken to St. Vincent's with severe trauma to his left eye. He scanned the rest of the report, making notes as he went, looking for the murder. He was just about to give up when he came to the list of evidence collected at the scene. The first notation was, "Eyeball, left, floating in whiskey glass," but it was the second which piqued his interest. "Bill, twenty dollar, serial number matching bill from North Central Bank Robbery, case number MC447399.8. Cross reference: multiple homicides, case numbers HC2791.45-HC2791.49".

Rob quickly checked the name of the lead officer on the homicide cases and was not surprised to find Lieutenant Ferdinand's name on all five of those reports as well. That explained her involvement with the bar fight case. Suddenly, for the first time since being banished to the land of night court cases, drunks, hookers, and wife beaters, Rob was interested in something. Opening the homicide reports, he quickly scanned them. He remembered the case. About a month ago, an elderly woman living in a nondescript lower class neighborhood had complained of a foul odor coming from the little frame house next door. Instead of a meth lab, the responding officers had turned up a multiple homicide. An interesting enough story, due to the incredibly violent nature of the murders, but when it came out that the victims were the bank robbers they had be looking for, and that the money was missing, it became the hot story of the year.

He would have to be careful that Morton in major crimes didn't find the connection in the cases. Not that he would look at the bar fight, and the five homicides at the little house on forty-third was probably cold enough he wouldn't be checking there. Nonetheless, he knew he would have to work quickly and quietly to stay ahead on this one and, perhaps, salvage his flagging career and self-respect. He wasn't sure how this was going to play out, but his instincts told him that there was something big going on.

Some days, he wished for a little glimmer of his mother's abilities. Just a little peek into the not too distant future would be so helpful, if not for the consequences. When Rob's mother had foreseen the death of his older sister, Marie, in a fire and had not been able to contact her it had been the final straw. Marie had moved away a few days before her eighteenth birthday, and had severed ties with her family, except for her little brother. He had known how to contact Marie, but his mother had not asked him, choosing, instead, to keep her premonition from him. Ironic, as he was the only member of the family who could have warned Marie that the water heater in her basement apartment was leaking gas and the only one who took his mother's premonitions and predictions seriously enough to act on them.

Rob shook his head, refocusing his attention on the story before he started remembering his mother's rapid descent into depression, and the night her inner demons chased her to the middle of the fifteenth street bridge and into the icy waters below. The first thing he needed to do was dig up all the background information he could on Lieutenant Alisha Ferdinand, the bank robbery, the murders of the robbers, and the assault. That was after he filed his assignment for the Metro Crime Page. If he neglected his assigned drudgery, he knew his editor would come around to see what was taking up all of his time and pass the story on to Alex Morton, with a thank you, but no credit for uncovering the connection between the crimes. He quickly scanned the entries, wrote up the more sordid parts and emailed the file to the Metro Desk, then he went to work.

He didn't want to use the paper's server. That would leave a trail Morton or anyone else could follow, so he grabbed his laptop and headed out to the cafe on the corner. They had about the worst coffee in the city, possibly in the world, but a good Wi-Fi connection. As he dashed out into the late morning sunshine, Carl Robbins, the city Political Beat reporter, called out, "Gotta ghost to catch, Paulpry?" He had suspected it had been Robbins who had bestowed the Ghostbusters lunchbox on him, and vowed to make him eat it one of these days.

He stepped out into the sunny day, with the laughter echoing behind him from the other reporters and staff who had heard Robbins' joke. He didn't care, he was focused. A little of the Rob Paulpry from the past was reawakening. He felt the old electric sensation coursing through his body and mind once again. It was good to be alive. Reporting was all he had ever wanted to do and now, for the first time since the Madame Blageur fiasco, he felt the thrill again. He practically sprinted down the street to the top of the seven steps to the Koffee Kup Kafe, which was located in the basement of the Granneman Building.

At some point since his fall from grace, Rob had stopped thinking of himself as a real reporter, and felt more like a secretary or scribe, taking down information for those more exalted than he. Suddenly, the drive was back, his interest was piqued, and he was a reporter again! When he was starting on a story like this one, he rarely knew where the trail was going, but there was a feeling. He had tried to describe the feeling many times without success. It was a combination of fear of the unknown and hunger to know. The more obscure the trail, the more doggedly he pursued it. Rob had to admit to himself that this trail was pretty obscure, even for him. He worried that his skills had gotten too rusty in the months he had spent reciting lists of drunk drivers and petty larceny calls.

He ran down the concrete steps and burst through the glass door of the Koffee Kup Kafe. The words were written on the door from top to bottom, with the first letters lined up. Back when he had been doing real reporting and had met a source or subject here, he would joke to himself about going to his KKK meetings. Much to his dismay, he saw that Gloria was working behind the counter today. All right, dismay was probably too strong a word. In his current world, Rob should probably be glad for every friend he could find.

Gloria was a nice enough girl, a few years younger than Rob, a little on the plump side. Pretty face framed by dark hair with streaks of pink, blue, or purple, depending on her mood, with a huge crush on Rob. Her eyes were the brightest greenest he had ever seen, but there seemed to be something behind them. Something vastly sad and haunted. She referred to him as "our personal star reporter" and wouldn't leave him alone to get any work done. In a way, Rob liked the attention and did nothing to dissuade the girl, even though he was not interested in the least in her flirtations. "Rob," she called from behind the counter, "you've been away awhile!" Rob had to admit to herself that she had a very pretty voice, and thought she could sing well. When he first met her, he had commented on this and she blushed and giggled, saying she only sang in the church choir. "Go ahead and grab a booth," she told him, "and I'll bring you your usual."

As he sat down and logged onto the wireless server, Gloria carried over a chipped red mug bearing the KKK logo and a carafe of what passed for coffee (maybe it was actually "koffee", whatever that was) and picked up the bills he had laid on the table. "Working on a story?" she asked. Rob replied as politely as his growing impatience and curiosity would allow and pointedly turned all of his attention to the screen of his laptop. After lingering another long moment, Gloria sighed and walked back around the counter. There were no other customers here at eleven o'clock in the morning, which meant two things for Rob. Relative quiet in which to work, and frequent visits from the infatuated waitress. 'Yin and Yang,' he thought ruefully.

Rob started his research by looking for all of the news reports about the bank robbery and homicides of the culprits. Going back to the beginning, he had discovered was the only way to start an investigation like this. If you wanted to find the end of the trail, he believed, you had to retrace the entire route. The story as it had progressed to date was a pretty bizarre and mysterious affair. The robbers had gotten away clean. In order to avoid the dye packs the tellers were supposed to slip into the money, they had secured each bundle of bills in its own plastic sandwich bag. Many people did not know that the dye packs were disguised to look like a bundle of bills. When the packs went off, the dye was mostly contained. The police had found them, and a few dyed bills, in a dumpster a few blocks away. These guys were smart.

They had not spent any of the money, had not spoken at all during the robbery, left no fingerprints, and had timed their attack for closing time, forcing their way in as the manager was locking the doors. The tellers had been caught completely by surprise away from their stations and alarm buttons. Someone, however, had found them.

The reports from the murder scene were particularly grisly. The violence with which the murders had been committed was something almost superhuman in nature. The police had tried to keep the more gruesome details out of the press, but information was like water, it can only be contained under specific conditions and the police department was far from hermetically sealed. The owner of the little house was a nondescript man, living a nondescript life. He had jumped at the chance to give interviews about what he had discovered that hot summer day after neighbors had reported an overpowering odor from the house he had rented to one John Smith for six months, cash up front. Fifteen minutes of fame later, he had gone back to being nondescript. Rob made a note of his name and address. He'd probably like another taste of fame, and Rob could promise him that, even if he had to lie to do it. It's not that Rob Paulpry condoned lying, as a rule, but sometimes you had to do what you had to do to get the story. He had said on many occasions that he only lied when it was absolutely convenient.

Having tracked the story itself back to its start, he turned his attention to Detective Lieutenant Alisha Ferdinand. He remembered the basic story of her meteoric rise through the ranks of the department, but he just knew there was more to her story. There was always more to anyone's story and no one could root out the skeletons in the closets like Rob Paulpry. Jotting notes and sipping the disgusting coffee, generously sweetened to take the edge off, Rob tracked Lt. Ferdinand's career back to her days in the academy. He then tracked her father's career, read about her mother's death from an unspecified illness when Alisha was a child, then found something particularly interesting. It was one line in an interview with her about an unrelated case, the reporter brought up the incident in which she had killed a stoner who had tried to take her badge from her. In her very short answer, she mentioned her psychologist. Of course, it was department policy to see the shrink following a shooting, but this interview had taken place more than two years after the shooting. Rob knew that for the sessions to continue even six months was unusual, but two years hinted of deeper issues and this troubled him a bit. Not that Rob didn't have his own share of deeper issues, but all he had a license to carry was a loaded question. He hated guns, feared them almost pathologically, in fact. He wasn't really sure where his aversion to firearms had started. There had never been any in his house, his mother had used a bridge to commit suicide, and, surprising as it may seem, he had never been shot or even shot at. Nonetheless, the mere thought of any kind of firearm sent shivers up and down his spine and caused him to clench up as though expecting a hail of bullets.

"You okay, Rob?" It was the sweet musical voice of Gloria, admirer and possibly the only remaining fan of 'Rob Paulpry, Ace Reporter'.

"I'm fine, Gloria, just working on something," he replied, trying to sound calm and polite, but get the message across that he wanted to be left alone. He had no wish to alienate his entire fan club by being too abrupt. Just then, the bell over the door jingled and a tall, lanky cop walked in, stopping Gloria before she could ask anything more.

"Hey, Sarge," she called. "Grab a stool, I'll get your regular right up." She walked off singing what sounded like a slightly distorted hymn softly. There was definitely something in the way she sang it that seemed off. Not wrong, but, rather somehow more right than usual.

Rob shook his head, "Must be the toxins in this poison," he mumbled, forcing down the last of the bitter coffee and leaving some more cash on the table. He collected his notes and shoved them into the pocket inside his laptop case and headed out. Gloria was deep in conversation with the police sergeant sitting at the counter and didn't even wave goodbye to him. "Oh, well," he thought. "Fame is fleeting and the public is oh, so fickle." Chuckling, he headed down the street. He had no particular destination in mind, but walking helped him think.

He had quite a number of the puzzle pieces spread out in his mind. Now came the task of putting them all together, starting with the border. As a child, he and his mother had spent many winter evenings piecing together puzzles on the dining room table and Rob had always looked at stories or problems as jigsaw puzzles to be solved. It was almost Zen-like for him, calming his mind and giving him focus.

Rob knew a lot about Zen, and just about every other kind of mind-calming practice in existence. As a young man in college, he had tried to find anything to help him focus and keep his private demons at bay. He knew first-hand what could happen if they got out of control. He had vowed at his mother's funeral that he would not end up like her. He feared that possibility even more than he feared guns. He had read that mental illness could be hereditary. Even though he knew full well that his mothers descent into despair had been the result of her "gift" and not mental illness, he was afraid, and he did not like being afraid.

He moved along the street, navigating his way through the noon-time throng on autopilot. His mind was working on the puzzle. He felt like he had just found a corner piece when he was jolted back to awareness by the cell phone on his hip. Rob considered the telephone to be an annoyance at best, a necessary evil most of the time, and was convinced that cell phones were the work of the devil himself. The paper required all of their reporters to carry one. Back in his heyday as the golden boy, Rob frequently turned his off. Now, in his current state of disfavor, he dared not. "Paulpry," he said into the phone after ascertaining that it was the paper.

"Paulpry, where the hell are you?" It was Helen Corydon, Editor and Pain in the Ass in Chief. "Another long lunch hour, I see. Get your worthless carcass back to your desk, I'm not paying you to wander around the streets pretending to be a real reporter. That crap you submitted this morning was thin even for you. I need five more column inches by one o' clock." She hung up at that, apparently satisfied with the amount of humiliation she had dished out.

Rob looked around to get his bearings. He had never been lost in the city. He grew up here, roaming the streets and had spent the greater part of his adult life scouring nearly every alley, boulevard and sidewalk following stories, piecing the puzzles together. He was standing on the corner of Fourth Avenue and Wabash street. Calling up his detailed mental map of the area, he plotted the shortest and longest routes back to the paper. Despite the temptation to do otherwise, he chose the former. Now that he had his route back to the paper programmed into his mental GPS, he turned his thoughts back to the story.

Of course, he really didn't know what the story was, or if it would pan out to anything more than some low-life thug having found a bill from the robbery and, toasted out of his mind on meth or PCP, assaulting a drunk, and leaving the bill behind. But, he had that old, familiar feeling, and couldn't just let it go without at least a little more digging. Rob was firmly convinced that there was no such thing as a true coincidence, and all of this seemed a little too coincidental. How had the unnamed murderer managed to track down the bank robbers when the police and FBI had nothing? Where was the rest of the money? Finally, what was the connection between the murders and the assault? There had to be a connection. Nothing was that random.

As he passed back by the KKK, he saw through the dirty basement windows along the sidewalk that the cop was still at the counter, talking to Gloria. They both looked up and seemed to watch him as he went by with, Rob noticed, that same haunted weariness in their gazes. "Don't be silly," he told himself and turned the corner on Seventh, back toward the paper.

Inside the 'Kafe', Sergeant Porter turned back around on his stool at the counter. "Are you sure about him?" Gloria asked, her ethereally musical voice resonating in the small space. The cop just nodded, drank his coffee, and rose from his stool.

"You were, also, not that long ago," he said from the doorway. Gloria bowed her head and smiled sheepishly. She cleared up the dishes and worried that she had let her attraction to Rob Paulpry cloud her judgment. That wasn't supposed to happen, but this had been brewing for so long, she just wanted to be done with it. Shuddering with the implications, she finished tidying up, singing a very, *very* old hymn to calm her nerves.

CHAPTER THREE

Al was grumpy. Given the choice between not sleeping and facing Caine again, she had, for the past three nights chosen sleeplessness. Sure, she could take the damned pills, lord knows she had enough of them stocked up, but she hated the hangover worse than not sleeping. Everyone in the precinct knew to stay out of her way when she was like this. Everyone except Frank, that is. Frank knew her better than anyone else in the department and could get away with behavior which might have resulted in bodily injury to anyone else who attempted it.

"Jimmy's statement," he announced, dropping a stack of papers and a styrofoam cup of coffee on the desk next to a frustrated Al. She had been trying for fifteen minutes to access some files on her computer without much success.

"Who the fuck is Jimmy, and why am I interested in anything he has to say?" she growled, punching the keys on her keyboard again. "Piece of crap won't take my password!" Frank reached over and tapped the caps lock.

"Try it now," he suggested calmly. Al hated it when he was calm in the face of her rage and frustration. She hated it even more when he solved a problem like that, simply, as if she was a child again, trying to learn to tie her shoes. As she typed in her password again, and saw with chagrin that it was accepted, Frank continued. "Jimmy is the main character in The Floating Eyeball Mystery," he reminded her. Al forgot all about the files on her computer and picked up the sheaf of papers and styrofoam cup and, taking a large gulp of coffee, began reading.

Not too much was different from the bartender's version of the story. Jimmy had brushed up against his attacker's arm reaching for the peanuts, apologized as the big man had turned toward him, and tried to peer under the brim of his hat. "You eyeballin' me?" she read aloud.

"I noticed that too," Frank said, sitting down in the chair next to her desk. "The DI's in boot camp used to say that to us if they thought we were looking at them. I'm running down military records for a match. It's a long shot but, who knows." Al turned the next page to the equally unhelpful forensics report. No fingerprints on the twenty dollar bill, not even the bank robbers. Likewise, none on the glass or the eyeball. She paused for a moment, wondering just how they had tried to lift prints off the eyeball, shook her head, and read on.

"No prints," she muttered. "Did Jimmy or the bartender mention if the guy was wearing gloves?"

"I asked both of them and they both swore he wasn't," Frank answered. Al glared at him. "Hey, don't shoot the messenger," he joked, throwing his hands up. Al shook her head and smiled. "And Al," he coaxed with his Uncle Frank voice, "get some sleep, you look like three day old stir fried shit."

"I love you, too, Frank," she answered.

Frank shrugged and stood up. "Well, off to fight crime and/or evil. Call me if you get anything new." He headed back out of the Homicide bull pen as Al attacked the reports. He knew that Captain McElroy had grounded her to her desk until she was caught up. Al was a damned fine detective and often grumped that she had not joined the force to be a secretary. The captain had heard her too and knew that this was the only way to get the reports done. He had confided in Frank that he would also rather have Al out on the streets, but he had superiors, too.

Frank turned back at the doorway and watched her for a moment. He was worried about her. She had the look he remembered all to well from the bad old days. It was the dreams again, she wasn't sleeping. He was tempted to talk to Dr. Morrissey, if not for the vivid memory of what had happened the last time he'd done so. Instead, he walked on down the hallway shaking his head. Better to have her tired and still talking to him. That way, maybe he could help. His biggest worry was that, when she got like this, she looked too much like her mother toward the end.

Al plowed through the reports. She was three weeks behind and, in this city, that was a lot of reports. It never ceased to amaze her how many people were killed by their fellow human beings and the amazingly stupid reasons they gave for doing so. The report she was working on when that thought came fell into the category of the stupidest of the stupid. A man had killed his wife for bringing home the wrong brand of cat food. He had beaten in her head with the can. When Al had arrived on the scene, he was sitting in the kitchen, covered in her blood, petting the stupid cat. She had nearly lost it when they had been taking the husband out and the cat had jumped up on the kitchen table and started licking the blood off its coat.

Besides the gory nature of the scene, Al hated cats. They couldn't be trusted and Alisha was surrounded by too many people in her life who were untrustworthy, she didn't need a sneaky animal around. Besides, there was too much work involved. Al had never been much of a caretaker, at least not since her mother's death. What was the use? No matter how good you were, or how much care you gave, the end was always the same...

"Al?" Detective Cooper's voice brought her upright in her chair, reaching for her weapon. She realized she had been dozing. "Hey!" he cried, throwing up his hands in mock fear. "Don't shoot, I have good news. You're only supposed to kill the bearer of bad tidings!"

"Sorry," Al mumbled, relaxing back down into her chair, "I was concentrating."

"My gramp used to say he was checking his eyelids for pinholes," Cooper joked.

"Did you have a reason for being here and interrupting me?" Al asked, pointedly. "Or did you just feel like sharing stupid, boring family stories?"

"Sorry. They finally ID'd the two bank robbers in the living room of the house on forty third. The ones who had suffered the head-on collision. Turns out they were brothers, last name, Abell."

For some reason, a shiver ran down Al's back at this information. She took the report from Cooper and started reading. After standing in silence for a moment, he realized he had been tuned out, and headed back to his desk. Ferdinand could be one weird bitch, he thought, but she was the best, he had to admit.

The first page in the stack was the autopsy reports. What had caused the delay in identifying the corpses had been the fact that the brothers had removed their fingerprints with battery acid, had never had their DNA entered into any database, and had never seen a dentist. X-Rays of Martin Abell had finally provided the clue. He had a pin in his right middle finger from a fracture thirty years ago. It had taken time to run down the serial number on the little piece of metal from the records of the now defunct rural hospital in Arkansas. Then, it had taken more time to find a family member, an aunt, to ID the bodies.

Both men had died as a result of blunt trauma to the heads, wounds which matched up perfectly to each other. One of them had hand-shaped bruising on his ankles. As improbable as it seemed to be, someone had picked up Martin Abell, who stood six-two, and weighed two forty, by the ankles and swung him with enough force to cave in both his and his brother's heads, killing both men instantly. The force of the impact had caused the attackers hands to shift, which rendered the bruising useless in identifying the brute who had wiped out the gang. Though all of the evidence suggested only one attacker, Al found this hard to believe. The Abells and their gang were tough, well armed, experienced street thugs. Somehow their attacker or attackers had managed to surprise and dispatch them without any of them even getting off a shot, or mounting much in the way of a defense. There were, according to the coroner's reports, almost no defensive wounds. It was almost as if the men had lined up and allowed their killer, or killers, to do his, or their, worst.

The next two pages were their rap sheets. Neither man was a stranger to the criminal justice system. Multiple arrests for violence against women, petty larceny, of the smash and grab variety, and assorted lesser offenses. Obviously, neither of these two were the brains behind the bank job. Al had never had any dealings with the two, but there was something about that name, Abell, that bothered her. She couldn't quite get a handle on it.

Just as she was starting on the next report in her long list of unfinished business, he phone rang. She knew she should be annoyed, but she was secretly relieved to be interrupted. 'Anything to avoid paperwork,' she thought to herself as she lifted the handset off the cradle. "Detective Ferdinand?" a male voice on the other end of the line inquired.

"This is she," Al answered shortly. She was always careful about giving out too much in he way of either information of emotion over the phone. At least until she knew who was on the other end of the conversation.

"This is Rob Paulpry, from the Times Republican," he said. Al hated reporters even more than she hated cats. In fact, she was convinced that all reporters were reincarnated alley cats. They both got their sustenance from digging through the garbage, but reporters were harder to get rid of. "I have something I'd like to discuss with you, if you have the time."

She knew who Rob Paulpry was. Every cop in the city knew him. Of all the lowlife pains in the ass who reported the news in the city, he was the worst. She hadn't heard anything from or about him since the fiasco with the phony medium and had hoped he had moved on or, even better, died. "Mr. Paulpry," she began, letting everything she felt about him and his kind creep into her voice. "In case you haven't noticed, as you seem to have been out of circulation lately, there are a great many important things with which I have to deal. Not the least of which are all of the murders in this fair city of ours. So, no, Mr. Paulpry, I do not now, or for the foreseeable future have the time to discuss anything with you. Why don't you try me about six weeks after the apocalypse?" She slammed the phone down and bolted up out of her chair, heading for the front desk. Some desk sergeant was going to get a piece of her mind. They all knew better than to let scum like Rob Paulpry interrupt her when she was stuck at her desk. Rounding the corner, with a lung-full of invective ready to explode from her chest, she saw Sergeant Porter just taking off his light jacket and shaking the rain from it.

"Hello, Lieutenant," he greeted her. "Is there something I can do for you?"

"How long have you been here," she asked, some of the wind dying, visibly, from her sails.

"Just arrived, why?" he asked.

"Who was here before you?"

"That would be Sergeant Foster," he replied. "I came in early to relieve him, his wife is having a baby." This finished deflating Al's anger. "Is there a problem?"

"No, just hold my calls, I'm trying to catch up on my reports," she answered, lamely. As she turned to head back in to her desk, Porter spoke again, halting her.

"The captain asked me to remind you of your meeting with Dr. Morrissey tomorrow," he said. Before Al could reply, the telephone rang and he answered it. As the frustrated detective headed back to her desk, he said into the mouthpiece, "Thank you, Gloria, your timing is impeccable, as always. Now we must be patient, the process has begun."

Al stomped back to her desk, still fuming. She couldn't remember who Sergeant Foster was, but when she saw him again, he was going to learn just what she thought about reporters and those who gave them access to her. Sitting back down at her desk, she forced herself to become completely immersed in the reports, determined to be back out on the streets tomorrow. After her appointment with Dr. Morrissey, that was.

Rob cradled the pay phone. It was getting increasingly difficult to find them any more, but he was convinced they were safer than the cell phone. He had read a number of articles about how easily cell phone traffic could be intercepted. Besides, his belonged to the paper and he really didn't trust the powers that be at the Times Republican. Thank God, the KKK was such a throwback. The pay phone was on the building beside the door and was always in working order whenever he needed it. It almost made him believe in divine intervention. Of course that would require belief in a divine being, which Rob absolutely lacked.

He blamed his atheistic world view on experience. He didn't know how anyone could look at the world and everything that happened in it since the dawn of time and believe that anyone was in charge, especially a perfect, loving, and sentient God. Looking up from his ruminations through the glass door of the Kafe, Rob saw Gloria talking on the phone. She caught sight of him, smiled and waved. He waved back and started up the concrete steps as she hung up the phone and started wiping down the counter. Somehow, Rob knew she was singing.

As he gained the bright sunlight of the rain-wet street, Rob started pondering his next move. His ambush hadn't worked. He often found that if he surprised someone while they were engrossed in their familiar surroundings, bearding the lion in his den, as it were, he could get them to let slip some morsel, some tidbit of information. He could see that Lieutenant Ferdinand was not going to be so easy. Time to step up his game. He would backtrack the cases, do some interviews, contact some of his old sources, providing they were still around and feeling communicative, and see what turned up. Then, he would approach the irascible Homicide detective with information she did not possess. No cop could resist talking to someone with information about a case. But, with Rob Paulpry, that information had a price, and he always got more than he gave out.

He checked his watch, he wanted to make sure he got back to his desk on time, he didn't need Helen the Barbarian calling him and looking into his activities. He hurried back into the offices of the paper just as a dark cloud momentarily obscured the sun. He was not so preoccupied that he missed the coincidental symbolism of that. If he read it in a novel, he would dismiss it as trite and contrived. But, he reasoned, the universe is often trite and contrived. Another argument, in his opinion, against an intelligent higher power.

Gloria sang for many reasons. Sometimes it was for the sheer joy of singing, other times out of habit, or to express her feelings in a way that speaking could not. Today, it was out of doubt and nervousness. The song she sang as she wiped down the counter hadn't been sung in centuries, but had always been one of her favorites. Very few people outside linguistic academia would even be able to identify the language, and fewer still translate the words of the song. Gloria knew and understood everything about the hymn and it soothed her nerves. As always, it had been her responsibility to bring the players into the game and subtly guide their actions, but this time was different. She loved and cared for every being she came into contact with, it was her nature. But Rob Paulpry struck a resonating chord deep within her very being. Perhaps it was because of the monumental importance of this stage of the game. The stakes were the highest they had been in millennia. Perhaps, she reasoned, it was because she had been allowed a glimpse into his past. The past that most people were unaware of, the past of previous times, the roles he had played before...

"Enough," she chided herself. "You know your role, and now must play it out as it lays, the die has been cast and there is no going back." She finished cleaning and went into the back. There would be no more customers this afternoon, and she needed to rest. Had there been anyone outside the little coffee shop, and had Gloria allowed it, they would have seen a soft, golden glow emanating from the kitchen area as she passed through the swinging door to her rest. But what the outside world observed was strictly controlled. No one even ever noticed the complete lack of any other staff in the restaurant, or the fact that everything was always perfectly tidy and clean, lacking even the food odors a greasy spoon should, by all rights have. No one who looked at, or the few who actually came into the diner (a limited and strictly controlled number) ever remembered that the diner had been closed for a number of years following a fire. Of course, no evidence of the fire could be seen by the patrons. If Gloria chose to, she could still see what the restaurant actually looked like, but preferred to see it as she wanted everyone else to see it.

Rob sat at his desk and stared at the computer monitor. Ostensibly, he was going over the crime reports, filling in the Police Blotter for the past twenty four hours. In reality, he was going over and over what he knew so far about the secret case, as he had started calling it. He had managed to discover the identity of two of the bank robbers. They were a pair of lowlife brothers, Martin and Lewis Abell. Obviously, their parents had thought the names to be funny. Some people had a sick sense of humor. No wonder the brothers had turned out the way they had. He hadn't been able to access the coroner's report yet, but, given the description of the crime scene, he was betting that it was very interesting. Whoever had taken out the bank robbers had been some seriously bad dudes. He couldn't believe, despite the police reports hinting at one attacker, that a single individual could do this much damage. None of the gang had even gotten off a single shot at their attackers. Not that they didn't posses the firepower, they had an arsenal lying around the little house, all loaded and within easy reach. Maybe superman was running around out there. All Rob had to do was find Lois Lane.

"Daydreaming, Paulpry?" It was the nails on the blackboard voice of Helen Corydon that jolted Rob out of his reverie, and nearly out of his chair. "Take your naps at home, I need the Police Blotter in ten minutes." She stalked off through the bull pen, wreaking havoc as she went. Helen rarely came out here. Rob decided he needed to be extra careful about covering his tracks. The fact that she had sneaked up behind him at his desk meant she had a hunch he was up to something. She was a royal pain in the ass and a cold-hearted bitch of the highest order, but she still had her reporter's instincts. He hunkered down and knocked out the Blotter in five minutes and sent it on its way along the electronic pathway to the press room. Ten minutes later he was in his car headed down Quigley toward the Fourteenth Precinct.

The fourteenth was in a part of town frequently referred to as "The End". Formerly a blue collar neighborhood, it was now nothing less than a blighted war zone. The square brick buildings which formerly housed various industries which shipped their wares on the river were dilapidated husks housing meth labs, shooting galleries for the new generation of heroin addicts, and filthy mattresses used by the lowest level of crack whores. Even the river was a sluggish trickle thanks to the Midvale Dam. The dam generated over-priced electricity for which the towns downstream paid dearly and had created Lake Cooper.

The lake was named for the state senator who had been behind the creation of the dam. He had convinced the voters that everyone would benefit from it. The only ones who had benefited were Senator Cooper and his rich cronies who owned the land which had become the lake and had built their palatial summer houses on the lake's twelve miles of shore. It was a playground for the rich. Meanwhile, downstream, the river had become a trickle. Railroads and then the interstate had eliminated the river trade, and The End had come to pass. The neighborhood had been christened with its current appellation in the sixties when the hard-core druggies had moved in. The original hippies hadn't been too much trouble and had referred to the area as "The End of the Rainbow". Once the peace-loving hippies had been supplanted by the violent, hard-core addicts, only part of the name had survived. Now it was "The End of the World", or "The End of Hope", but usually just, "The End".

Though they had a presence in the form of the Fourteenth Precinct, the police did little to even attempt to stem the flow of illegal activity down here. Their real goal was just to keep it confined to the ten or so square blocks which made up The End.

Occasionally, when things got too out of hand, or threatened to spill out of the neighborhood, they would make a sweep and clean up some of the two-legged vermin that infested the area. But that just made room for the next batch and caused even more problems when the ones removed were released from custody and tried to reclaim their territory.

Suddenly, a light caught Rob's eye and snapped him out of his musings. Light was anathema to the denizens of The End and, as far as Rob knew, the area wasn't even electrified any more. He stopped his car in the middle of the street and looked at the new church on the corner. The lighted sign out front read, "The Basilica of St. Luke". He hadn't heard of a church going up down here, but he had been out of circulation for a while. "Good luck," he whispered at the edifice and pulled away, not noticing the tall, broad-shouldered priest in the old-fashioned cassock and broad brimmed hat watching him from the doorway, his face hidden in shadow.

Alisha' Journal
May 9, 2010

*I gave in last night and slept. It was an accident, I didn't mean
to doze off. In my dream, I was getting married. I felt happy. The
wedding was outdoors, the weather was beautiful. Ever since I was
a little girl I had imagined myself having a beautiful outdoor
wedding. The priest was smiling as he performed the ceremony. I
glanced to my left, behind the groom at his attendants and that's
when everything went to hell. There were two groomsmen. The
Abell brothers, looking just as they had the day we found them,
battered and days dead in the living room of the little house. I could
smell their bloated corpses. As they smiled, maggots and beetles
spilled from their mouths. I looked back at the priest who was
smiling expectantly, and realized he was waiting for me to say
something. Then I noticed the street sign behind him. It read,
"Nod". None of this was making any sense to me, so I looked, for
the first time, at the groom and awoke screaming. It was him. I was
marrying the Bad Man.*

CHAPTER FOUR

Dr. Kevin Morrissey sat in his tiny office on the fifth floor of police headquarters reviewing Alisha's file. It was the thickest one in his battered, institutional green file cabinet. Usually, with an officer-involved shooting, he saw the officer for a few days to a couple of weeks and released them back to duty. Then there would be follow-up visits at six months and a year, but Lieutenant Ferdinand was different. He looked down at the thick file lying on the scarred top of his grey metal desk. It contained all of her past records from the time she was twelve years old. Once, when Dr. Morrissey had been called out of his office during a session with Alisha, she had, in an uncharacteristically whimsical moment, scrawled "War and Peace" on the front of the file.

As he was studying Alisha's handwriting and musing once again about what a Freudian psychologist would say about her prank, there was a firm knock on his door and Lieutenant Alisha Ferdinand entered the office. She looked as though she hadn't slept for a while, and like she was not in a mood to discuss it. "Welcome to my ivory tower," he said, by way of a greeting. The Ivory Tower was what the rank and file cops called his little, nearly airless office on the top floor of the headquarters building.

"Can we just get this over with?" Al asked. "I have been flying a desk for three days catching up on paperwork and I need to get out on the street and clear the cobwebs out of my brain." Desk duty explained some of her mood, but not the apparent lack of sleep. Dr. Morrissey hoped it wasn't the dreams again. He just sat quietly, waiting for Alisha to speak. He knew better than to press her or start off asking questions. Alisha Ferdinand had more and thicker defenses than he had ever encountered and the last thing he needed was to set off her mental alarms by probing too soon. Especially when she was in a mood like this.

Finally, she broke the silence. "Fine, I know the drill. Yeah, I look like three day old stir fried shit. Like I said, I've been on a desk and you know what that does to me." Dr. Morrissey nodded. "Well, I had a dream last night," she started, reluctantly. Dr. Morrissey tried very hard to suppress his excitement. Alisha's dreams and her delusions about them being prophetic would someday be an important paper or book for him. There were many documented cases of delusional people who believed that they could see into the future, but few of them persisted as long as Alisha's had. Her dreams had all the earmarks of classically reported precognition, the symbology, the vagueness of the visions, and the sincerity. But, she hadn't talked about them for some time. "I was sitting at my desk, doing paperwork. I was almost finished when the computer beeped and started spilling a stream of unfinished reports out of the monitor like the damned thing was puking on my desk." Morrissey was disappointed. It was obvious she had made that up, and hadn't even put as much effort into it as she usually did.

"If you are going to start those games again, Alisha," he said to her, tiredly, "we are going to be here a long time. You know, you're my only appointment for the rest of today." He always blocked off the entire afternoon for Alisha. The one time, early on in their time together that he had interrupted her because of another appointment, she had treated it like a betrayal and had not opened up again for weeks. The tough, determined Lieutenant Ferdinand was as fragile as an egg behind her facade and he had learned how to peel the layers of the facade back, a little at a time, without cracking the shell underneath. He had never gotten all the way through, although in the beginning he had come close, but Alisha's defenses were phenomenal.

Al knew that she would have to do better than a computer vomiting up forms, but she was so tired, and it was the first thing to come to mind. "Sorry, Doc," she began, resorting to charm. "It's been a rough week with some weird shit, and I'm just tired. Nothing unusual, just tired." Dr. Morrissey lay down his pen, took a sip of his rapidly cooling coffee and waited. Much of his success in the field of clinical psychology was a direct result of his patience.

While he waited, Dr. Morrissey thought back on the events which had led him here to this place at this time. He had been a med student, doing a rotation in the ER of a metropolitan hospital, when a patient had come in with a gunshot wound. This was not too unusual for a Saturday night. It was also not unusual for a police officer to accompany the patient, either in an attempt to find out who had done the shooting, or as the arresting officer. In this case, it was the latter.

The nineteen year old kid had stolen a car and was joy riding downtown when the rookie officer on his first solo patrol without a training officer had pulled him over. The kid had jumped out of the car and turned toward the rookie cop, raising his right arm. There had been the glint of streetlights off something shiny in the kid's hand, and the young officer had done what his training said to do. He had fired three shots, aiming at center mass. The joyrider had fallen to the street, the beer bottle in his hand shattering on the pavement.

When the attending pronounced the kid dead, Morrissey had been standing next to the young cop and had caught him when he collapsed. He spent the next five hours talking to the distraught peace officer, reassuring him that he had been right to pull the trigger and that it was not his fault the young man was dead, but the result of his own actions in stealing the car. When the IA sergeant had arrived, Morrissey had given the young cop his number, but had never heard from him. He read in the papers that the rookie was cleared of wrongdoing in the shooting. The kid's family tried, unsuccessfully, to sue the department, and the rookie had quit the force and left town.

When Kevin Morrissey had told his father, a well-known cardiac surgeon, that he had decided to go into psychiatry, Dr. Andrew Morrissey had hidden hid disappointment well, but when his son took the job here with the police department, he had tried very hard to talk him out of it. Sure, he could make more money in private practice, but he couldn't get the memory of that rookie cop out of his head. He had never regretted his decision.

So now, here he sat with the most interesting case in his career. Homicide Detective Lieutenant Alisha Ferdinand, the woman with the Bad Man in her dreams. Her case was not only interesting because of the complexity of her delusions, but the depth and conviction of her belief in them. The trauma of her mother's death due to alcoholism had no doubt been the catalyst which had triggered the dreams. Her belief that the dreams were prophetic were, unquestionably, an attempt to order her world and control the future in and in doing so, prevent any more surprises, such as the sudden death of her father. Alisha Ferdinand's psyche was one big and heavily layered onion and Dr. Kevin Morrissey was determined to peel every single layer away and get to the core of it.

"So," he prompted, "whenever you are ready to tell my the real reason you haven't been sleeping..."

Al was trying very hard to focus. Her lack of sleep, frustration at spending the last few days on her desk, and the residue of the dreams were coming together and creating a soporific fog in her mind. She just wanted to curl up and go to sleep. This was the kind of mood and frame of mind in which she could all too easily let things slip to the psychiatrist. She had not taken the sleeping pills the night before in hopes that she could just doze, but she realized her mistake when she awoke from the dream. If only she had taken the pills the night before. She was too foggy from lack of sleep to think clearly, and now Dr. Morrissey had caught her in her lame attempt to put him off the track.

"So, have we seen the Bad Man lately?" he asked suddenly. She started at the mention of him and the shrink saw it.

"About a week ago," Alisha began, carefully. The dream about the drug raid would probably set off fewer alarms than the others. She told him about the Bad Man, dressed as the officer leading the raid shooting the others and turning his weapon on her, but she left out the name she had read on the name tag. It seemed to work, they discussed what this meant and how she felt about it. Before she knew it, Al was walking out of the minuscule office, leaving Dr. Morrissey scribbling his notes about the session.

When Alisha walked out of the office, Dr. Morrissey knew that there was more to her current state than the dream she had related. He had a bad feeling. Finding himself with a couple of free hours, he left his office early. He shook his head as he locked the door. Alisha's conviction that she was psychic seemed to be rubbing off on him, he had the strange and frightening feeling that he might never see her again.

Rob Paulpry was having similar feelings of doom. He knew going into his investigation that he had been off a beat for a long time, but it seemed his skills had atrophied more than he had expected. He was running into one brick wall after another in his search for more information on the bank robbers. Last night, the desk sergeant, a long, lanky cop named Porter, had stonewalled him, not even letting him past the desk, so he knew he needed a way to get to Lieutenant Ferdinand that would allow him to climb the stone wall. His plan was a simple one. One which he had used many times in the past to get reluctant members of the police to talk to him. He would offer a simple trade. He would gather information from the street that the police didn't have and offer a quid pro quo. It always worked because he could use the threat of publishing his findings and, if the cops tried to threaten him with obstruction or withholding evidence, he was prepared for that as well. He would simply claim he had been bluffing, that he had no new information. No one could prove what he didn't know.

However, his brilliant plan seemed to have hit a dead end. The neighbor who had complained about the smell of the corpses in the little house had moved, leaving no forwarding address and the house itself remained sealed off with crime scene tape. Proof that it was still considered an active investigation. The owner of the property was livid with the police as he couldn't rent or sell the property. He told Rob he'd had plenty of offers for both. Apparently, there were a lot of sick people out there who were eager to live in a house in which multiple murders had been committed.

Undaunted, Rob stopped by the pay phone outside the Kafe and called Spike Friedman, the lowest of the bottom feeders with whom Rob had ever dealt. Spike was, once upon a time, a good Jewish boy from the suburbs. Somewhere along the line, he had discovered drugs, guns, and prostitutes. His street name came from the metal spikes he'd had implanted in a row on top of his head. Spike's mother answered the phone, "God," Rob thought, "She's still alive?"

"Good afternoon Mrs. Friedman, this is Rob Paulpry from the Times Republican, is Lennie home?" Rob had learned early on to use the punk's given name when talking to his mother, with whom Spike still lived. Despite what seemed like a small criminal empire, Spike wasn't really very good at what he did. His drugs were poor quality and only out of towners ever bought from him, and then, only once. His girls were constantly being arrested and costing him bail and court costs. In short, Spike was always flat broke and more than eager to sell information to Rob. The only trouble was that Spike was so desperate that his information could just as readily be a construct of his imagination. Rob verified everything before paying the worm.

Spike came on the line. Rob could picture him, skinny, pale, and wearing a yarmulke to cover the spikes, of which, as far as Rob knew Mrs. Friedman remained unaware. "Well, well, well," Spike started. "If it isn't my esteemed colleague in the information distribution game. How are you, Mr. Paulpry?" Rob could tell from the tone of Spike's voice that his mother was still within hearing of the phone conversation so he couldn't resist needling his dubious source a little.

"Hey, Lennie," he began. "How's business. I noticed you've been spending a lot of time in night court with your girlfriends, and rumor has it that the certain head of a certain Hispanic drug gang who would very much like to talk to you about some missing blow."

It was very quiet on the other end of the line for a moment, then, Mrs. Friedman obviously left the room.

"Look, Paulpry," the hood began in his "Spike" voice. "You got no call hasslin' me. You been out of the loop since you were conned by that fake psychic. Word on the street is you've lost whatever magic you had once upon a time. The famous Rob Paulpry, Ace Reporter is washed up! So, if anybody's got the right to be callin' and hasslin' somebody, it ain't you, so if you want somethin' it's gonna cost plenty! And don't call me Lennie!"

"So sorry, Spike. Look, if I'm bothering you at a bad time, or you just don't feel like talking, I understand," Rob replied, his voice full of honey. "Tell you what, I'll just call Rafael Ramirez and see if he can help me. I'm sure he would for a fair trade of information, like a certain address in a certain upscale suburb..." By living with his mother well out of the area in which he did business and somehow keeping it a secret, Spike had managed to keep one step ahead of all of the other street rats he had pissed off repeatedly over the years. If Ramirez or any one of several dozen real thugs ever found out where Lennie hid out, there would be hell to pay. Rob would never divulge that information because he would never endanger Mrs. Friedman. But, Lennie didn't know that for certain.

"No need to go to a second-rate source like Ramirez when you have someone like me, someone with street-level information. Ramirez is management, he's lost touch with the real street," Spike replied, in a much more congenial tone. Rob had him, but couldn't resist toying with him a little more.

"I don't know, Spike, if you have more important things to be doing..."

"Nothing is more important than my old friend, Rob Paulpry," Spike replied. "What can I do for you?"

"What do you know about the bank robbers killed in the little house on 43rd a while back?" Rob asked. He found that asking a question point blank and by surprise could sometimes get him a kernel of information for free.

"Now, there you go again, Robby," Spike replied. "Expecting something for nothing. All quid with no pro quo. No answers until we discuss price."

"Of course," Rob answered. "But, as usual, I'll have to check the authenticity of the information before I pay for it." Rob hated dealing with Spike. He looked around during the moment of silence. A homeless man reeking of cheap whiskey shuffled by on the street above, staggering into the rusty iron railing which served to keep people from taking a header into the concrete stairwell.

"Well," Spike said, at last, "two of them were brothers..."

"Martin and Lewis Abell," Rob finished for him. "Come on, Lennie, give me something everyone doesn't know already. I'm sure Rafael has better information, and at a cheaper price. In fact, he'd probably trade me info for info." Just then, a spider crawled across the buttons of the pay phone. Rob blew it away and watched as it swung from its silken thread in the breeze.

"OK, then, talk to Willy Raines," Lennie supplied. Rob suspected by the change in his informant's tone of voice, his mother had come back into the room.

"The gun-runner?" Rob asked.

"Yeah," Spike growled. "He's pretty pissed about the whole deal. The Abell's got their pieces from him and still owed him five large when they went and got themselves killed. Word is that he knew them before, well enough to trust them on the deal."

"Thanks, Spike, that's a new piece of information. I'll check it out," Rob answered.

"Then you'll pay up, right?" the whiny hood simpered.

"Pay?" Rob asked. "I don't remember discussing any payment."

"Paulpry you son of a syphilitic whore!" Spike exploded. "You tricked me!"

"Calm down, Spike," Rob told him in his most placating tone of voice. "Have I ever stiffed you? Meet me tonight, say eleven, at MacMurphy's Tavern." Rob hung up the phone without waiting for an answer, he knew Spike would be there. As Rob climbed the pitted, stained concrete steps back up to street level, he noticed there were probably ten people in the Koffee Kup Kafe. He'd never seen it so busy. Shrugging, he turned left and headed back to the parking lot at the paper to get his car. Willy Raines was smarter than Lennie Friedman, he'd have to approach him a little more carefully and tactfully.

Al stepped out of the department headquarters into the afternoon sunlight. She stopped for a moment beneath the ginkgo tree beside the entrance to the parking ramp and breathed deeply. Her sensitive nose picked up the underlying city smells of car exhaust, filth and decay even though the pavement and air had been scrubbed clean by another storm in the wee hours of the morning. Resting her hand on the rough bark of the tree, she remembered reading once that ginkgo trees flourished in poor soil and air. That was why they were often used in city beautification projects. She was snapped out of her reverie by a thrashing noise in the branches over her head. Snapping her gaze upward, she saw a smallish, scrawny, sickly-looking cat, with a ragged left ear that looked like something had chewed on it a long time ago. It was black with small patches of orange, white and tan in its coat, tortoise shell, she believed the coloration was called. The creature looked as though it was starving and was clutching a bird in its jaws. The cat's prey was not quite dead and writhed and croaked piteously. Pinning the bird to the branch with a forepaw, the cat began tearing at its flesh before killing it.

An involuntary retching sound escaped from Alisha's throat. Looking up from its now mercifully still prey, the feline stared right into her eyes and hissed, its mouth and the white patch on its chest covered in the bird's blood. Alisha fled to her car, resisting the urge to draw her weapon and shoot the damned cat.

"Perfect," she thought as she sat behind the wheel, calming herself. "First, I tip Morrissey off that he's back, now this". It was Al's firm belief that one should never ask what could happen next, because the universe, in her experience, had a sick perverse sense of humor about such things and would show you. But she couldn't help wondering...

Rob was late for his meeting with Spike, but he knew the scrawny hood would be there, eagerly awaiting his payday and running up a tab the reporter knew he would wind up paying. He couldn't believe Lennie's tip had paid off so well. For once, the little punk had known something of real worth and Rob now had enough information that even the unapproachably bitchy Lieutenant Alisha Ferdinand would have to talk to him.

As he rounded the corner onto sixteenth, Rob saw flashing lights at the tavern. He pulled his car over a block down and hurried to the mouth of the alley, slipping through the crowd of cops and the curious to peek around the wall of the building into the passage between the bar and the long ago closed dry cleaner. Just as he was carefully craning his neck to see better without drawing the attention of the large cop standing just on the other side of the crime scene tape, he caught a break. On the other side of the crowd, there was a commotion and the big officer went to help quiet it down.

Rob ducked under the tape and sneaked around the edge of the small group of detectives gathered in the pool of light spilling from the open alley door of the tavern. They were talking to the bartender and didn't notice him. As he circled around to where he could see what was lying on the filthy pavement, he heard the bartender say, "I was just taking the trash out and found him." Looking down, Rob saw something he couldn't, at first, identify.

Looking more carefully, he realized that it was a body. The corpse was so brutally twisted and pounded out of shape that it looked to Rob as though the life had been literally wrung out of it. The face was caved in and the amount of blood and the large area over which it was spread spoke of great violence. Stepping to his right to get a better view of what was left of the victim's face, Rob felt something under his foot. As he stepped again, he thought he had a rock lodged in the tread of his shoe. He reached down and removed the item, noting that it was metal, not stone. Looking more closely at it, he let out an involuntary cry. He was holding a small metal spike coated in blood. He had seen this item before, sticking up out of the head of one Lennie, "Spike" Friedman.

Suddenly, he heard a voice behind him. The speaker was female and the voice had a sexy, sultry, world-weary quality about it while, at the same time, carrying a cold edge, like a very sharp knife just withdrawn from a freezer. "Who the fuck are you?" Turning, the reporter came, at long last, face to face with Lieutenant Alisha Ferdinand.

CHAPTER FIVE

Most people, when left in an interrogation room at the fourteenth precinct were nervous and frightened. Rob Paulpry was neither. What others looked upon as an inconvenience and, guilty or not, an injustice, Rob saw as an opportunity. Lieutenant Alisha Ferdinand didn't know it yet, but he had leverage. He was in possession of information she desperately needed. In a strange way, he was saddened at the death of Spike. But, also realistic enough to know that it was only a matter of time before Rafael Ramirez and Los Diablos de la Noche, his gang, found the little weasel. He just hoped they hadn't managed to find out about Lennie's mother. But, with him out of the picture, she was almost certainly safe from their street justice.

Just as Rob was thinking about Mrs. Friedman, the door opened and the lovely Lieutenant Ferdinand entered the room, accompanied by the older, rumpled sergeant who had handcuffed him, with what Rob had felt had been unnecessary roughness, in the alley behind MacMurphy's. He had seen news photos of Lieutenant Ferdinand and had even seen her on the television news a few times, but none of this had prepared him for the reality of her. She was quite possibly the most strikingly beautiful woman he had ever encountered. She was small, compact, he would say. Curvaceous, but not due to an excess of fat. She was obviously quite fit. Of all the things Rob imagined he would like to do with Alisha Ferdinand, hand to hand combat was definitely not on the list. He would have the reach on her, but between the muscularly fluid way she moved and a certain feral glint in those amazingly green eyes, the woman was flat-out intimidating. Couple that with what he knew of her history, and Rob knew how any confrontation would come out.

"Mr. Paulpry," she began, somehow making his name sound like a profanity. "First of all, thank you." This surprised Rob, no mean feat. "You correctly ID'd the victim in the alley. The print from his right thumb, the only useable one he still had, came back to Leonard, 'Spike', Friedman." Despite the detective's tone, Rob felt that the interview was actually going well so far. "I understand you were acquainted with the deceased?" Rob nodded his head in reply. He knew better than to start speaking. He suspected that Ferdinand was quite possibly nearly as good as he was at eliciting information, so he would have to be careful. One of the techniques he had used on many occasions was to compliment or thank his subject for something to put them at ease, then ask a seemingly innocuous question to get them speaking. Once you started someone talking, it was easier to get them to reveal more than they intended.

They sat for a long, silent moment, staring at one another across the scarred top of the green-painted metal table. Though neither of them spoke, volumes were communicated across the silent wasteland of Interrogation Room One. The atmosphere was so charged that the big sergeant began to fidget. Finally, she broke the tension. "What else do you know?" she asked point blank, without breaking the almost hypnotic eye contact.

Now, for the bombshell. "I know you have two cases which seem to be linked, though you can't figure out how." For the first time since sitting down opposite the reporter, Lieutenant Alisha Ferdinand's gaze flickered. He'd scored a hit.

"Go on," she encouraged gently, letting just the right amount of smokiness creep into her voice and leaning in a little closer.

"God," Rob thought. "She is good." Aloud, he said, "Now, Lieutenant, if I did know anything more, mind you, I'm not saying that I do. But, if I did, what would the benefit be to me in just spilling it all right here, for you?"

"Well," the lieutenant replied, leaning a bit more and shifting so that the top of her blue blouse, which Rob noted complimented her skin tone beautifully, gap open, "besides doing your civic duty, I might not arrest you on suspicion of murder and obstruction."

Leaning in toward her and blatantly looking down into the shadows of her cleavage, Rob replied, "Cute mole". It had the desired effect. The disheveled sergeant grabbed him by the collar and slammed him back in his chair, and the lovely lieutenant leaned back in hers, with a little smirk on her face.

"Let him go, Frank," Al instructed the beet-faced older cop. "If he does know anything, he can't tell us if he can't breathe." With a final shake, like a cat killing a rat, Frank let go of Rob. The reporter was grateful as he had been starting to see sparkly spots before his eyes. He coughed and massaged his throat. "Frank," Al instructed, "go get Mr. Paulpry something to drink." When the still-glowering sergeant hesitated, she added, "Don't worry, Mr. Paulpry will play nice, won't you, Mr. Paulpry?" Rob nodded. "And, besides," she added, "if he doesn't, I'll hand him his ass." Rob believed not only that she would, but that she could. Frank left the room, giving the reporter one last dagger-filled look.

"Nice guy," Rob said when the door closed. "You two been going together long?"

"Dear old Uncle Frank," Al replied, smiling slightly. "He's just protective of me. What about you, Mr. Paulpry, May I call you Rob?" He nodded, warily. "Well then, Rob, you indicated that you may have some information regarding a couple of my cases. Now, I feel it is not only your best interest, but in the common interests of both of us and society at large for you to share that information, don't you?"

"Well, Lieutenant, may I call you Alisha?" Rob replied. "Well, Alisha," he continued without waiting for her to answer. "It does seem that there may be information to be shared, but sharing implies a two way exchange, and I'm not certain you are ready to hold up your end of that deal. However, if you were to answer a couple of questions first..."

"How about this," she countered. "How about I let you spend the night in the holding cell with a few of the other lowlifes we've rounded up tonight. Perhaps you could make a new friend or two who would be more than willing to share with you. In fact, I happen to know of one particularly amicable soul down there right now who would love to be your special friend."

"Sounds like fun," Rob answered, beginning to enjoy the game. "In fact, the last time one of your brothers in arms decided to extend the hospitality of the holding cell to me, I got leads on two good stories. See, more than anything else, the residents of your cell really like to brag, especially to a reporter who can get their true story out. You know, tell the world how they were framed and mistreated by your colleagues..."

Just then, Sergeant "Uncle Frank" came back into the tiny, green room with its metal table and chairs bolted to the floor with a folder and a cup. Setting the coffee down in front of Rob, he handed Alisha the file. "ME's preliminary," he told her, ignoring the reporter. "Pretty intense."

"The Diablos are pretty thorough and creative when it comes to doling out their version of justice," Rob commented, downing a swig of the cold, stale coffee. Both cops continued to ignore him, poring instead over the papers and photos in the file folder. Rob leaned in, trying for a peek at the report and was rewarded with a flat-handed slap to his forehead. "Hey!" he yelled. "That's brutality, aren't there cameras in these rooms?"

Both officers looked at him, deadpan, and replied in unison, "Budget cuts". Rob sat back, finished the black swill in the styrofoam cup, picking the grounds from the bottom of the cup off his tongue and brooded.

Looking at him with a smirk, the Sergeant said, "I spit in it, too."

"I thought I tasted bacon," Rob shot back, getting great satisfaction at seeing the big cop bristle then being restrained by the diminutive detective.

"Let's leave our cub reporter here to stew for a few minutes," she told the burly older man. Rising from her chair, they left the interrogation room. Alone, Rob fiddled with the handcuffs and strategized the best way to turn this to his advantage. Then he realized the folder containing the ME's report on Spike was still on the table. He slid it over to himself and opened it. The first page was the preliminary report. It catalogued the injuries Spike had suffered in the last few minutes of his life, Rob just scanned this quickly and turned to the photos underneath. The first showed what was left of Spike's face and the second the trauma to his hands. It was the third photo that was nearly too much. It showed the damage inflicted on the front of Spike's skinny chest. It looked like a bomb had gone off inside his ribcage. Rob picked up the photo. The moment he touched it, Rob Paulpry received his first psychic vision, and finally understood his mother.

He saw a huge figure in a broad-brimmed hat silhouetted against the meager light of the alley and then there was a gigantic hand reaching for him, felt the agony of numerous broken bones, smelled blood, vomit, and urine and then, felt a sharp, crushing pain in the center of his chest, as though someone was squeezing his heart. He could actually feel the fingers of his assailant inside his ribcage, slowly compressing his heart, as though squeezing out a sponge. Drenched in sweat, unable to breathe, he finally managed to cry out, just before losing consciousness.

Closing the door to the interrogation room, Al asked Frank, "What do you make of that report?"

"Well," Frank replied. "I know one thing. Peter Parker in there didn't do it." He leaned against the wall, looked down at the worn beige floor tiles, and sighed. "I'm getting too old for weird shit like this."

"What do you mean?" Al asked. "Just another case of murder we won't be able to pin on Rafael Ramirez." Frank shook his head. "What?" she demanded.

"He didn't want to put it in the report until he was sure, but the ME is pretty sure there was only one assailant," Frank replied, slowly looking up into Al's face. "COD was blood loss due to his heart being crushed."

"So the perp...what, stomped in his chest?" she asked.

"No," Frank replied, almost in a whisper. "He stuck his fingers into Friedman's chest and squeezed his heart until it exploded. Al, it's the guy from the house on forty third, it has to be. There can't be two SOB's out there like that. At least I hope to hell there can't!"

"The Case of the Heartbroken Hood," Al ventured. Just then, there was a cry and a thud from within the interrogation room and both cops rushed in to find Rob Paulpry, his head on the table, hand clenched to his chest, drenched in sweat and moaning. The photos and papers from the ME's report were strewn across the table and floor. "Call an ambulance," Al snapped at Frank. He punched up dispatch on his cell phone as she circled the table, muttering, "I didn't think you could have a heart attack without a heart."

Rob sat up and took a loud, gasping breath. Looking down, he saw that his hand was clenched in the front of his shirt, the two cops noticed it, too. With a dazed expression on his face, Rob said, "He squeezed the life out of him..." Al and Frank exchanged a look.

"How'd you know that?" Frank demanded. Looking at Al, he said, "It wasn't in the report."

"I saw it... and felt it..." Rob replied, weakly. Just then, Al remembered something.

"Frank," she said. "Cancel the ambulance, I think Mr. Paulpry is going to be all right, aren't you, Mr. Paulpry?" He nodded, feeling as though he was coming back to life. "Bring us some coffee, Frank," she finished, looking warily at the reporter as the color slowly returned to his face.

"But..." Frank started.

"Sergeant McDonnell, please do as I ask." Frank dialed dispatch again and headed out the door. "Hot coffee, please," she requested. "For both of us." After the door closed, Al looked directly into the frightened reporter's eyes and asked, "What the hell just happened?"

Rob was starting to get his brain functioning again. "Just took a little nap," he muttered. Alisha slammed the photo of the ruined chest cavity of Lennie, "Spike" Friedman down on the table in front of him.

"Don't screw around with me, Paulpry. I have enough on you to hold you for this murder. We both know there's no way in hell you did it, but I can still hold you for seventy two hours without charging you unless you talk." She slid the photograph over closer to him and was rewarded by seeing him recoil from it, as though trying not to touch it. "Come on, reporter," she almost purred, "you've seen lots worse, haven't you. Weren't you the first one on the scene when the old brick plant burned down killing a dozen or so squatters?" As she waited for an answer, Al looked at Rob Paulpry, really looked at him for the first time. She noticed a haunted look in his eyes she didn't think had been there before. It was a look she recognized. She had seen it many times before on her own face after being awakened by the Bad Man. Softly, she asked, "What did you see?"

Still dazed, Rob answered without thinking, scheming, or planning. "A big guy, wearing a broad-brimmed hat looming over me...him. He squeezed his heart like a lemon! Who does that?" Suddenly, Al remembered something from the stories surrounding Paulpry's fake psychic debacle.

"Your mother," she started, bringing the reporter straight up in his chair. "She could see things, as I remember. Was it something like that?"

"So you do read my stuff," Rob replied, beginning to recover.

"Back when you had stuff to read," she replied. "Was it a vision?"

"How would I know, I've never had a vision!" Rob snapped back. "Look, I'm not saying that I have material information in an active case, just like you're not saying that you have information that could help me. So, the only solution I see is that we work together. A fair and free exchange of information. I'll tell you what I know which may or may not be related to any case other than Spike's murder, and you give me my story as it unfolds." Al started to speak, but Rob held up his hand to silence her. "I won't publish anything until you give me the go ahead, and you won't talk to Ribley, or any other reporters that come sniffing around." Into the ensuing silence, the reporter added, "Look, I know what a lowlife Spike was, probably even better than you do, but I liked him. Let me help catch that monster. If not for me, or even Spike, for his mother."

"I can't make any promises, until I get at least an idea of what you have," Al replied. Given her opinion and experience with reporters, especially the sensationalist, headline grabbing ones like Mark Ribley, she was surprised at how she was feeling. She knew Frank wouldn't come back in until she opened the door, "hot coffee" was their code word for "get out and don't come back". It was a good thing he wasn't in here right now, he'd never let her live down going soft of one of the human alley cats that were, in her opinion, reporters. The air in the room took on an almost palpable thickness from the tension which had developed since Frank left. It wasn't sexual tension, more along the lines of two jungle cats circling one another, each looking for an opening while keeping the other at bay. Finally, Paulpry spoke.

"I know that the murder of the bank robbers on 43rd, the bar fight the other night, and probably Lennie's murder are somehow tied together. I also know what Lennie was doing in the alley behind MacMurphy's. Enough to pique your interest?" he asked calmly. Rob was recovering slowly from his flash, vision, whatever the hell it was, and was actually beginning to feel in control of himself and the situation once again. He did have the fleeting thought that, if what he had undergone was a vision like his mother had experienced, he took back every wish he had ever made for a glimmer of her abilities. No wonder it drove her out of her mind. He still had the explosive, crushing feeling in his chest and, in the back of his mind, the fear that comes from the knowledge that death is speeding toward you with no way to stop it. Lenny's final emotion, he surmised. He hoped that he would be able to shake the feeling. He wasn't certain what carrying something like that around in his head for the rest of his life would do to him. More to the point, he was afraid he knew exactly what it would do to him. He had seen what it had done to his mother.

He wondered if his mother had gone to her death with the final, agonizing moments of his sister's fiery death in her consciousness. The coroner's report said that Marie had experienced flash burns to the back of her torso and limbs before the smoke had overcome her. She had been in the basement of the apartment house doing her laundry when the pilot light on the water heater had ignited the cloud of gas in the utility closet. Feeling the pain in his chest, Rob shuddered, thinking of his mother feeling those burns and that terror for the final eight months of her life. The lovely lieutenant interrupted his decidedly morbid musings and, for the first time, surprised him. "I'm interested. Let's hear what you have, then we'll talk about helping each other."

Frank Porter was not very happy with being excluded from the interrogation room while Al grilled the reporter. He knew how she felt about his type, but for some strange reason, he didn't trust the two of them together in that interrogation room. He had a good gut where she was concerned and had managed over the years to steer her clear of trouble on more than one occasion. His gut told him that Paulpry was trouble. More so than your typical reporter. He didn't know what it was about the man, or more precisely, about the two of them together that worried him so much. Alisha could handle her own with any suspect in an interrogation. He remembered when the huge biker who had just beaten his girlfriend to an unrecognizable pulp had decided to come over the table at her. The scumbag was easily three times her size, but by the time Frank had heard the commotion, dropped the coffee cups and run ten feet, bursting through the door like Superman, Al had reduced the tattooed brute to a sobbing mass of flesh at her feet. So, why was he so worried about one scrawny reporter? He knew it didn't make any sense, but his gut was his gut and he trusted it.

Just as Frank decided that he had given the two of them enough time alone and started down the short hallway with its chipped and peeling green paint, the door to the interrogation room opened and Alisha and the reporter walked out together. Something was different. He could see it on both of their faces. The fluorescent light just outside the interrogation room had burned out about a month previous and had yet to be repaired, so they stepped out into a pool of shadow. As they walked toward him, emerging from the gloom, Frank could see a change, especially on Al's face. He didn't like it.

Turning toward the weasel of a reporter, Al shook hands with Paulpry and said, "I'll be in touch".

"I'll do the same," the reporter replied. Then as he walked past Frank, he nodded with a faint smirk of a smile and said, "Sergeant".

Al turned and headed down the hallway in the opposite direction toward the Homicide bull pen, Frank rushed as quickly as his age and bulk would allow to catch up. He overtook her in the doorway at the other end of the hallway. "What the hell happened in there, Al?" he asked, a little out of breath.

"Mr. Paulpry and I came to an agreement. We are going to share our resources on this one. Consider him a consultant," she answered, too calmly, Frank thought.

"I don't like it," he stated flatly. "And since when do you ever call any reporter Mister?" Al didn't answer, she just patted him on the shoulder in that infuriatingly condescending way she had and pushed open the door to the squad room, leaving him alone with his concerns. He stood looking at the door for several minutes then turned to leave. Looking down, he noticed a piece of paper on the floor. Picking it up, he saw that it was a flier for Bingo at St. Jude's. Frank had been a good Catholic boy, less a good Catholic man, he had to admit, but he'd never heard of that church. The address wasn't far away, across from Eden Park right in the middle of The End. Looking at the card with the circled number, he muttered, "Somebody fucked up". Then he noticed the notation in Alisha's unmistakable scrawl, 'Check it out'. He had to wonder what it was all about. Not wanting to talk to her just now, he decided to leave the flier in her mailbox on his way out. Maybe tomorrow he would talk to her. Tonight, he would just worry.

CHAPTER SIX

It was Dr. Morrissey who had first suggested to Al that she keep a dream journal. He said that writing down the dreams would accomplish two things. It would allow her to deal with them in the rational light of day. Also, by dating the dreams and referring back to real events, she would begin to realize that the dreams were not, in fact, prophetic. That it was just that her perception of the timing of the events and the dreams had gotten confused. He couldn't have been more wrong. As she flipped back through the most recent pages and compared the dreams to the notes on the run of weird cases, it was obvious that the dreams were warning her, or trying to tell her something, or, more likely, taunting her.

With the journal lying open on her lap, Alisha tried to string together the pieces of the puzzle. First, the dreams. How did they relate to each other and the cases. One was simple, she saw the symbolism in most the dreams easily enough as it related to the weird goings on in her life. The rest was still tenuous at best. It was easy enough to link the bar fight with the murder of the bank robbers, there was the twenty the killer left behind. Plus the way the drunk had been attacked was in line with the brutality of the killings. Likewise, the killing of Lennie "Spike" Friedman was carried out with the same ferocity. But that was where the thread snapped. What about the marriage dream, or the drug raid, or the damned Bingo game?!

It was the reporter, Paulpry, who had caused her to go over the dream journals again. Talking about his mother and her dreams and how he had been the only one who understood and believed in them. So now, here she sat, a bottle and a half of Merlot later, surrounded by her notes and reports, staring at the pages of the journal, more frustrated than before. She looked at the clock hanging over the kitchen window and saw that it was two thirty in the morning. She needed sleep, but feared it, too. She did not want to dream, but she was afraid not to. The final piece of the puzzle might be hidden in the next dream. She could take one of Morrissey's fucking pills, but what if the dreams had a sequence which would be interrupted by a night of dreamless sleep? There were too many possibilities.

As she started to look back down at the pile of papers surrounding her, Al caught movement outside the kitchen window in her peripheral vision. Instinctively, she reached for her weapon, which never left her side, even at night...especially at night. Moving very slowly, she withdrew the pistol from its holster and turned toward the window and froze. It was a cat! Not just any cat, but the one she had seen in the tree outside Police Headquarters after her last session with Dr. Morrissey. She recognized its markings, size, the ragged left ear, and its eyes. Mostly the eyes. It was staring in at her, wet and shivering in the chilly rain. Not doing anything, just staring, and, for some reason, that frightened Al almost as much as the Bad Man. It had apparently climbed the tree at the corner of the building and walked on the narrow ledge which ran under the windows upon which some of her neighbors tried growing herbs, vegetables and, once, pot. Apparently unaware of who lived a few windows down.

"Go away!" she shouted at the bedraggled feline. It just blinked and sneezed. Alisha rose rather unsteadily from the couch and crossed over to the window, intent on shooing the scrawny, flea-ridden, disease-infested thing away. Halfway across the room, she realized that she still had her weapon in her hand, cocked, with the safety off and a round in the chamber. Laughing out loud, she eased the hammer down, flicked on the safety and laid the Glock on the counter.

There were bars outside the window, but the little cat was skinny enough to get between them and, as Alisha approached, it stretched up, putting both of its front paws on the window glass, almost as if in supplication. Alisha reached up to rap on the glass, in hopes of scaring the nasty little creature back out into the night. But, for some reason, she unlocked the window and slid it open. The wet, shivering bedraggled little cat jumped in as if it owned the place. Al jumped back with an involuntary cry. "Great, Lieutenant," she chided herself. "You'll take on the biggest, meanest drug-addled punk on the street, but you're afraid of a little kitty!" She reached to grasp the cat and fling it back out into the night just as the wind shifted, blowing a spray of cold rain into her face. She suddenly had a mental image of her grandmother, the religious pragmatist, saying, "All living things deserve our respect", as she picked up a hairy, gross looking spider and threw it outside. Moments before, Al had been poised to smash the thing into pulp with her geometry book.

Looking at the unkempt feline bathing itself on the counter, she reached up and closed the window. "All right, cat," she said, the word cat coming out like an invective, "you can stay the night. But once the rain lets up, you are out of here." Looking in the refrigerator for something to feed it, she found some tuna salad and milk and put them out on saucers. "Jesus," she muttered. "First Paulpry, now this!" The cat, purring like it had something broken inside, little squeaks and rusty sounds mingled in with the normal sounds, tucked into the milk and tuna. Al picked up her weapon and weaved unsteadily down the hall toward her bedroom.

She slept that night. Once she awakened to the squeaky, chirpy, grinding purr of the cat in her bed. For some reason, she did not fling the horrid thing across the room. Instead, she murmured, "I hope you don't have fleas," and went back to a deep, restful and thankfully dreamless sleep. She awoke about seven the next morning, muzzy-headed from the wine, with only a vaguest recollection of the night before. Stumbling toward the bathroom, she stepped in something cold and gooey. Looking down, she yelled, "Cat shit!" at the top of her lungs, suddenly remembering the feline.

"What the hell was I thinking!" she asked the universe, very loudly. Al had decided many years ago that the universe, or any power that existed beyond her mortal ken was, at best, hard of hearing and, most days, completely deaf. After cleaning off her foot and the mess on her hallway carpet, she went in search of the cat, intent on taking it straight to the city pound. If it stayed there its allotted seven days and was euthanized, it was not her fault. Someone else would bear the brunt of the Karmic debt for its demise. The cat, however, seemed to have other ideas. It was gone. Al peeked and poked into every nook and cranny for two hours, but the wretched little feline was nowhere to be found. The doors and windows were closed tightly and locked, the closet and cabinet doors were shut and there was precious little furniture under which it could hide. It was simply gone. After her fruitless search, which did serve to burn off the worst of her hangover, she decided she must have gotten up in the night and evicted the flea-bearing little trespasser. "Good," she stated firmly as she headed for a shower.

Rob Paulpry always slept in on Sunday. He hadn't always done so, but, since his downfall in the journalistic world, he rarely had reason to get up early on his day off and scour the alleys and crack houses for a lead. After everything that had happened last night, he was amazed he had been able to sleep at all. He still could not get the image of the mangled body of Spike scattered around that alley like a broken bag of garbage out of his mind. Rolling over to look at his alarm clock, he saw that it was ten a.m. The morning sunlight was a little brighter coming in through the windows of his small bedroom than it had been in several days. Rob took this as a good sign. He knew he'd feel better if the rain would let up for a while. Preferably before the snow set in. Years ago, Rob had come to the conclusion that he was solar powered. If he didn't see the sun for a few days, he simply ran out of energy, on both a mental and physical level. Off in the distance, he heard a siren which brought his thoughts back to the lovely Detective Lieutenant Alisha Ferdinand. She was a puzzle, for certain, and obviously did not like him or anything he did or stood for, but there was an odd feeling of kinship there. He couldn't explain it, but he felt it deep down. Thinking of her reminded him of the flash (which was what he had decided to call it, 'vision' seemed too...neat, for lack of a better word) he had experienced when he looked at the photos of the carnage in the alley behind MacMurphy's. Not wanting to relive that experience, he pried open his eyes and looked around himself. It was an early morning ritual he had practiced since he was a child, reorienting with the real world he called it.

When he had inherited the little two bedroom house from his Uncle Ted, the sound of sirens was not common in the nice, neat little residential neighborhood. That was one of the things he liked the most about the house. Its location was far removed from the cesspool in which he swam for his daily bread. An isolated island of sanity in his otherwise wildly insane world. But in the past few years, the craziness had begun creeping closer. Just a month ago, there had been a raid on a meth lab just two blocks behind his cozy little suburban bungalow. He lay in his bed staring up at the pale yellow ceiling, his eyes tracing the familiar crack which had run across the ceiling for as long as he had been in the house. He tried to put everything into some sort of order, but the pieces just would not fit together.

Despite her promise of cooperation, Detective Ferdinand had not been very forthcoming with information. She had, of course, promised more and Rob had to admit to himself he had withheld several key pieces of knowledge. It was how the game was played, each side only giving out what they had to in order to keep the partnership working to his or her own advantage. He had to admit, that Alisha Ferdinand was one cop who could easily get him to spill more than he intended. Not only was she that good, but she was gorgeous and knew how to use it. "Careful, Robby, old boy," he cautioned himself. "You wouldn't want to let her get too far ahead in the game."

With some effort, he hauled himself out of the warm cocoon of his bed and padded down the hallway to the bathroom. He had never bothered to redecorate the house and it still bore the unique stamp of his Uncle Ted. Everyone knew that Uncle Ted was gay and that his "roommate", Phil, was much more than a roommate, but Rob was the only one who was honest about it. He had loved his uncle and

Phil, too, because he made Ted happy. Whenever he was there for one of his all too infrequent visits, he jokingly referred to Phil as "Aunt Phil". When Phil died, something in Ted died, too. It was Rob who had bullied the few and scattered members of the family into letting Ted be buried next to Phil. He had purchased the plots and double headstone himself. Now, sitting at the 1950's grey and red Formica-topped table in the tiny kitchen, he felt the loss all over again.

Shaking his head, he got up to steal a cup of coffee from the half finished pot and reasoned with himself that this was a reaction to Spike's death. Whatever he thought of the little rat, Spike had been a part of his life for several years and, in a perverse way, Rob knew he was going to miss him.

Frank was worried about Al. She had always been a little sketchy, but had a quick and brilliant mind and good judgment. He was not doubting her intelligence this morning as he sipped a cup of burnt coffee at his desk in the bull pen, but her judgment. He couldn't believe that she had taken up with that lowlife, Paulpry. After their meeting last night, he had done some digging into the reporter's past. His mother had killed herself. She had walked to the center of the Fifteenth Street Bridge in the middle of February and jumped into the river. No note, no explanation, nothing. Her daughter had died in a fire not too long before, so it was assumed that was what had triggered the suicide. There had been rumors that she was some kind of psychic, and apparently her son believed all of it. When he had been taken in by the fake medium, which Frank considered a redundant phrase, his career had gone to shit. Yet, here he was, a consultant, Al had called him, on a string of very high profile and, frankly, weird-ass fucking cases.

Frank was almost worried enough to talk to Dr. Morrissey, the department shrink, but not yet. He felt he needed to keep the lines of communication open and knew that Al would find out and shut him out if he went to the Doc. So, Frank worried. What else could he do?

"Well, for one thing," he muttered to himself, "you can go home and get some sleep." He left the half filled styrofoam cup of cold coffee on his desk and headed toward the door. As he passed by the mailboxes by the front desk, Frank noticed the Bingo flier he had tucked in Al's box on his way out last night. He had never made it home. He was too confused and worried to relax, so he had gone back to the alley behind the tavern where the Friedman punk had been beaten to an unrecognizable pulp. He hadn't been able to learn anything more at the scene, so had returned to the precinct and brooded over a stack of overdue reports.

He pulled the flier out of Al's box and stared at the obvious mistake in the Bingo card and decided to swing by the church and check it out. He didn't have a clue how the flier related to any of the cases, but it bothered him and was something he could actually do. Hell, for all he knew, Al had taken up Bingo, or worse, Catholicism.

He waved to Sergeant Porter at the desk, who said, "Good morning, Sergeant McDonnell," and then, "be careful." Frank thought that an odd thing for the lanky, perfectly pressed, buttoned down desk sergeant to say. He grunted an unintelligible reply and headed out into the parking lot, still shaking his head. In all the years he had been on the force, Frank had seen a lot and experienced some strange shit, but this was like a perfect storm of weirdness. He'd never seen anything like it, not all at once like this anyway. As he pulled out of the lot and nosed his car in the direction of Eden Park, Frank felt a chill pass over him. His granny had always said it was someone walking on your grave. Frank laughed to himself. More like too much coffee, too little sleep and too much worry about Al.

There had been many times in his long life that Porter had been forced to remind himself that it was not his place to interfere with events, but to let them unfold. At times like this, it was difficult. He liked Sergeant McDonnell and hated to see anything happen to him. He was not certain that anything was going to happen, so much depended on free will, but he had a bad feeling. He could ask

Gloria, and, if she looked in the right direction, she could tell him, in perfect detail exactly what, if anything, was about to befall the sergeant. But, since they were forbidden to interfere with free will, they would both be helpless to prevent any calamity which came as a result. She would be upset by the information and might lose her focus at a crucial moment. No being ever loved its fellow creatures more than Gloria but, sometimes, that unbounded love could be a detriment to their task. He would remain silent on the matter and simply send out a prayer. Gloria would be upset with him for not doing something, but, in the end, she knew the rules and understood their necessity.

Porter's reverie was interrupted by his replacement, Sergeant Stan Robertson, loudly slamming his log book down on the desk and asking, "Well, Porter, what's the scoop?" Sergeant Robertson did not like Porter. He felt he was too put together and squared away to be real. He preferred his cops look more like him or Detective Sergeant McDonnell, who he had passed on his way in, rumpled, slightly askew, in other words, real. He secretly suspected that Porter was a fag. Not that there was anything wrong with that, as long as they kept to themselves. He didn't even have a problem with them on the force. He felt that the nineteenth precinct was the best place for them. The nineteenth had McCleary St. with its row of gay bars and the Temple of Eros Bath House. Vice had tried for years to shut the temple down, but could never get the evidence that there was anything but consensual sex going on in there. Of course, in Robertson's opinion, that should be enough. It's not that he cared who had sex with whom, but that was just unnatural. Five years ago the state legislature had stricken down the laws against consensual sodomy as unconstitutional and Robertson still felt queasy whenever he thought about it.

He took report from Porter and settled in. He liked day shift on Sundays. The drunks were all either sleeping it off in the drunk tank, or an alley somewhere, the perverts were in bed with each other, and the God-fearing were in church. Sundays were generally nice and quiet which was how Stan Robertson liked it. He was usually nursing a hangover on Sunday morning and this Sunday morning was no exception. It wasn't one of the real skull-splitters he sometimes had, but it had teeth to it all the same.

He didn't see himself as a drunk, just a regular guy who had a stressful job, an alimony spending bitch of an ex-wife, two greedy kids he never saw or heard from except when they wanted something, and a generally crappy existence which was, of course, no fault of his own, at least in his own opinion. He deserved the occasional, make that nightly, drink to relax. His drinking was not compulsive or destructive. It was medicinal.

As there was no one in the lobby at the moment, Stan took the opportunity to take a dose of medicine from the large thermos jug he carried for just that purpose. "Ahh, mother's milk," he sighed contentedly, took the sports section out of the paper on the desk, put on his, "Don't fuck with me" face, and settled into the creaky old wooden swivel chair with his scuffed and worn shoes up on the desk.

Gloria unnecessarily polished the counter at the Koffee Kup. It was sparklingly clean already, but it made her look busy and, besides, she enjoyed doing what many others felt were menial tasks. She had a broader view of things than most and understood that there were no truly menial tasks, that every action was meaningful and the repercussions from everything rippled out through the cosmos, creating vast changes in the fabric of what most people considered reality. So, she polished the counter.

She looked up as the bell over the door jingled. It was one of her few regulars, Mr. Albert Stone. Gloria knew that was his real name, though he had never given it to her. Mr. Stone had been on the streets since his family had perished in a horrible house fire, for which he had blamed himself. He had been intending to install the smoke detectors the following weekend, when he returned home from his business trip. Albert had not been one of those stereotypically self-centered, negligent, career-centered men about whom you hear. He was a true family man. His wife, Ella and two daughters, Sam (Samantha, though she did not like to be called that), eight years old and Lucy (just Lucy), ten, were truly the center of his world. The only reason he tolerated the frequent absences for business was because he was providing a good life for his girls. When he had pulled down the street in the nice residential neighborhood on the north side of the city and had seen all of the emergency vehicles, his chest clenched and a great emptiness had opened up within him, as though everything had been sucked out, leaving him hollow. He hadn't called from the train station to let them know he was home, it was two days early and he was hoping to get home before anyone was up and have breakfast ready for them. He'd often thought that maybe, if he had called, he would have awakened his wife and they might have escaped, or if he had gotten the smoke detectors up or a host of other reasons he had come up with over the years to blame himself.

He had not told Gloria any of this, she just knew. It was part of her to know, because one could not truly love all beings as she did without knowing everything about their pasts. She could, if she wished, have even known all about the future of any creature she encountered, but Gloria had vowed long ago, very long ago, not to peek forward unless it was of the utmost urgency to do so. Too often, the possibilities of the future were just too much for her to bear. She never saw just one outcome when she dared look ahead in time, but all of the possibilities of every possible choice that could be made. The farther ahead she looked, the more possibilities opened up, and whatever she saw, she was powerless to interfere.

Warily, Albert sat down at the counter and Gloria put a plate of scrambled eggs and bacon with a side of whole wheat toast down in front of him along with a steaming mug of coffee. Like everyone else who came into the Koffee Kup, Albert never questioned the miraculous rapidity of the service or the lack of a cook in the kitchen. Of course, Albert never questioned or commented on anything. In fact, he had not spoken for eight years. He had walked away from the plot containing the remains of his wife and daughters, leaving his car parked on the little gravel drive of the cemetery and had not spoken a single word since, not out loud, anyway. Most people didn't even see Albert when they encountered him on the street. Those who did, wrote him off as worthless, Gloria knew better. All beings had a place in the grand scheme, even if it was not readily apparent.

As Gloria was refilling Albert's cup, the door jingled open again and Porter walked in, and Gloria knew he was worried about something before she even looked at him. Of course Porter was the one being she could not read like a billboard. It was necessary, she knew, but, still, it frustrated her. He nodded and said hello to Albert, who of course, did not respond aloud, took his regular stool, and sipped the mug Gloria set in front of him. His expression verified her first impression, but he remained silent, as she knew he would.

Alisha's Journal,
May 15, 2010

I was at a funeral, a Catholic funeral. With all the Catholic cops she and her father had known, she could recognize one instantly. The church was dark, incredibly, eye-strainingly dark. The priest in his old fashioned cassock and wide-brimmed hat came down the aisle swinging his censer and flinging holy water left and right from a ridiculously oversized aspergillum. As he neared where I sat, I saw that the censer had flames licking out of it and was putting out huge clouds of smoke. The priest drew abreast of me, swinging and flinging smoke and water. The smoke from the incense hit me first and I thought I was going to throw up. Incense smoke had always bothered me due to my acute sense of smell, but this was different, it smelled like a pile of rotting corpses in the Summer. As I tried to rise, I felt the droplets from the aspergillum strike my arm. They were warm and viscous, not cool and liquid like they should have been. Looking down, I saw, in the sudden flare of the candles on the ends of the pews, that it was blood. Now that there was more light, I saw the rows of uniformed officers around me. This was a cop's funeral. Behind the priest came the casket, draped in the ceremonial flag, with a gold badge resting atop it, the deceased had been a detective. As the coffin passed, there was a thump as though a wheel had run over something in the aisle and the badge slid off into my lap. Looking down, I immediately recognized the badge number, it was Frank's badge! The priest looked down at me and laughed an all too familiar laugh. It was the Bad Man. Over the laughter, I heard the thumping again and again, and cries from inside the casket.

CHAPTER SEVEN

Frank parked on the street on the east side of Eden Park and looked up at the church. He would have sworn on a stack of bibles and anything else you wanted him to that there had never been a church here. But the building was old and worn, the stone steps had that sagging look they get from decades of footsteps wearing concavities along their centers and the wood framing the door was faded and a little splintered in places. In short, at least as far as the outward appearance, the building had been there a long time. Even the three brass address numbers were darkly tarnished with verdigris around the edges. 416 South Nodaway, Frank checked the address on the Bingo flier, it was the right place, but something just felt very wrong to him. The street sign on the corner had been damaged at some point in the past, half of it was missing, so it just read, "Nod".

Frank got out of his car and crossed the pothole-filled ruin of a street and approached the broad worn steps. Suddenly, there was a man in front of him, a street person, filthy and reeking. He looked at Frank with tears in his eyes and shook his head. Frank stepped around him and the man moved to intercept him, holding his hands out in front of himself, he appeared to be trying to prevent Frank from entering the church. "Move along, buddy," he growled, flinging a handful of change in the derelicts direction. Surprisingly, the bum ignored the money and continued to impede Frank's passage. "Look," Frank explained, less than patiently, "unless you want to spend the night down in the holding cell at the Fourteenth, move...out...of...my...way!" He gave the shaggy, silent, homeless man a shove. It wasn't a hard shove, more in the manner of a gentle nudge. The filthy man stumbled back, landing on his butt on the lowest step and just sat there, staring up at the cop with tears streaming down his face. "Oh, come on, I didn't hurt you," Frank cajoled, his anger momentarily spent. Digging into his pocket, he pulled out a twenty and shoved it at the man. "Get yourself a meal or a bottle, or a fix, whatever it is you need." Once again, the pitiful man just ignored the money and looked pleadingly at the gruff detective. Frank just shook his head. "Look, fella," he said, "I don't know what your problem is with me, or the church, or, maybe, God, but I'm goin' in there, so why don't you just beat it."

Albert Stone just sat on the step and watched the big cop climb up to the portal, tears running down his cheeks to disappear into his matted beard. This was going to be bad, he knew it somehow. He had the same empty feeling he had experienced a lifetime ago when everything had been pulled out from under his feet. He had no idea how he knew it, or what had brought him here to this place to try and prevent what was coming. There was great evil emanating from the phony church like a dark cloud, how could the cop not feel it? Albert silently wept bitter tears.

Frank climbed the thirteen steps to the door of the church and tried the handle. Surprisingly for this neighborhood, it was unlocked. He pushed the door and it groaned open on rusty hinges. Inside, the building was dark, very dark. Frank found a light switch on the wall and tried it. It was one of the old push button ones. He pushed the two buttons in and out a few times with no effect. "Figures," he grumbled. "Hello," he called. "Anybody here? Police, I have a few questions." In the answering silence, Frank suddenly realized he didn't actually have any questions. At least, not any that made any sense. He had the Bingo flier in his pocket with the fucked-up numbering, but what was he going to do, accuse the priest of running a crooked Bingo game? His eyes had adjusted enough to the gloom inside the building to make out details. The entire place spoke of much use, but in the distant past. There were signs that, at least in recent years, the church had been largely forgotten and abandoned. The faded runner in the aisle, once a deep crimson, was threadbare down the center, but covered with about an inch and a half of dust. The pews looked tired and disused. They, too, were covered in dust and cobwebs with a few hymnals scattered about in the seats. He noticed, too, that it was unbelievably cold inside the church, like a walk in cooler or freezer. He could see his breath. Frank had just about decided no one was, or had been here in a very long time and was turning to go when he felt a tremendous impact on his back. Someone had hit him!

Turning around as he straightened, Frank reached for his weapon and saw the biggest priest he had ever seen. He was wearing an old fashioned cassock like the one Bing Crosby had worn in those old movies and a wide-brimmed hat which obscured his face in shadow. Somehow, the huge bastard had crept up behind him while he was musing over the condition of the church. "Hold it, Padre, I'm a cop," he said, pointing at the badge hanging in its leather holder out of his jacket pocket.

In a gravelly, deep bass, the priest said, "I know who you are, Detective Sergeant Frank McDonnell. Otherwise I would not have been able to call you hence and give you the message."

"Message?" Frank replied, now thoroughly confused. "What message and for who?"

"For whom," the priest corrected, reminding Frank of the priests and nuns at the Catholic school he had attended as a boy. "For the one you hold dearest," he went on, cryptically. "She is the one I want...no, need." She? Did he mean Al? Suddenly Frank was more afraid than he could ever remember being, but he hid it as well as he could.

"I know you down to the very essence of your being." The huge priest was advancing slowly as he spoke. "I know about your career, about your pitiful life outside the precinct, about your relationships, all of them, but, particularly the one with her. The only woman you have ever loved. You believe that it is a paternal love, like an uncle, but deep inside you know better. It is a burning intense desire, you wish to possess her, but know you never will. So, do you know why you cannot possess Alisha, Uncle Frank? Because she is mine. Is and always has been from the moment of her birth and for centuries before." The giant clergyman was making no sense at all. Frank could tell he was off his rocker. Keeping his weapon trained on the slowly approaching figure, he reached for his radio to call for backup. Before he could get the walkie to his mouth, it was slapped from his hand and sent spinning across the abandoned church to shatter on the door of a confessional.

"Just stop right there," he commanded, unable to figure out how the big sonofabitch had gotten so close to him so fast. "I'm going to have to ask you to step back and get down on your knees with your hands behind your head, facing away from me."

The priest laughed, and the sound sent waves of cold fear through the detective's soul. "Kneel? Before you?" Again, the laughter. "I kneel before no being. I tire of this game," he announced. Suddenly the priest's huge hand closed over Frank's gun hand, squeezing with tremendous force, he felt bones breaking and heard a cry, which he realized a moment later had come from his own throat. The priest's other hand grabbed the left side of his jacket, ripping his shield from his pocket and flinging him away like a rag doll. Frank landed on top of one of the pews, tipping it over and pinning his leg beneath it. Again, there was the sickening crunch of a broken bone, but Frank managed to keep from crying out this time. Instantly, it seemed, his assailant was upon him again, lifting him up with one hand, no mean feat as Frank had put on some pounds over the past couple of years and weighed in at a good two twenty five. Holding Frank up in the air like a toy, the priest punched him in the face repeatedly, shaking him hard, like a dog worrying its favorite toy whenever he tried to defend himself. The priest carried the cop to the doorway and flung him out to land hard on the steps, the back of his head bouncing on the worn stone. Frank's vision, already blinded by the sunlight after the gloomy interior of the church, sparkled and started to fade. The last thing he saw before blacking out was the priest leveling Frank's own weapon at him. He heard the concussion, and everything went black.

Seeing the police detective come flying out the door of the church, Albert knew what he had been sent here to do. At first, he had thought it was to stop him from entering the church, but that wasn't it. In a way that was comforting to Albert because it meant he had not, after all failed in his task. He saw the evil creature masquerading as a priest step out and raise the pistol to shoot the policeman. At the last possible instant, Albert Stone fulfilled the destiny set out for him longer ago than he could imagine. He rose up from the step and placed himself directly in the line of fire.

At the Koffee Kup Kafe, Gloria cried out and Porter stiffened. The policeman looked into the tear-filled eyes of the waitress and spoke into his radio. "Shots fired, officer down, 416 South Nodaway." Gloria turned without a word, though there was much she wanted to say and began singing an ancient dirge.

Albert knew he was dying. The bullet in his chest burned like a white-hot poker. But, he did not despair or fear the approach of death. The important part that made him Albert Stone had died eight years ago. As he felt the world slipping away and the sunlight began to fade, that cold, dark, empty place in the center of his being which had once housed his soul, filled with light. The warmth flooded him and he was at peace. As he slipped into oblivion, he could hear the sweet, angelic voice of Gloria, the waitress at the Koffee Kup Kafe singing in an ancient tongue, what he knew was his funeral song. In the final moments of his corporeal existence, Albert Stone became himself once more and understood everything. As he slipped away, he was filled with peace, joy, and satisfaction at having played his part.

Al heard the call as she was headed into the precinct and whipped her car around, flipped on the light and siren, and plunged headlong into The End. Arriving, at the address, her heart froze in her chest. Sitting across the street from the church was Frank's car, and on the steps leading up to the edifice, the coroner was zipping a body bag. She leapt from her car, leaving it running and the driver's side door hanging open and dashed up to the steps, looking frantically around for Frank and muttering, "No, no, no..." under her breath.

Her headlong flight was suddenly halted as someone threw their arms around her. Raising her foot to stamp on her attacker's instep, she heard a familiar voice in her ear. "It's not him, Lieutenant," said Rob Paulpry. Rob had caught the call on his scanner and had arrived on the scene just as the paramedics were loading Frank into the ambulance. He was somehow conscious, though one of the medics said he didn't know how he had even survived the beating he had taken.

Frank saw Rob and called him over, glaring down the medic who had tried to tell him to lie still and let them load him into the rig. He whispered, "Pocket". Rob saw a folded piece of paper and, looking at the paramedic, who held up his hands, withdrew it. "Give it to Al," the sergeant had ordered him. "The priest is after her, tell her to be careful." The medic gave Frank an injection and he quieted down enough to allow them to load him and speed of toward St. Luke's.

Rob explained all of this to Detective Ferdinand as she stood on the steps of the church, taking in the scene. "Stay here," she commanded Rob and walked up the steps. "Who's in the bag?" she asked the tech from the coroner's office who had just loaded the body bag onto his gurney.

"A derelict, no ID, but it looks like he saved Sergeant McDonnell. Took a bullet for him."

"Did anybody see the priest?" Al asked.

The tech shook his head, "Place looks like nobody's been here for a long time, if you ask me," he replied, motioning to one of his colleagues to help him carry the gurney down to the van.

She looked down at the paper in her hand, the one Frank had instructed Paulpry to give her. Unfolding it, she saw that it was the Bingo flier she had lost. Frank had written, "Not right" in the margins and drawn an arrow from G-48 to the 'N' column. Al felt a cold chill slither down her spine. Then she heard an argument from down at the bottom of the steps, a uniform was trying to remove the reporter from the scene.

"Officer," she called. When the young cop looked up, she said, "It's OK, he's a consultant, he's with me." She hoped it was not a mistake bringing the reporter in on this strange series of cases, but, somehow, it felt right. Her dad had always encouraged her to trust her gut. "Paulpry," she called as she descended the steps. "I'm going to the hospital to check on Frank, meet me in an hour at the precinct." She didn't wait for an answer, she knew he'd come. She sprinted up the street to where her car sat, door open, still running and jumped into the driver's seat. Looking down as she fastened her seat belt, she saw two objects lying on the seat, both covered in blood. One was Frank's sidearm, the hammer still cocked. It took her a minute to recognize the other, it was his shield, but it was bent and mangled. It looked like someone had crumpled it like you would a used tissue.

Always a cop, despite her feelings, she threw the transmission into park and flagged down one of the crime lab techs who was just loading his kit into his vehicle. The tech photographed everything, unloaded the gun, verifying that there was one round missing and that the shells matched the casing they had found on the steps. Frank's assailant had tried to shoot him with his own weapon. He bagged up the pistol and badge, gave Al some advice on cleaning the blood out of her upholstery and she sped off toward St. Luke's. 'The Case of the Pugilistic Priest,' she thought wryly as she pulled away, 'Frank would like that one'. Then the tears started.

CHAPTER EIGHT

Rob headed straight for the Fourteenth Precinct. On the way he pulled his electronic umbilical cord out of his jacket pocket and dialed the paper. When Jeannie, the secretary who worked at the front desk, answered, he told her he was sick and didn't know when he'd be back in, then he asked her to have Morton cover his assignments. That'd teach the sanctimonious SOB. Then, he turned off the cell so that Helen couldn't call him back. He knew he'd have to tread lightly and use every trick he had learned over the years to keep this story for himself. Sure, there had already been a two paragraph piece on the fold of page two about Lennie's murder and the incident at the church would, no doubt, be covered. But, the real story was his, all he had to do was figure out what in hell it was.

Given the extent of his injuries, Rob felt pretty certain that the same attacker who had killed the Abells and Lennie had been the one who worked Frank over. But the rest just didn't make any sense. Why did Frank call him 'the priest'? Why was he apparently after Lieutenant Ferdinand?...There were a lot more questions than answers at this point and Rob did not like it. He liked answers, and he liked getting them before anyone else. He needed to be back in the game, out in the field reporting real stories, not tied to a desk combing through reports of hookers and bar fights. He knew that this story would give him back what he had lost, his job, his self-esteem, and mostly, his credibility. All he had to do was untangle it and figure out just what the hell the story was. Even with the confused mess of this story, Rob felt good, like he was back in the game at last. His mind was clicking along on all cylinders (some of which he hadn't used in quite a while), and the fog was lifting.

As he drove through the dilapidated streets on the outskirts of The End, toward the Fourteenth, he noticed the light was dimming out. Dark clouds were reclaiming the sky once again, promising rain. Rob shivered, though he wasn't cold.

Frank was in surgery when Al arrived at the hospital. The nurse she cornered didn't know anything except that it would be awhile before he came out and that he was listed in serious condition. Al knew that not even her badge would get information out of the hospital staff in this day of medical privacy, but she and Frank had taken care of that. She was listed on all his information as his niece and contact person and he was listed as her uncle on hers. No one ever questioned them about it, but the fact was they were the closest thing to family that either of them had. Sometimes Al felt loved and comforted by this, and sometimes she just felt sad. Today she just felt worried.

The nurse promised to come out and tell her as soon as she had any word. Feeling frustrated and helpless, Al went out to the waiting area and paced for awhile, then she decided to make some calls. Her first call was to the lab. The head CSI on duty today was an old friend of her father's, Mitch Gunderson, he answered the phone on the fourth ring. "Gunderson," he sounded harried and more than a little grumpy, understandable given the circumstances. He softened his tone when she identified herself. Of course, it was too soon to have much in the way of answers. What he could tell her was that all of the blood on the pistol and badge belonged to Frank, that he agreed that the badge looked like someone had crumpled it, he surmised that the attacker must have been high on PCP. How else could he have exerted that kind of force and done so much damage to Sergeant McDonnell?

The strangest thing, however, was that, in going over the crime scene photos, something had jumped out at him. Though it was obvious that the assault had occurred inside the church, there appeared to be only one set of footprints in the many years of dust. As far a he could tell, the footprints were all a match to Sergeant McDonnell's shoes.

Al thanked him, elicited a promise that he would call her first as soon as he had any more information, hung up her phone and paced some more. She hated waiting. It was her least favorite part of the job. The little waiting room was typical. Bland beige walls, ugly, industrial grade indoor/outdoor carpeting on the floor, and five highly uncomfortable chairs. The lighting was bad and the stack of magazines on the little round table in the corner were older than the Merlot she had been drinking the night before.

The young nurse she had spoken with earlier bustled by with a navy blue jacket on over her teal scrubs, apparently going home for the day. Al stopped her by stepping into her path. The poor nurse was startled so badly that she dropped her purse. "I'm sorry, Miss Ferdinand," she stammered.

"That's Lieutenant Ferdinand," Al corrected, pulling her jacket aside to show the girl the gold badge clipped to the waistband of her pants.

"Yes, Lieutenant," the nurse corrected, obviously intimidated. That was exactly the effect Al had wanted. She didn't have time for being nice. Frank was somewhere in this God-forsaken death factory, his attacker was out somewhere in The End, and she felt helpless. She hated feeling helpless. "Mr....I mean Sergeant McDonnell," the nurse corrected quickly, "just got out of surgery. He's up in ICU. They are watching his intracranial pressure because of the head wounds. They were able to pin the fractured femur and repair most of the damage to his hand. He stable, for the moment. The doctor said your uncle is one tough cookie to have survived a beating like that."

Before the girl could finish her sentence, Al was striding off toward the elevator at the end of the hall. She knew they wouldn't let her stay in ICU, but she had to at least see him. As she stepped out of the elevator on the seventh floor, she experienced one of those weird time warp feelings. For a moment, she was a teenager again, visiting her grandmother. The hospital had bent the rules considerably, allowing her to come up to the Neuro ICU with her father, but it would be the only chance to say goodbye. Her grandmother had experienced a severe stroke a few days before, and the doctors had been unable to stop the bleeding in her brain.

Al shook her head to clear it, this was no time for her to slip into the past. Gram was gone and Frank needed her now. The nurses station was centrally located with the rooms encircling it. The front walls of the rooms were glass with curtains which could be pulled for privacy. Three of the six rooms were occupied. Al glanced at the whiteboard behind the desk and noted that Frank was in bed four.

He looked like hell. His head was swathed in bandages, his face was hardly recognizable it was so swollen and bruised, and he had IV's, monitor wires and an oxygen tube running from him to various bags, sockets and machines. His right hand was propped up on a foam wedge and bandaged, with wires through his fingers connected to rubber bands which pulled the fingers into a curled position. His left leg was also elevated. "Oh, Frank," she murmured with tears in her voice.

"Miss," came a voice from behind her. Startled, she turned quickly, her hand going to her pistol. "Hey," said the older, tough-looking nurse, "Don't shoot the messenger." The nurse was unfazed by the presence of the young woman with a gun in her ICU. "Look, honey, Amy called up and said she thought you were coming up here. The rules say no visitors, but since you're family, I decided to give you a few minutes, but you really have to go now. The surgeon is due to check back in with him any time now and if he finds you here it will be both our asses." Al couldn't help but like the nurse.

"Is...Is he ..." she started, unable to finish.

"Is he going to be all right?" the nurse whose name tag Alisha saw read B. Badke, RN, finished for her. "That's in God's hands right now, all we can do is our best, and the best way you can help him is to get out of the way and let us do our work. But a few prayers probably wouldn't hurt." Al thanked the woman and, after making sure they had all of her contact information, headed back down the hall to the elevator.

Leaning her forehead against the cool metal of the elevator door, Al just stood, not pressing any buttons, or moving for a few minutes and let everything that had happened wash over her. The murder, the assault on the drunk, the killing behind the bar, the cat, the reporter...the reporter! She suddenly realized she had left Rob Paulpry waiting for her back at the Fourteenth for, she looked at her watch, five hours! He had probably gone home, she reasoned to herself, but dialed his cell just to make sure. It went straight to voice mail. "Paulpry," she said into the phone, "I hope you got smart and went home. Call me at the precinct tomorrow and we'll talk."

As she put the phone back into her pocket, she felt something there. It was the Bingo flier with Frank's cryptic notes scrawled on it. What the hell did it mean?

Rob Paulpry had always thought of himself as a patient man, but Alisha Ferdinand was stretching his definition of patient to the limit. When he'd walked in, he had startled the desk sergeant, who appeared to be dozing in what looked like an alcohol induced state. He'd nearly fallen off his chair, and had not been particularly hospitable. He didn't believe Rob was there to see Lieutenant Ferdinand, had refused to call her to verify, and then, had proceeded to ignore him, turning on the previously silent scanner and pretending to be busy. That was all right, Rob knew how to play the waiting game.

Five hours later, he felt like he was losing the game and decided that Lieutenant Ferdinand was not going to show up after all. She was probably still at the hospital with the sergeant. He headed out the door, to the obvious relief of the slovenly desk sergeant, who he saw reaching over to turn off the scanner, and crossed the parking lot in the late afternoon gloom to his car. The clouds seemed to be setting right on top of the building and were darker than ever. Rob felt the old tingle. Call it his reporter's intuition, a hunch, whatever, he knew something was about to break. Knowing full well that it would probably be nothing more than Helen the Barbarian screeching at him for calling in to work, he turned his cell back on. There was only one message. In some perverse way, that made Rob fell neglected and unwanted. There had been a day when he couldn't leave to take a piss without ten people looking for him.

Much to his surprise, the caller was not Helen Corydon, Editor from Hell, but Lieutenant Alisha Ferdinand, telling him to call her tomorrow. Well, that was a start. From what Rob had been able to glean from his investigation thus far, that was the closest any reporter had ever gotten to her. He drove aimlessly for a while, between the hunch and his hurt feelings over not being missed, Rob knew he couldn't just go home. However, he had no idea what to do at this point. As he meandered the streets around the outskirts of The End, he went back over everything he had learned so far. More to the point, he went over what he hadn't learned. He had no idea how the bank robbery, the murder of the Abell brothers, the brutal slaying of Spike, and the attack of Sergeant McDonnell were linked. But he knew that they were.

Finally, he pulled into a convenience store in a well lit, affluent neighborhood a few blocks from The End. There was a police cruiser parked near the entrance and he could see the officer inside talking to the pretty young woman behind the counter.

In the elevator, Al pulled the folded paper out of her jacket pocket and looked it over once again. There was the familiar Bingo card, with G-48 circled and Frank's cryptic note and arrow. At the bottom, was the address of the church, 416 South Nodaway, under that, something she had somehow missed before, the name of the priest. It read, "Fr. Lucius Caine".

Al really did not remember getting home. After finding that name on the paper where she was certain it had not been before, she must have gone on auto pilot. One moment she had collapsed against the cool wall of the elevator, and the next, she was unlocking her door. Opening it, she had the unmistakable feeling that something was wrong. One of her instructors in the academy all those years ago, had taught the recruits what he considered the three rules of surviving as a cop. Rule one: "Listen to that little voice in the back of your head, it's always there for a reason." Rule two: "Never, EVER give up your weapon." Rule three: "You ain't T.J. Hooker." She supposed, as she drew her weapon and reached for the light switch, that if he was still teaching, he was using a new reference, or not. Alisha envisioned scores of young recruits scurrying to the video store only to discover William Shatner in one unbelievable situation after another.

Turning on the light, Al saw two things. The first was the damned cat sitting on the floor at the end of the coffee table. The second pushed aside all of the revulsion and anger at the presence of the animal. On the table were three objects, only one of which she had ever seen in her apartment before, the large baggie full of the sleeping pills she had dumped into it over the years in order to fill her prescription and keep Dr. Morrissey off her back. Though she had no idea how the baggie had gotten out here, it was the other two items she found the most disturbing. The first was a bible, it had a black cover with a name embossed in gold on the lower edge of the cover. The second was a bottle of the cheap rot gut bourbon that had been her mother's preference, with the cap off. Walking carefully over to the table, she looked down at the bible, reading the name on the cover. For only the second time in her entire life, Al fainted.

CHAPTER NINE

The first time Al had fainted was when she was fifteen years old. Her paternal grandmother had tried to fill in for Al's mother after she died. She had been there for her, listened to her, been as much of a mother as she could. After her mother's death, her grandmother had moved in with them to help her father. She had been the only adult female in Al's life in whom she felt safe confiding everything.

Grams didn't judge, only listened, gave advice when it was actually needed, and, most importantly, especially after the dreams began, believed her. With her broad views of religion, magic, and parapsychology, Grams was willing to admit any possibility. So, when her granddaughter had told her she had foreseen her mother's death, she had not tried to talk her out of the notion like all the rest of the adults she had told. Instead, she had said, "I'm so sorry you had to experience that." Just like that, she had accepted Al's explanation.

In the three years immediately following her mother's death, Al had spent many nights in Grams' room when her father was on duty. They would talk about everything, and laugh, and sometimes cry.

Grams had done a far better job of explaining about the changes in her body as she matured than the doctor or his nurse. Doctor Miller was a kind and caring old gentleman, but not so good with 'The Talk' when he was giving it to a pubescent girl. He tended to cover his nervousness with a brusque, businesslike manner which, frankly, had frightened Al. His nurse, Amy, was a little better, but still, Al left the office feeling like she was missing important parts of the puzzle. Grams had filled in the rest of the picture, in Technicolor!

She and Grams had a deal. They each promised to always be completely honest with each other. It wasn't always easy, or comfortable, but it was the only relationship Al had ever experienced which was built entirely on honesty. When her father had picked her up at school and told her that Grams was sick, in the hospital, and might not make it, Al had felt betrayed. Of course, she realized quickly, Grams hadn't betrayed her. She had no more known that this was going to happen than her granddaughter had. The dreams never seemed to warn her when she needed it. She thought that if she had dreamed this was going to happen, she could have warned Grams and maybe something could have been done to prevent it.

The worst part of the whole ordeal had been not being able to see Grams for four days. Al could not remember ever going that long without seeing her, especially in the last three years. When her father had finally threatened, begged, and cajoled the hospital staff enough, they had relented and let her up to the ICU to say goodbye. Of course the stubborn girl had refused to admit, even to herself, that this was the reason for the visit. She was going to have a talk with Grams. She needed to tell her she had been right about Jimmy McGee and Kathy Farraday, that she had gotten a ''A' on the Algebra final she'd been so worried about, and that she missed her. Despite her father's best attempts, Al was completely unprepared for what she saw when she arrived at the cubicle off the nurses station.

At first, she thought that it was a colossal joke. Grams wasn't there. There was just some shriveled husk of a woman lying in the hospital bed connected to various machines with tubes and wires. It was like something in a haunted house. She looked up at her father to ask what it was all about and saw the tears standing in his eyes. "We need to say goodbye," he choked out in a harsh stage whisper.

"No," she had cried out, turning back toward the figure on the bed.

"Yes," came a familiar voice from the chair in a dark corner of the space. Peering into the depths of shadow, Al saw Grams. She started to call out to her, but Grams put her finger to her lips, silencing her. Then she looked up at Al's father and the nurse.

"We'll leave you alone for a minute," her dad had said, ushering the nurse out.

"We don't have much time," Grams said. "What you see on the bed isn't me."

"I knew it," Al said, relieved, but was halted by Grams' raised hand. She always did that when she sensed anyone was speaking when they should be listening and it always stopped her granddaughter in her verbal tracks. Looking more closely at the figure on the chair, Al noticed a subtle glow around her, a faintly phosphorescent nimbus. "Grams," she asked quietly, "what's going on?"

"Your father is right, honey. It's time to say goodbye. I have been hanging on here until we could have one, last talk." Again, the raised hand as Al started to respond. "You have to listen, right now, Angel. I don't know how much longer I can hold on." Al nodded.

"First of all, you're going to have to be there for your dad when I'm gone," Al started to cry at this, but Grams silenced her. "No tears," she said. "We've talked about this. Remember the story about the Rabbi on the docks watching the ships going and coming. My troubles are almost over. Yours are still unfolding. I should be crying for you." Al nodded, drying her tears.

"That's better. Now, you remember what I told you about God and the devil, and good and evil? How they're all actually just a part of every one of us? Well, from where I am right now, I can see a few things. I don't know what is going to happen in the future, exactly, but I have glimmerings of things. Watch out for him, Alisha. Watch out for the Bad Man. Don't believe anyone who tries to tell you he's not real. I've seen him. I don't know who or what he is, or how he came to be, or why he is drawn to us, but he has been pursuing the women in our family, those with The Gift, for longer than you would believe.

I can look back easier from here and with more clarity than looking forward, and, though I can't see exactly how it is all going to happen, I can give you one piece of advice. You can't let your guard down where he is concerned, not for the briefest of moments. Also, he will always tell you the truth, but it will be a twisted version saturated with his own sick desires. Listen carefully to him, but dig through to the real truth and you will know what to do. Be brave, I'll be watching." Al nodded again, not trusting herself to speak and feeling suddenly very frightened and alone.

"He is the only being I have ever encountered who does not have even a tiny spark of goodness and light within him. He is made completely of the darkest stuff found in the deepest realms of our souls. We all have a bit of that, but he is all darkness and no light. But you, my precious angel have more light than anyone. If there is one person who can beat him, it's you."

She just sat and gazed at Al for a long time, then, cocked her head, as if hearing something far off. "Give me a kiss, sweetie, I have to go soon." Al started over toward the chair, but Grams shook her head and gestured toward the bed. Looking closely, Alisha could see now that the figure beneath the sheets was Grams, ravaged by the stroke and subsequent bleeding into her brain. She crossed to the bed and gently kissed the sagging, wrinkled cheek, reverently. Looking up toward the chair, she watched as the apparition sitting there slowly faded down to a single point of bright white light and was gone.

She wasn't aware of fainting, she remembered later hearing a high pitched noise and feeling something cold and hard strike her on the cheek. The next thing she recalled was being in her father's arms as he wept. She wanted to tell him it was all right, that Grams was OK, but knew he had to grieve, so she just held him and they wept together.

Rob sat in the convenience store parking lot for a long time, listening to his police scanner and going over the facts in the case so far. There was something missing. Granted, there were threads tying everything together, but they were tenuous at best. Somewhere, buried in all of this was the unifying link. He had the odd feeling that it had something to do with Lieutenant Alisha Ferdinand. She was the only connection to all of this. At least the only one he could see so far.

A sharp tapping on his side window snapped Rob out of his reverie. It was the cop he had seen inside talking to the clerk. "Everything all right here, sir?" he asked. Rob assured him that everything was, indeed all right, showed his ID and press pass and explained that he was working on a story. The officer shone his light into the back seat, a veritable trash pile to the naked, untrained eye. Rob could see him considering the monumental task of searching through it all. Instead, he called in his personal information and license plate number and advised him to go home. He was making the girl in the store nervous sitting out in the parking lot. Rob thanked the cop, closed up his laptop and, with the officer still standing beside his cruiser watching him, backed out of the lot. He wasn't sure where he was going, he just drove for awhile. Before he knew it, he saw the Granneman building coming up on the right.

He pulled into a parking space in front and saw Gloria out beside the building, bent over. He got out of his car and walked over to her. Hearing his approach, she straightened and turned toward him. "Good evening, Mr. Paulpry," she said, smiling her bright smile. At the corner of the building, Rob saw a scrawny little cat with a torn ear lapping milk out of a saucer.

"That's a pretty rough customer," he joked.

"Oh, she's one of my regulars," Gloria replied. "They're all pretty disreputable." She laughed and held the door for him. Rob laughed along with her at the small joke at his expense and followed Gloria inside, crossing to his regular booth. He opened his laptop as she brought a cup of coffee and a full carafe over to him. Setting them down on the chipped Formica, she asked, "Breaking a big story?"

"More like, it's breaking me," he replied. He turned to his computer screen to let Gloria know he wanted to be left alone to work, grabbed a handful of sugar packets, ripped them open and stirred the sweet granules into the coffee. As usual, the coffee smelled burned and even felt thick as he stirred. He looked intently at the screen of his laptop, but was not thinking about anything that was displayed there.

He was thinking about the conversation he had the with the pretty homicide detective in the interview room the night before. Alisha Ferdinand was mostly interested in Rob's mother and her visions. She had read and remembered his series of articles about the "Mystic of Fourth Avenue". She would not tell him why she was so focused on that part of his life, but reacted more than usual for her when he mentioned his mother's dreams. He knew there was something about them that stirred up something in her, but didn't know what. He also had no clue where to look to find out. then, there was the business with the Bingo flier. What the hell was that all about? The more he tried to look into things, the more questions he uncovered. But he wasn't looking for questions, dammit! He wanted answers.

He decided to stop looking at the crimes for a moment and look at the information outside them. There was an apparently abandoned church that no one could exactly remember ever having been there before, a Bingo flier from the same church, with apparently some numbering flaw on it, a twenty from a bank robbery which showed up in a bottom of the barrel dive of a bar, and a homicide detective who was more interested in his mother's prophetic dreams than what he knew about her cases. None of it seemed to tie together. The only other common denominator was the vicious nature of the murders and assault, but that didn't seem to tie in with Lieutenant Ferdinand.

Rob's mind was spinning in so many circles he was getting dizzy. As he rubbed his eyes, he heard the sound of a plate being set on the table. Looking up, he saw Gloria. "I know you didn't order it, but you looked hungry," she said. Rob suddenly realized that she was right. He hadn't eaten anything all day. He tucked into the omelet, toast, hash browns and bacon like a starving man. The food helped. He felt a little calmer and less confused. He decided he wasn't going to get anywhere sitting there with his laptop. It was time to call it a day. He would go home, get some sleep, meet Lieutenant Alisha Ferdinand at the Fourteenth tomorrow and make her tell him what was going on. He had to admit to himself, however, that he couldn't imagine anyone making her do anything. He still had a few good cards he had not yet shown. Time for a little quid pro quo, he decided.

As he rose to go, leaving a twenty on the table, Gloria called to him from behind the counter, "Be careful, Mr. Paulpry. There are a lot of bad people out this time of night." He smiled and waved to her. On the way to his car, he thought what a strange young woman she was. He couldn't remember when she came to work at the diner, and never seemed to have a day off or even to go home. Oh, well, he had stranger fish than that to fry right now. He started the car and turned on his police scanner out of habit. When he heard Alisha's voice requesting backup at the church, Rob felt his stomach clench and his heart leapt into his throat. He nearly sideswiped a fire hydrant as he peeled out in a tight U-turn and headed toward The End.

The first thing Al noticed when she came to was that the cat was gone, again. Gone, too, were the pills and the whiskey bottle, though there was a ring on the coffee table where it had sat. The bible, however, was still there. Steeling herself, she picked it up and read the gold lettering on the cover. it read, "Martha Mae Wilson," her Grams' maiden name. She recognized it though she hadn't seen it in years. It was the bible Grams had been given as a girl upon her confirmation in the Presbyterian church she had attended with her family. There had been Wilsons in the church since its founding and her father was mortified when his middle child had stopped attending. She had tried to explain that she wasn't turning away from religion, just finding her own path. Al had assumed that the bible was packed away in the storage unit with all of the things she had kept from the apartment when her dad died. How had it gotten here? And what was with the booze and pills? Had she imagined it?

The ring on the coffee table could be from something else, but she didn't have any square vases or pitchers, and the bible was still there.

Confused, she went into the bathroom to wash her face. Opening the cabinet beneath the sink, she pulled up the loose board and checked. The pills were there, sealed in their baggie, just like they should be. That settled it for her. Somebody was screwing with her and she was damned well going to find out who and make them regret it. She stormed out of her apartment, making certain that the door was locked, though it had been locked when she came home, hadn't it?

The first place she would go was the self-storage facility where her unit was. She had to see if it had been broken into and if there was any evidence pointing to who was trying to mess with her mind. The unit was locked up tightly and, when she opened it, everything inside seemed to be in its place. She shoved the keys pack into her pocket and felt the Bingo flier there again. She knew where she was going next.

There was light inside the church, illuminating the expanse of red stained glass in the front of the building. The light seemed to flicker, as though it was coming from candles. She parked her car across the street, noticing that she was parked just where Frank had been, and moved carefully toward the door. It was as likely as anything else that she was just going to surprise some teenagers partying in the building despite, or because of, the crime scene tape across the door. The door opened inward as she remembered, so the building could be entered without disturbing the tape. As she arrived at the entrance, she saw the chain and padlock the police had put on the door lying off to the side. No doubt the trespassers had used bolt cutters, kids, she thought sourly. It could be junkies shooting up, she reasoned. Either way, she proceeded carefully.

Entering the vestibule, she noticed a strange, fetid smell. No doubt the combined odors of dust, rotting carpet, dead mice, and God knew what else. Peeking in, she saw what must have been a hundred candles burning everywhere. They were old, cheap candles and let off a greasy smoke that she realized was part of the odor. She did not see anyone, so she waited in the shadows for a moment. Finally, impatience won out. Stepping out into the wavering, guttering light, she pointed her pistol and flashlight into the building, sweeping from side to side as she called out , "Police! All right, whoever you are, you are trespassing on a crime scene. I want you to come out right now and keep your hands where I can see them."

There was no reply or movement. "I mean it, come out right now!" Then, way up near the front of the church, she heard a scuffling sound and caught a motion. She took one step forward orienting her pistol on the spot. "I see you," she called. "Come out, right now!" Then, all at once, every candle blew out, and he flashlight failed. In the pitch black, she heard footsteps and a door ahead of her to the right opened.

Silhouetted in the wan light coming through the door was a big figure, quite possibly the biggest Al had ever seen, wearing a broad-brimmed hat. Her insides clenched with fear, but her reflexes and training took over. She called for backup and ran after the fleeing figure. The door stayed open, giving her enough light to pursue him, but she bashed into the end of a pew, regardless, and was still cursing as she stepped out into the night. The clouds were still heavy and low in the sky and as she tried to spot her quarry, lightning lit the night. In the momentary flash, she saw him running into an alley a block over, across an empty lot. She gave chase, flinging her useless flashlight aside.

It couldn't be him, she reasoned as she ran through the light mist which had begun to fall, greasy on her skin. He only existed in her dreams. Suddenly, her Grams' last words came back to her. What if she was right? What if he was real? She didn't have time for this nonsense right now, she chided herself. Whoever she was chasing might or might not have any answers for her, but was probably the one that hurt Frank, and she was not going to let him get away. She reached for her radio, but it was gone, she must have dropped it when she crashed into the pew. She was on her own.

She reached the mouth of the alley and flattened herself against the wall. She carefully peeked in. There were a couple of lights on inside the buildings on either side, so there was a little illumination, but she could not see any motion and the far end of the alley was totally black. She called out, "If you're in there, you need to step out where I can see you with your hands above your head." There was no response, no sound at all. She knew she had seen him run in there. She should wait for backup, but he might get away before they found her. Without her radio she had no way to tell anyone where she was, then she had a thought. "Stupid," she said, and took out her cell phone.

She dialed the precinct. The phone rang seven times and was picked up by the answering machine. Answering machine? When had they installed an answering machine, and where the hell was the desk Sergeant? She left a terse message and started to scroll down her contacts, when her phone died. "Sonofabitch!" she rasped out under her breath. She had no choice, she started down the alley, keeping to the wall and carefully checking out every doorway and shadow. The doors were all locked up tightly and she saw no evidence of any living thing. She arrived at the darkness at the end of the alley. Moving even more carefully, she edged into the blackness and came up against a brick wall. It was a dead end! She was turning around when she heard breathing and felt two huge hands grab her shoulders in a painfully tight grasp.

Al managed not to scream, but couldn't move. Her arms were pinned to her sides and she was completely immobilized. Then she felt herself being lifted off the ground and flung against the wall at the end of the alley. She landed on her knees, with the air knocked out of her. As she knelt in the wetness, trying to remember how to breathe, she heard the sound of her weapon sliding across the pavement. It bumped into her knee. "Pick it up," said a nightmare voice.

Rob arrived at the church, squealing to a stop. The Lieutenant's car was parked on the street, but there was no sign of any other police presence. He ran up to the door of the church. The crime scene tape and heavy police issue chain and padlock were in place. The mist was getting heavier, turning to rain as he circled around to the back of the building. He found a back door, likewise taped and padlocked. He called out, "Lieutenant Ferdinand, are you here?" There was no answer. As the rain began falling more heavily, he noticed something in the empty lot behind the church, a light on the ground. Running over, he found a flashlight. It was one of the big ones favored by the police, nearby lay a police issue walkie talkie. He was suddenly very worried and even more afraid.

Al picked up the pistol, still gasping for air. The voice spoke again, "You want it to end? The fear, the sleepless nights, the pain... There are two ways. Fulfill your destiny, come with me and be mine as you are meant to be. You have always been mine, as your mother before you. She hid from me in a bottle, you hid behind that worthless piece of tin clipped to your waistband." Her hand went, involuntarily, to her badge.

"The other way I think you know. I gave you a hint earlier tonight, now, here we are. Kiss your lover, or kiss the barrel of the gun. Which will it be?" Suddenly, as the rain intensified, Alisha felt the barrel of her pistol against her mouth, pushing slowly, almost sensually between her lips. She could smell the gun oil and taste the metal. Tears were streaming down her face, mixing with the rain, now a downpour. She did want it to end, but not his way. But the temptation was there, as it had been for years. One pull on the trigger, then, blessed relief.

He spoke again, as though he was reading her thoughts. "That's right, Alisha, relief. It's the only way." She felt her finger tightening on the trigger. It would be so easy.

She threw the weapon from her shouting "No!" He laughed in the darkness, then, silence, and she knew he was gone. She was wracked with sobs and drenched, kneeling in the alley. She vomited, and the smell of it mixed with the other disgusting odors, assailing her sensitive nose. She was revolted, cold, and hurting, but she was alive, and somehow, she knew she had won, if not the war, at least a battle. Looking toward the end of the alley, she saw a bright light. Was he coming back for a second round? Scrabbling in the mixture of filth and rain, she located her weapon and pointed it toward the approaching light and rose.

Rob found her, stumbling down the alley in the downpour, her weapon trained on him. "Lieutenant, it's me, Rob Paulpry," he shouted, trying to be heard over the rain. There was a terrifying moment of indecision when Rob sincerely believed she might shoot him, then she lowered her weapon. He ran over to where she stood unsteadily. She fell against him and passed out. He managed to carry her back to his car and get her into the passenger seat. "Take me home," she sobbed.

Alisha's Journal
May 18, 2010

I was sitting in Dr. Morrissey's office, but everything was wrong. I felt small. The proportions in the room were skewed. My chair was tiny, almost like I was sitting on the floor, but my legs reached the floor normally. The desk was huge, dwarfing me further. Behind it, Dr. Morrissey's chair was like a small skyscraper, I had to crane my neck to see the top of it. The back of the chair was toward me, something Morrissey never did, and he was speaking. Like everything else in the office, his voice seemed wrong. It was deep, loud, and grating. It was the voice of the Bad Man. The chair turned toward me as he was saying, "I'm glad to see that you've made your choice, Alisha. I've waited for so long, and now, I shall finally take you as mine." As the chair turned, the light shifted in the room and I saw that the desk was not a desk after all, but a mausoleum, ornately carved with sick images of pain, torture, and suffering. He stood, impossibly tall, and reached toward me. Then I heard Grams' voice telling me that there were always an infinite number of choices in any situation. Looking up at the looming figure, frozen mid-reach, I said calmly, "No".

CHAPTER TEN

For the first time since she was 12 years old, Al awoke from a dream of the Bad Man without screaming. She was still frightened, she could hear her heart pounding in her ears, but she felt calm, empowered, and hopeful. Quickly, she recorded the dream in her journal. She had learned over the years to do this before she was completely awake or she would lose pieces of the dream. It had become so much a part of her routine, that she could write down a dream before she was aware of anything else in the world around her. Once finished, she closed her eyes and did some deep breathing exercises to calm herself. When her pulse rate and breathing returned to normal, she heard another sound. It was her apartment sized washing machine spinning out a load. Alisha had done a lot of weird things in her life, but sleep laundry was a new one. As she threw back the covers, a rotten, rank smell assaulted her.

The bra and panties she wore were damp and reeked like raw sewage mixed with vomit, her hair was matted and stunk and her mouth tasted like she'd been on a four day drunk. Then, in a flash which caused an attack of vertigo, it all came back to her; the church, the alley, everything. She lay on her bed trying to sort it all out. Judging from the condition she was in, it wasn't a dream. So many times in her life, the line between her dreams and reality became so easily blurred, but this was real, she decided. Then she heard someone talking in the other room.

She listened for a minute to see if she might have left the television on, but the sound was definitely a man's voice speaking in the living room. She reached over to her night stand for her pistol and found that it wasn't in its place. Where was it? She panicked for a moment, then, calmed herself. Getting up as quietly as she could, she picked her robe up off the end of the bed and slipped it on. She applied pressure to the bedroom door as she cracked it open, to prevent any noise. She couldn't see out into the living room, but she could hear more clearly with the door cracked open. Listening, she was able to identify the voice. It was not, as she had feared, the Bad Man, it was, "Rob Paulpry," she shouted, flinging the door open. "Just what in hell are you doing in my apartment?" The startled reporter sat on the floor in a rumpled sweat suit with the logo from Pepperdine University emblazoned across the front of the shirt, playing with the cat. "And why did you let that thing back in?"

It took Rob a minute to realize just what Al was talking about. Given her state when she had stumbled out of the alley the night before, he was not surprised that she didn't remember him gingerly taking her weapon with two fingers and a shudder and more than half carrying her across the wet, slick clay of the empty field, around the church and dumping her in the passenger seat of his car. But he wasn't sure what he had let in. "You mean him?" he asked, gesturing at the cat, who was now sitting calmly licking his hindquarters. "He was sitting on my chest when I woke up this morning."

"So you just brought him here with you?"

"You really don't remember anything about last night, do you?" Rob asked. Al didn't answer. She hated admitting anything to the reporter. It wasn't that she didn't remember what had happened in the alley, but she didn't want to give him any information without first finding out how much he already knew. She stalked into the kitchen and poured herself a cup of the coffee Paulpry had obviously made.

She took her cup and headed for the bathroom for a shower. The door had barely closed when she whipped it open again and shouted, "Paulpry, what the hell is this?" Rob dashed down the hall to see what was going on.

Al stood in the hallway gesturing into the bathroom at the plastic bin on the floor. Smirking in spite of the glare in her eyes, he replied, "It's a litter box. I cleaned up your cat's little present in the hall this morning and fixed him a place to go."

"It's not my cat," she snarled, "and who told you to buy cat litter?"

"I didn't have to," Rob replied. "I had it in my car."

"That figures, you *would* have a cat." just then, the timer on the washing machine buzzed.

"Do you mind?" Rob asked, pushing past her to put the laundry in the dryer. Al saw her clothing mixed in with his and shuddered, feeling oddly violated. "No, I don't have a cat, but I do have bald tires on my car," he answered, as he stuffed the laundry into the dryer and added a fabric softener sheet. "In the winter, cat litter helps with traction if you get stuck." He closed the dryer and started out, freezing as Al saw the thing that put the whole morning over the top and shrieked at him.

"My pistol!" He'd had no idea what to do with her weapon the nigh before, so he had gingerly laid it on the sink. He figured rinsing it off would not be a good thing, but wasn't about to try to do anything else with the vile thing, so, there it lay, coated in filth from the alley and damp from the rain. "Get out of my bathroom," the livid detective fairly growled at him. "But don't you dare leave this apartment!" Rob backed carefully out into the living room, thinking it would take a bomb to get him out of this apartment right now.

She picked up the weapon. It still reeked of the alley. The hammer was cocked and the safety off. It was a minor miracle, as Grams would say, that the fool reporter hadn't shot himself. She carefully lowered the hammer, ejected the magazine and jacked the slide, cupping her hand around the ejector port to catch the round. Leaving the slide locked open, she lay the pistol back on the sink and climbed into the shower, turning it as hot as she could stand. As an afterthought, she reached out and locked the bathroom door. Living alone, she often just left the door open as she showered, but they were out there, the reporter and the cat. She was unsure which one of them she trusted the least.

Rob rolled up his sleeping bag and sat on the couch. He watched the cat lapping at he milk he had poured for it for a moment, then he looked down at the bible on the coffee table. Next to it, he noticed a square ring, as though a bottle or vase had been set there. The ring surprised him, given the otherwise fastidious condition of the apartment. He wet his finger and rubbed the sticky ring. Smelling it, he was intrigued. It was cheap bourbon. Rob Paulpry had spent a lot of time in the grips of Demon Rum in his younger days and knew the various poisons at a glance or a whiff. He hadn't noticed a bottle of bourbon when he was looking for the coffee earlier. "She probably hides it," he commented to the cat who was sitting out in the middle of the floor bathing.

The cat had surprised him as much or more than anything else this morning. He was sure it was the same one he had seen Gloria feeding outside the diner. He didn't figure Alisha Ferdinand for a cat person, and obviously, she wasn't too taken with the feline, either. "So, what are you doing here?" he asked, but of course received no more than a twitch of the cat's ragged ear. He heard the shower stop and braced himself for the onslaught. He just hoped and prayed she didn't bring the gun. She did.

Al stalked out of the bathroom, her hair still wet, carrying the pistol and her coffee cup. She put the weapon down on the coffee table and crossed to the kitchen for more coffee. Even obviously empty and open, the pistol made Rob nervous. He got up and crossed over to the chair across the room. Al, seeing his obvious discomfort, shook her head. Reaching into the top cupboard over the sink, she retrieved her gun cleaning kit, poured coffee into her mug, and crossed back over to the couch. She spread a cloth out on the table and picked up the pistol's magazine. Shucking the bullets out, she carefully wiped them down, standing them up in a row on the table, then carefully cleaned the magazine itself. That accomplished, she moved on to the pistol.

Rob watched the process with that familiar nervous feeling in the pit of his stomach. He didn't know why guns made him so nervous, but they were the one thing in the world he truly, deeply and sincerely feared. Seeing the beautiful cop handling the weapon with such calm and efficiency did nothing to allay his fears. Finally, he stood and headed to the kitchen, anything to put some distance between himself and the gun. "Mind if I make some toast?" he asked. Al shrugged and waved the pistol, momentarily pointing it his direction. Rob nearly peed his pants at the sight of the muzzle briefly pointing at him.

Al knew it was cruel and irresponsible to point her weapon at the annoying reporter, but she just could not help herself. She was mad at him, though she really didn't know why. She heard the buzzer go off signifying that the dryer was finished, which reminded her that she would need to wash her sheets. Her damp underwear had transferred the stench of the alley to them. Then, she had a realization. She closed the slide of the pistol with a loud, metallic clack and slid the magazine into it, enjoying seeing Paulpry jump at each of the sounds, then, holding the pistol casually, she stood and said, icily, "Mr. Paulpry," he turned toward her nervously. "You undressed me," she finished with menace in her tone.

Despite the knot of fear in the pit of his stomach caused by the presence of the firearm in the hands of a very angry Detective Ferdinand, Rob managed to stammer out, "Would you rather I put you in bed like you were? You smelled like a homeless wino, garbage and puke." Just then, the toaster finished, and the bread popped out. Al thought the reporter was going to have a heart attack. He jumped a good foot off the floor, then exploded. "Look, lady, you might be the toughest cop from here to the Pacific and beyond, but I pulled you out of that alley, drove you home, even washed your clothes! The least you could do is either put that gun away or shoot me! I am trying to help you here!"

"Trying to help your career, you mean," she shot back.

"The two are not mutually exclusive," he replied.

"I'll be the judge of that. Oh, and you can relax about the pistol," she gestured toward the coffee table, at the row of bullets still standing there, "it's empty. Now, bullets, or no bullets," she placed the pistol on the counter and moved back toward the couch, "gun or no gun, you are going to tell me everything that happened last night. Then you are going to tell me everything you know about these weird-assed cases and how they connect. If you don't cooperate fully, I am going to run you in for obstruction, trespass, kidnapping, and attempted sexual assault."

Rob knew she had him backed into a corner and that he had to do something to regain his position in the negotiations. Then, he remembered something she had said as they slipped and stumbled across the wet vacant lot last night. Calmly, he turned toward her and asked, "Who's the Bad Man?"

CHAPTER ELEVEN

Sergeant Robertson sat in the back corner booth in the bar. He was quite thoroughly buzzed. All hell had broken loose at the Fourteenth last night. First, he'd had to put up with that slimy reporter hanging around all afternoon, like the high and mighty Lieutenant Ferdinand would have anything to do with a lowlife like him. He knew Paulpry had been lying and had taken great pleasure in watching him slink off like that. Then the shit had hit the fan.

Sure, he'd turned the scanner off, everybody did. He told the Captain that it wasn't working right and that he'd just been about to fill out a maintenance request on it. Of course, when Captain McElroy had turned the stupid thing back on, it had worked perfectly. It was no wonder Stan Robertson hated gadgets. They always fucked with him, just like every person he had ever known.

It had been that way most of his life, starting with his father. Henry Robertson had been a big man. He'd worked hard all his life, it had made him big, strong, and angry. Henry had worked construction, the rail yards, the highway department, you name it. It seemed there was always a new job, because, just like his son, people had always fucked Henry Robertson over. Somehow, they always found some excuse to let him go. No wonder he'd turned to drinking. Stan's mom had been no help, always making his father angry. She could set him off quicker than anything, then always cried about how he treated her when she got what was coming to her. That was the big difference between father and son. Henry Robertson always made sure the assholes got what was coming to them. Stan, however, had trouble standing up for himself. That had earned him more than a few tastes of his father's ire. Unlike the whiners on the TV talk shows, Stan Robertson had used the well-deserved lessons from his father to become a better man. He was a sergeant on the police force. He carried a .357 magnum in his uniform holster, a sweet little .38 snubby in his ankle holster as backup, had a razor sharp switchblade in his pocket and two sawed-off twelves at home. Stan Robertson was ready to kick ass and take names. As usual, however, the administration chose to screw him over and put him on a desk.

When Stan had joined the force, his dad had laughed a loud, whiskey-soaked, derisive, braying laugh. "You, a cop? You little piss ant, what the hell makes you think you can be a cop? You're afraid of your own freakin' shadow!" Without thinking, Stan Robertson had rounded on his hulking, drunken father, catching the big man squarely on the jaw, knocking him backward over the coffee table. He'd run out with a vitriolic string of curses trailing him down the rickety wooden stairs. He'd never gone back. Six months later, when they'd found his father lying in a heap at the bottom of those stairs, his neck broken, Stan's primary emotion had been relief.

He had requested the Fourteenth right out of the academy. That was where all the action was. He started first day on patrol letting the pimps, whores, drunks and crack heads know who was in charge. It was great! Until the rich daddy of the poor little junkie he'd busted sued. The brat had it coming in his BMW and his Brooks Brothers suit. He'd resisted, plain and simple, yelling that he didn't have to go with the cop because his daddy was some high muckety-muck lawyer who could buy and sell any cop he wanted to ten times over. Robertson felt like he'd kept his cool pretty well up to that point. "Not like your old man, pig. What'd he do for a living, pimp out your old lady?"

Yeah, he'd lost it. It had taken a lot of surgery to put the kid's face back together, and his daddy really was connected. The only thing that saved the department and his job was the fact that the kid had pulled a gun. An unregistered .38 snubby which had been reported stolen from a gun shop two years earlier. Robertson chuckled remembering planting the piece, carefully making sure the unconscious punk's prints were all over it. To placate Mr. Lawyer Daddy, the sergeant had been assigned a desk. Was it any wonder he drank a little? But, there was no reason for Captain McElroy to call him a drunk.

One of the rookies had brought his duffel into the McElroy's office while the captain was reaming him and the thermos had fallen out, rolling to a stop at the captain's feet. Before Robertson could stop him, the captain had opened the jug and sniffed it. Of course, he had protested that it wasn't his, that someone was trying to set him up, like they had always done his dad. Captain McElroy had reached into his desk and pulled out a portable breathalyzer like the patrol cops had in their cars and held it out. "Prove it," he said.

Robertson had complied. What else could he do? Taking the plastic mouthpiece between his lips, he had blown. It had been a while since his last sip, and he hadn't had enough to register, he told himself. The look on the captain's face when the device had beeped, told him otherwise. Fucking gadgets! That was when that bastard, McElroy had called him a drunk! Stan wasn't a drunk. He knew drunks, he'd been raised by one and had busted more than he could count over the years. He wasn't a drunk!

Just as he slammed the shot glass down on the table as punctuation to this thought, Stan heard a deep voice from somewhere behind and far over his head say, "Of course you aren't a drunk, Sergeant Robertson. But, they want to make you look like one and discredit and ruin you just like they did your father, don't they?"

His right hand sliding around to the grip of the magnum in the pancake holster in the small of his back, Stan turned his head, craning his eyes and neck upward to see who was speaking to him. Through the alcoholic fog coating his optic nerve, he saw the biggest human being he had ever encountered. "Fuck off," he slurred at the hulking figure. The big man was wearing a broad brimmed hat and Stan couldn't see his eyes. He didn't like it when people hid their eyes from him. It usually meant they were up to something, or trying to do him over. The stranger didn't move, just stood there, so Stan growled a little louder, "Didn't you hear me, I said, fuck off!"

The giant chuckled, actually laughed at him. Seeing red, Stan whipped his hand around and pointed at the huge figure with his...finger? Calmly, the stranger reached his hand out and dropped the magnum on the table. "Calm down, Stan," he said, slowly. "I am here to help. Put the gun away and let's have a drink and talk. Time is short if you want to save your career. We have to act before the captain can file his report, don't we?" Stan nodded dumbly, staring at his weapon as the mammoth figure squeezed his bulk into the other side of the booth. He had to sit sideways, his long legs sticking out of the booth.

Stan just sat and continued to stare. His piece still lay on the table where the big bastard had dropped it. Finally, he reached out to pick it up. His hands were shaking. He cursed himself silently for his weakness, for letting the stranger see it. Putting the gun away, he reached for the bottle on the table...bottle? Where the hell had that come from. He hadn't bought it and he was pretty sure his companion hadn't set it down there. "Drink up, Stan," his new friend said. "We have much to discuss and more to do. I know things, Stan. I know about your father and how he treated you. He was wrong, you know. You're not a coward, you're just careful. You're much smarter than he was, wasting all his time tilting at windmills, picking fights he could not possibly win. Not you, Stan, you choose your battles much more wisely, waiting for the right time. I know, I have done the same thing, for longer than you can imagine. But now, it is time at last. My time."

Stan drank the shot of whiskey in front of him. Had he poured it, or had his new acquaintance? The big guy knew what he was talking about. The longer Stan listened to him, the more sense he made. Maybe it was Stan's time, too. He felt relaxed as the strong liquor coursed through him. He'd never had anything like it. Somehow, inexplicably, the whiskey was lifting the fog. Everything was becoming clearer to him. He looked over at the stranger, who laughed. "Wonderful, isn't it?" he asked, gesturing toward the now nearly empty bottle. Where had it all gone? "It is very rare and expensive, distilled from the apples of a certain tree in Africa. The natives say it gives clarity and knowledge to those who drink it. Let's them know what is right and what is wrong. now that you are feeling it's effects, let us turn to your problem."

"Who are you?" Stan finally managed to stammer out.

"I am your only friend, Stan. The one who will help you prove them all wrong. Your father, Captain McElroy, the pimps, punks, and lawyers, all of them. They will see who the boss is, the big man. They will know the name of Stan Robertson and fear and respect it as they should."

"Y-your name?"

"I have had many names over my long life, but you can call me...Caine."

Porter looked up from his cup of tea. It was an ancient blend only he drank and only Gloria brewed. The plant from which it was made had grown in a lush and verdant valley which had been desert for more years than anyone alive could remember. Gloria met his gaze and he read the fear in her eyes. "It had to happen, we tried to save him," he told her. "Some will not be saved." As a tear trailed slowly down Gloria's cheek, Porter finished his tea. With things advancing as rapidly as they were, he knew not when, or if, he might ever have another cup. So much hinged on factors beyond his, Gloria's, or anyone's control. Free will was both a blessing and a curse. "It was his choice," Porter said softly. "You know what happens if we meddle in free choice."

"He has no such qualms," Gloria replied bitterly. It was an old argument. Porter had lost count how many times they had discussed the same subject, always with the same conclusions. But, knowing the right path did not always make it easy to take. One could easily argue that the intent behind actions could possibly make the difference in their outcome. No matter the purity of intent, however, as soon as any being started imposing his or her will on others, the intent as well as the entity began to change.

Neither Gloria or Porter spoke, they did not need to. The debate was carried out in silence in the empty diner. Then, Gloria began to sing a lament for lost souls. As Caine reached across the table and placed his hand upon the head of the misguided policeman, there was a shift in the universe, as if someone had moved some great cosmic game board the merest fraction of the tiniest part of an inch. "It has begun," Porter announced.

Rob was fairly certain that, for a brief moment, he was very close to at least great bodily harm, if not death. He looked around as Lieutenant Ferdinand fixed him with a stare equivalent to a harpoon. He was trapped in the little kitchenette. No way out except for the small window over the sink. No weapon except the empty pistol on the counter, and there was no way he was going to touch that. In short, Rob Paulpry feared for his life.

Then, he was rescued...by the cat. It jumped onto the counter from the window sill (When had it gotten up there?), rubbed against his shoulder, hopped down, padded across the floor until it was exactly halfway to Al on the couch, sat down, and stared at her.

There occurred the longest moment of silence Rob had ever experienced. It probably only lasted a few seconds, but it seemed like forever. Then, still staring at the cat, almost as if the creature had hypnotized her, the detective asked, "How do you know about the Bad Man?" Her voice was so calm that it was, in a way, more frightening than her anger had been.

Even more unsettling was what he saw in her eyes. For the first time since he had met her, Alisha Ferdinand looked afraid. It was there, in her eyes, stark, consuming terror. Looking at her, Rob became afraid. If there was someone out there so bad that he could frighten the unflappable Lieutenant Ferdinand, he was someone to be feared and avoided. According to her muttered ramblings of the night before, the Bad Man had been in the alley with her. Just the thought that he might have barely missed an encounter with this figure made Rob want to sit down. Without thinking, he crossed the living room, followed by the cat, and sat on the opposite end of the sofa. The cat curled up in a ball in the center of the couch and promptly purred himself to sleep with that broken clockwork purr of his. Then, Rob told her all he knew. He started with what had happened the night before. He told her how he'd found her stumbling out of the alley and taken her home, and what she had said in her semi-delirious state. Then, he backtracked. He told her about finding the link among the cases, about Spike, Willy Raines, even about seeing Gloria feeding the cat outside the KKK. In short, he stopped being a reporter, stopped angling for information to make his story, and started being a person, a frightened, confused human being in need of a ally. Surprisingly, the first question she asked when he finished was, "Are you sure it was the same cat?"

"Yes," he replied. "I'd recognize that mangled ear anywhere. Now, it's your turn. If we are going to help each other figure this out, nothing short of full disclosure will do. Let's start with the Bad Man."

Al winced at the mention of the name. She had thought the name many times, heard it in her dreams forever, and had heard Dr. Morrissey say it aloud, but the reporter was the first person other than the good doctor and her Grams she had ever heard say it and, for some reason, that frightened her. It was as though he was holding something of hers, something private, intimate and disgusting. She remembered the seventeen year old girl who had killed her boyfriend for posting nude pictures of her in the locker room after she broke it off with him. Now she thought she knew exactly how that girl had felt. She almost felt like running over Rob Paulpry with her car, just like that girl had done her asshole jock ex-boyfriend.

"He's not real," she said. "At least that's what scores of shrinks, well-meaning friends, and family members, all but one, anyhow, have told me since I was twelve. I see him in my dreams." Al found that once she started talking, she couldn't stop. The story began pouring out, just like the first time she had told Dr. Morrissey. But this was different. Rob believed her. She could see it in his eyes.

She was used to seeing, clinical detachment, surprise, wariness, even fear. But this was the first time since Grams she had seen belief. She knew the reporter's past, how his mother had dreamed of the future, so it was not really a surprise that he believed her wild stories, but she was relieved nonetheless.

"May I see the dream journal?" Rob asked when she had finished her story. While she retrieved it, he sat and digested everything she had told him. When Al had first started talking, Rob thought that she was screwing with him. Ever since the Rose Smith debacle, he had been considered fair game for unrelenting harassment from his peers, friends, even strangers. So, it was easy for him to assume that anyone who mentioned dreams, visions, or psychics was taking a shot at him. He had even begun doubting his own memories and beliefs, until the other night at the Fourteenth, when he had touched the photo of what had been left of Spike's face.

Al could not believe she had opened up like that. And to a reporter! Now she was going to show him the journal. No one else had ever seen it. Even Dr. Morrissey thought she had stopped keeping it She had managed to convince him that she believed the dreams were just subconscious manifestations of her accumulated traumas, rather than glimpses of what was coming. If she could only decode them in advance. Maybe that was why she was showing the journal to Paulpry. He had some experience, believed at least in the possibility, and there was something else, too. The other night in the interrogation room, he had reacted to one of the crime scene photos. It was more than just normal revulsion, he had felt something. He had known something. Rob Paulpry had been afraid.

She returned to the living room with a thick spiral bound notebook in her hand. The cover was, incongruously, Rob thought, bright pink. The cardboard was missing from the back of the book and the whole thing looked 'a little worse for the wear', as his Uncle Ted had often said. Rob reached out his hand, but the woman hesitated, holding the book cradled protectively in front of her chest.

"Not yet," she told him. "First, you have to tell some stories and answer some questions."

Rob started to feign ignorance, to pretend he didn't know what she was asking, but then thought better of it. She had been completely honest with him, he owed her the truth. So he told her everything. He told her about his mother's dreams, the fire that killed his sister and eventually his mother, too. Then, he unwittingly lied to her. "But, I guess it skips a generation, because I don't have any of it. I've wished for some glimpse into tomorrow from time to time, but, nothing." He held his hands palms upward and shrugged.

"It is typical for men to deny precognitive powers," she responded clinically. "Historically, women have been the stronger seers. In many ancient cultures, it was believed that only women could have the power of foresight. Most often, it was linked to childbearing, but researchers have shown that there is no link to gender." Rob shook his head, obviously she had studied the subject in depth.

"So," she continued, "if you don't have the gift, what happened the other night at the precinct?" Again Rob considered feigning ignorance and, again, thought better of it. He did notice the way she sarcastically pronounced the word, 'gift''.

"I have no freaking idea," he stated plainly. "All I do know is that I decided at that moment, that if that was what it was like for my mother, to take back every wish I'd ever made for a glimmer of her abilities." Rob got up from the couch and crossed the room into the tiny kitchen for more coffee. The cat's golden eyes tracked him across the room, as did the female cop's brown ones. He was unnerved by the similarity in their expressions as they watched him. He brought the carafe back to the couch and refilled her mug without asking. When he had returned the pot to its burner and resumed his place on the other end of the couch, he finished answering her question.

"It was like I was there, but not just watching. I was Spike. There was this huge, shadowy SOB, and he reached out and wrung out my...Spike's heart like a kitchen sponge. Then I blacked out."

With a tremor in her voice, Al asked, "Did you see his face?" Rob shook his head.

"He was wearing a broad-brimmed hat, and it was dark." Unconsciously, Rob began rubbing his chest as the memory of that awful pain and the sensation of his heart being squeezed came back to him. He had been through a lot in his life, had experienced depression and feelings of hopelessness, but nothing like he'd felt holding that photo. There is no feeling like the certainty you are going to die and the hopelessness of knowing there is nothing you can do about it.

He looked up at Ferdinand and saw an odd mix of emotions on her face. Fear, sympathy, disgust, and, underneath it all, a resolve that went beyond steely. It was titanium. Then she seemed to make a decision. "I don't know what the fuck is happening, what started it, or how the hell this shit storm came to be, but we are going to end it."

"We?" Rob asked.

"That's right, Paulpry," she snapped at him. "You seem to be mixed up in this almost at much as me. I'm keeping you close so I can keep an eye on you. Who knows, maybe you can help." That was a difficult admission for the young detective to make, but she felt cut off and adrift. She never realized how much she relied on Frank, how much he steadied and supported her, how much she loved him. "That fucker has been messing with me for years, most of my life, in fact, but now he's screwing with family, and he's going to find out that's a line he should never have crossed."

"Where do we start?" Rob asked, feeling swept up in her emotions.

"First," she answered, "we go get my car, if anything is left of it, that is." Just at that moment, her cell phone rang. She had a short conversation in the hallway, out of Rob's hearing. He was actually glad for the break. It gave him a little time to regroup. He was still uncertain about what he had gotten mixed up in, but he was sure of one thing, he needed to see it through. He found he had even stopped thinking about the story, it wasn't the important thing any more. That thought scared him almost as much as anything else in the whole mess. The story had always been the important thing.

Al came back into the room, thanking the person on the other end of the phone call. "Come on," she ordered Rob. "You're taking me to the Fourteenth. That was the desk sergeant, someone called in about last night and one of the uniforms drove my car back there." Neither of them commented on the timing of the call.

CHAPTER TWELVE

Stan felt good. He'd never experienced a morning after a long night of drinking, ass kicking, and no sleep where he felt like this. Everything was perfectly clear to him; no headache, no cotton mouth, no nausea, just clarity, courage, certainty and a feeling of power unlike anything he had ever experienced. This was to be his day, Caine had said so. Today was the day he would show them all what you got when you fucked with Stan Robertson. A new day had truly dawned with the rising of the sun. He felt new, energized, fresh. If he was to be completely honest, Stan had to admit that he had *never* felt like this. He liked it!

Sergeant Porter sat at the counter in the Koffee Kup Kafe and turned to look out the window just as Stan Robertson shambled by. He looked drawn, haggard, disheveled. His uniform was wrinkled, torn, and sweat and vomit stained. Porter saw a familiar gleam in his eye, however and knew that he felt far different from how he looked. As Gloria came back in and caught sight of the unkempt policeman, her breath caught in her throat, and tears stood in her eyes. She, too, had seen the look before.

"He has made his choice," Porter said softly, taking the plate from her hands. "There is nothing we could have done, you know that."

"You mean nothing we *would* do," she replied.

"You know the consequences," Porter reminded the girl. "The moment we start meddling in free will, we become just like him." A tear flowed down Gloria's lovely face as she turned away from the window and Sergeant Porter, unable to bear looking at him or the world for a moment.

Sergeant Stan Robertson staggered on through the bright morning, clearing a path on the sidewalk. As people shied away from the filthy, shambling creature he had become, he saw them stepping aside in awe and respect. It was just like Caine had promised, he was finally getting his due. They could see his power, his strength, his total command. He barely registered that faggot, Porter sitting in the diner as he went by. He'd get his, too, but not today. Today, he had other fish to fry. Today, he would let everyone know who Stan Robertson was and what he stood for. His dad, the punks on the street, the rest of the cops at the Fourteenth, and, especially, that prick, Captain McElroy. He was going to learn the hardest lesson of all.

The calls about the filthy, staggering police officer careening down the street started coming in about five minutes before the door of the Fourteenth Precinct burst open. The young corporal who had been assigned desk duty in light of the events of the day before was on the phone with another distraught citizen whose child was still screaming in the background, she was crying that the "bad policeman" was coming after her. He had been trying to assure the woman, over the piercing shrieks of the child, that it was not a member of the force and that cars were on the way to the location to apprehend him. What he didn't tell her was that it was going to be a good half hour before any units could respond. The End had gone crazy. Starting at about four this morning, there had been a huge bar fight, with serious damage inflicted by what the few eyewitnesses left conscious and able to speak swore was a cop, assorted random assaults and even a few fires. The incidents were scattered across the width and breadth of the blighted neighborhood and the Fourteenth was stretched about as thinly as it was possible for it to be.

Robertson slammed the door open and saw the frightened face of the youngster at the desk. They had replaced him with this pup? The kid was barely out of diapers. He could see that the corporal was wearing his bullet proof vest under his pressed and shined uniform. He could also see the fear on his face. Stan liked the look of fear on the faces of anyone stupid enough to cross him.

The young officer recognized Sergeant Robertson, though he had never seen him, or anyone else for that matter, looking like the veteran cop did at the moment he burst through the door. He was filthy, for starters. His uniform was torn and tattered as though he had been in a brawl and it looked like he had puked down the front of his shirt. Then, he saw the large revolver in the sergeant's hand. Instinctively, he jumped up, dropping the phone and reaching for his own weapon.

Stan just laughed at the kid's bravado, couldn't the punk see he was out of his league? He raised his magnum and fired, hitting the kid square in the middle of his chest. The impact from the bullet knocked him backward into the filing cabinet and he slumped on the floor, still conscious, but dazed and breathless. Stan walked around the desk and saw that, despite having just been shot and his breath knocked out of him, the kid was still trying to get to his weapon. Stan fired again, destroying the kid's right hand. Then, he calmly stepped on his throat and began applying pressure gradually. The punk's eyes bulged and his tongue stuck out as Stan's weight pressed down upon his trachea. He beat ineffectually against Stan's leg with his left hand, clawing and kicking desperately for release. The hyoid bone in his throat gave with a soft pop and red, frothy blood began bubbling out of the corporal's mouth. Stan left him choking on his own gore and made his way back to the captain's office. Now, the real fun was about to begin. He'd show that sanctimonious, holier-than-thou son of a bitch who was in charge. He had very special plans for the captain. He couldn't remember if it was his idea, or Caine's, but, either way, it was going to be fun. Despite the clarity Stan was feeling, there was a sense of confusion as well when he thought too much about what he was doing. He knew he was right, and sensed that he had always wanted things to work out , if not exactly like this, close enough. At the same time, there was the voice of his new mentor, Caine. It seemed to be a part of his every thought, guiding him by saying the same things Stan had always thought, but never said aloud. As his thoughts whirled, Caine's voice came to him again, calming him, reassuring him that this was justice, and that Henry Robertson would finally be proud of his son.

Rob and Al rode in silence on the way to the Fourteenth Precinct. Though each of them was lost in his/her own thoughts, there was a sense of communication. It was as though in sharing their stories, some sort of bond had been formed. This thought amused Rob and sent a shiver down Al's spine.

Caine was pleased. His pet policeman was cutting a swath of fear and disgust as he strode toward his destination, havoc was being wrought by the pitiful, easily controlled creatures inhabiting his chosen domain in this cesspool of a city, all was going according to plan. Sure, there were a few loose ends, but they would soon be tied into a neat, festering little Gordian Knot, with no Alexander the Great to cleave it in twain. And, bound up in the middle of that knot, his prize, Alisha Ferdinand. Caine had to admit that he had not foreseen her allying herself with the reporter, but he was a minor nuisance at best. He was a bumbling fool, completely ignorant of his abilities. Most mortals would give anything for a fraction of the abilities he possessed, yet he ignored them and locked them away from himself. If Caine had any sympathy for these wretched, fragile creatures, he might feel something for Rob Paulpry besides disgust, but such was not his nature, never had been. Paulpry was a fool and would soon meet a fool's demise, while the girl watched. Then, finally, Caine would take her as his own.

For centuries, Caine had sought to possess one of her line. They all had the power he coveted. Even given all that he had learned over his vast existence, the future was still uncertain. With Alisha Ferdinand by his side, he could use her abilities to unlock the mysteries of tomorrow and thwart the plans of those who would oppose him before they were even fully formed. It would all be his. At last. As it should be. Caine smiled, and Alisha Ferdinand was overcome by a profound sense of dread and foreboding.

"You know, we cannot allow him to possess her," Porter told Gloria. She nodded, still reeling from the death of the young policeman. Violent cruelty still jolted her to her very core. After all this time, she still could not understand it. "Not understanding it is a good thing, " replied Porter, responding to her unspoken thought.

"Sometimes..." she began. Porter nodded, he understood. There were times when the lure of destruction was strong for him, too. The desire to lash out and wipe the slate clean. They both had the capability to wreak such havoc, but they were creatures of light and wholesale destruction was the purview of the creatures of darkness. They both understood that, if they ever gave in to the desire to destroy, they would join those ranks, leaving a void in their forces which might not be filled quickly enough to prevent the End of All Things.

Halfway to the Fourteenth Precinct, Rob had turned his police scanner on just for some noise in the too silent confines of his car. He was almost afraid to say anything to the silent Lieutenant Ferdinand as she stared straight ahead not even seeming to notice anything outside her own private thoughts. He had a feeling that, like him, she was going over the conversation they'd had this morning and everything that had led up to it. Neither of them seemed ready or willing to delve further into anything right at the moment.

The scanner went crazy. There must have been fifty active calls going on simultaneously. Both Al and Rob jumped at the noise. At the same time, Rob turned onto the ironically named Salvation Street, the main drag through The End and screeched to a stop. There was a huge bonfire in the middle of the street, with the wasted denizens of the abandoned buildings throwing anything they could get their hands on atop it as it blazed. As they sat and took in the scene, which reminded Rob of something from a post apocalyptic sci fi movie, a squad car rolled up, its lights flashing. The officer driving hit a quick pulse on the siren, hoping, no doubt to disperse the crowd around the conflagration.

The scruffy, burned-out band of arsonists stopped throwing debris on the fire, all right, but did not disperse. They started toward the squad car, surrounding it. Rob and Al heard the frantic call for backup from the young sounding officer in the car over the scanner. Al opened the passenger door and barked back into the car, "Get out of here". As she drew her weapon, and Rob started looking for his digital camera, everything went to shit. A wretched, skinny crack whore threw a cinder block through the back window of the police car, shouting, "Take that, you ugly sonofabitch!" When the driver leapt from the car, weapon drawn and turned to confront her, one of her cohorts (her pimp, maybe?), a big, Asian guy pulled a burning two by four from the fire and, raising it above his head, ran toward the young cop from behind. Alisha shot him. No hesitation, no warning, no second thought. The bullet tore through his chest, exiting the opposite side and struck something in the fire which must have been supporting most of the pile of burning debris. The entire flaming structure collapsed upon itself, sending a huge shower of sparks, gouts of smoke, and leaping flames in every direction. The crack whore ran down the street, the young uniformed officer turned toward Al, pointing his weapon in her direction. lowering it when she showed him her badge, and his equally young partner finally exited the car, drawing his pistol.

Over by the fire, things were in chaos. One of the rioters was engulfed in flames and ran, screaming, a few feet before collapsing into a smoking heap and the others picked themselves up and scattered through the maze of derelict buildings, twisted streets and black alleys. Rob never stopped snapping pictures. This story would get him back into the game for real. That is, if Helen the Barbarian would even look at it.

Al, meanwhile, was giving both of the young uniforms a serious talking to. Rob could not hear the words, but he could read the body language. She towered and the two younger officers cowered. Barking what looked like a series of orders, the detective turned on her heel and headed back toward the car. Rob quickly put his camera away and got back behind the wheel. "Get me to the

Fourteenth," she growled sharply. "And if you ever disobey me in a situation like that again, I will shoot you myself!"

Rob reached to turn off the scanner, but she stopped him with a look, listening intently. "Answer the fucking radio!" she shouted at the box under the dash. "Who the hell is on desk duty?" she demanded. "If it's that drunken idiot, Robertson, I'll throttle him like his mother should have when he was born!" He had no doubt that she could and would follow through on her promise.

Rob was still shaking. He had been through a lot in his career, but had never actually seen anyone shot before. Given his phobia about firearms, he really had hoped to live out his life without that particular experience. The worst part was the calm, calculated way she had done it, and the fact that she seemed unfazed by the incident. As he had pulled away from the fire, she had calmly replaced the round in the magazine of her weapon and now sat with it cradled on her lap. This was one cold, calculating female. He made a mental note not to push her too hard, and maybe not at all, in the future.

Weaving their way through the streets of The End, they encountered more chaos and mayhem. The detective's gold badge opened up barricades and got them waved around roadblocks. Rob couldn't help but wondering if someone had laced all the drugs in the blighted neighborhood with some hallucinogenic substance. Everyone in The End seemed to have simultaneously gone berserk, in the true meaning of the word. Ragged derelicts were charging at riot gun wielding police officers with knives, tearing up anything they could get their hands on and there were more bonfires scattered through the streets. "What the hell is going on?" he demanded aloud.

"Armageddon," Al quipped. Neither of them laughed. By the time they reached the Fourteenth Precinct, they both knew, without any psychic powers, that something was wrong. The gate to the parking lot was standing open, as was the door into the squat brick building. "Wait here," Al instructed Rob.

"Are you out of your mind, too?" Rob asked. "It's a full scale, fucked up riot out here and you have the only gun. You can shoot me if you want, but I am sticking to your ass like Velcro." She looked, for a brief moment like she might seriously be considering turning her weapon on him and Rob suddenly remembered his recent vow not to push her too hard.

"Keep behind me and do what I say," she growled, running across the abandoned parking lot and flattening herself against the pitted, grimy bricks. It took just a second for Rob to react and join her. "Keep up, I won't be waiting for you or coming back for you if we get separated," then, they were through the door.

Al's sensitive nose picked up the smell of death. Feces and blood. The desk was apparently abandoned, the telephone receiver dangling and beeping and the radio going crazy. Moving slowly and sweeping the room with her eyes, she made her way over to the desk. Rob stayed right with her. Looking over, they both saw the body of the young corporal. Rob noted that his hand was missing, his weapon still holstered, and the name tag on the blood stained uniform shirt read "Hartley". "Rick Hartley," Al supplied. "Explains why the radio wasn't being answered."

Rob then looked at the young officer's face and saw the look of terror on it. Blood covered the lower half of his face and pooled around him, his eyes bulged, his tongue was protruding obscenely and his eyes were wide, staring and bugged out of their sockets. On his throat, a vivid bruise was noticeable, even through the blood. The story had started writing itself in Rob's head, every detail catalogued analytically, to be sorted out later when he had time to sit and write. He knew on a gut level, that he would spend a long time trying to forget many of those details.

They moved carefully around the end of the desk and headed down the hallway. Here, too, the normally locked door was open and Rob noticed that the beeping of the off the hook telephone and the constant radio traffic from the base set behind the desk were the only sounds in the normally bustling, building.

Captain McElroy had been in the basement records room all morning. He wasn't on duty. It was supposed to be his day off, but after the mess with that jerkwad, Robertson, he was going to have to find a permanent replacement at the desk. The kid they'd sent over was too green. The fourteenth would eat him alive. So, here he was, on his day off, in the dark, musty dungeon. He probably should have gone home and left the decision for another day when the computer in his office crashed. Of course tech couldn't send anyone until the middle of next week. But, he hated putting things off. Maybe, if he had learned that lesson ten years ago, his wife and son wouldn't be living in Seattle and not speaking to him. She had accused him of being married to the job more than her, and, if he was honest, he would have to say she was right. Civilians just couldn't understand. Shaking off the maudlin thoughts, he bent back over the keyboard of the old, slow computer and pecked away. He wished he'd paid more attention in his high school typing class.

The basement was dark, damp, and lonely, but it was far from quiet. The steam pipes hissed and clanged, the water and sewer pipes gurgled, and the captain could hear what sounded like the scurrying of clawed little feet in the dark recesses. "Rats," he muttered. He hated rats more than just about anything. Right at the moment, he hated Stan Robertson even more than rats, but in a different way.

Robertson had always been a screw up. Trying to prove something to the world, McElroy supposed. He'd leave all that to the shrinks to figure out. Right now, he just wanted a hot, decent cup of coffee and to stomp the living shit out of Sergeant Stan Robertson. If it had been up to him, he would have booted him off the force after he'd planted that gun on the stupid spoiled rich kid he'd busted buying drugs in The End.

But, like so much else in his life, it hadn't been up to him. He hit print and leaned back in the wooden swivel chair while the old printer clacked and wheezed its way through the list he'd compiled of potential candidates for the desk job. One thing about the records room, it was in the far back corner of the basement so Captain McElroy was insulated from the comings and goings of the precinct. If he needed him, the young corporal could call him on his cell. But, for the time being, he felt protected from the usual madness.

The printer finally wheezed to a stop, spitting out the one sheet of paper. For all the time and noise, one would think the damned thing had to make the paper and boil the ink down from pine sap, or whatever the hell ink was made from, before it could print. He snatched the paper out of the tray and headed back up to his office. He'd drop the list on his desk then go out to check on the kid, remind him he was there if he needed anything.

Rob had only been more afraid once before in his life and that was the night in the interrogation room when he had touched the photo of the dead Spike and had that flash of the punk's last moments. He was beginning to think it might have been better if he had waited in the car after all. It wasn't just the dead desk cop, or the eerie quiet inside the Fourteenth following the bedlam outside, there was something else. If Rob believed in the concept of capital E Evil as a force unto itself, sentient and living, he would say it had been here. All things considered, maybe it had.

As he followed close behind Alisha Ferdinand, making their way through the empty police station, he found himself trying to piece the story together. He knew that this was his mind's way of coping with the terror he was feeling, but he didn't care. He'd take any solace he could find at this point. He went all the way back to the murdered bank robbers and started working forward, ending up with Ferdinand's dream journal and the mysterious Bad Man. Suddenly, something dawned on him. It had been there all along, he mentally kicked himself for missing it. He started to say something to her just as she rounded the corner into an office and stopped short, causing him to run into her.

Al was on autopilot, her reflexes and training were the only things keeping her moving. Her mind was a maelstrom of thoughts, memories and images. Her dreams came back to her, overlapping, flowing together, becoming a blurred jumble of noise and light. At the forefront of it all was the Bad Man, laughing and jeering at her as he always did in the dreams. This was all too crazy, it couldn't be him, he isn't real, no matter what Grams said. He's just a dream, she told herself over and over again, to no avail. She rounded the corner in the hallway and saw Captain McElroy's office door was ajar. She eased it open with her foot, peeked around the doorjamb, and froze in horror at what she saw.

As Captain McElroy came down the hall to his office, he noticed the smell. It was a mixture of blood, booze, sweat, and puke. Probably, one of the patrol cars had brought in a belligerent drunk who had anointed the hallway around the corner on his way to the holding cell. The glamorous life of a cop at the Fourteenth Precinct, Gateway to The End, he thought wryly. He'd always felt that a plaque with the Dante quote, "Abandon hope all ye who enter here", should hang over the booking desk. As he opened the door into his office, he heard a sound in the hallway behind him, then there was a bright flash behind his eyes as Sergeant Robertson's sap caught him neatly above his left ear.

McElroy fell like a ton of shit, and Stan grinned. No one else on the force even carried a sap anymore, but Stan liked the weapon. Made of braided leather with a lead head surrounded by just enough padding to keep from breaking bones, it could take out a punk easily with one well placed blow. Of course it was against department policy to hit a suspect in the head, lawsuits being all the rage, but Stan never had been one to play strictly by someone else's book. No, Stan Robertson had his own playbook, with just one rule, win.

When Captain John McElroy awoke, the first thing he noticed was the pain in the left side of his head. The second was that he couldn't breathe very well, and, finally, that he also couldn't move. As he carefully opened his eyes and his vision cleared, his situation became clear to him. He was standing behind his desk. His wrists were flex-cuffed to the security screen on the inside of the window and his legs were bound together and similarly attached to the steam pipe running along the floor. In his mouth was a piece of cloth he assumed was his handkerchief, bound in place with his tie. As he managed to raise his head and look up, he saw the disheveled, disgusting Stan Robertson, grinning at him. John McElroy knew then that he was about to die, and most unpleasantly. Almost as if he sensed the Captain's thoughts, Sergeant Stan Robertson grinned even bigger and started toward him. Captain McElroy started praying, and Sergeant Robertson started laughing.

As the door swung slowly open on creaky hinges, Al could not believe what she was seeing. It was like something out of one of those horror story comic books her cousin, Sid, had constantly read as a kid. She had always felt a little nervous around Sid and was privately relieved when his family moved out to the west coast and they lost contact. Captain McElroy was tied to the security screen on the window, quite obviously dead. It was apparent that he had taken a long time to die. Everything about the scene was a mockery of the crucifixion. His arms were bound, spread-eagled, to the screen, his feet tied together and to the steam pipe, his feet overlapping. The killer had driven the letter opener off the desk through his feet, pinning them to the floor. In the corner lay the stapler, covered in blood, there was a row of staples driven into the captain's forehead, symbolizing, she guessed, the crown of thorns, and a long laceration had been cut into his side.

As Al examined the body, she heard a sound behind her and saw the reporter heaving up his breakfast out in the hallway. For some reason, at that point, she stopped being a cop. She knew full well that she should stay on scene, secure the building, and call it in to headquarters, but something within her told her to leave. Turning from the ruined remains of her captain, she grabbed the still-retching Rob Paulpry by the collar and headed back out into the gray, smoke-laden morning. Shoving him roughly toward his car, she barked, "Follow me," and headed to her own vehicle, never pausing to see if he followed her instructions. He did. He didn't know why, but he did, and they headed back toward her apartment, taking a path which avoided the war zone around the Fourteenth Precinct.

CHAPTER THIRTEEN

Caine was pleased, which was not, in the grand scheme, a good thing for the universe. His latest convert had proved to be even more than he could ask. In all the time he had been playing this game, he had only been in possession of a few so depraved. He looked over at his acolyte and smiled a smile that had driven men mad for centuries. It was all beginning to come together. He could feel it now. It was finally his time.

Stan Robertson sat in the corner of the dark church smiling to himself. That prick, McElroy wouldn't be fucking him, or anyone else over any more. He took another swig of Caine's wondrous apple liqueur and closed his eyes. He relived the events of the day, picturing himself in all his glory. He was, in his own mind, at once both savior and avenging angel. He had saved the rookie kid on desk duty from having to endure the crap that life as a cop dished out. He would never have his career ruined for doing what needed to be done, or have to put up with assholes in charge like McElroy. 'Ahh...McElroy', he thought to himself. Vengeance was finally Stan's. He pictured himself in his glory, sweeping into the room and striking fear into the heart of the captain by virtue of his righteous power. Oh, how he had trembled to be in the presence of such holy wrath. In the end, Stan knew that Captain McElroy had seen the error of his ways and repented, but it had come too late, justice had to be meted out.

Caine looked once more over at his disciple sitting in the corner in a stupor with an idiotic smile playing on his filthy, blood smeared face. Yes, this one was special. For just a moment, Caine had the sadistic desire to take down the curtain of delusion and let in a ray of truth, just to see the reaction on the face of Sergeant Stan Robertson. But, he reasoned, he still needed him, and the reality of who he was, what he had done, and his future might unhinge the cop too much even for Caine to use him. He let him rest and revel in his distorted memories of the morning's events. Once he was finished with him, however, he would let the full weight of everything crash in on him and watch as it destroyed whatever was left of the pitiful human by that time.

By then, he would have the real prize. She will come willingly to him, he sensed it. Finally, all the pieces were in place. He had waited so long, at last, one of the Keepers of the Future would be his. Long ago, longer than human memory, the Keepers were held in high esteem. Their abilities were respected, nurtured, and honored. Then came the so-called "Age of Reason" and so many truths and secrets were lost, vilified, and swept under the rug. Not that this was all bad for Caine. The denial of the deeper abilities of certain minds made the owners of these powers easier prey. All but the Keepers. Even after their fall from exaltation, the women who kept the future were strong. Of course there had always been others not of the bloodline who had some inkling of the power, but it was minuscule in relation to that of the Keepers and burned out too soon. Caine had so many disappointing disciples over the aeons. So many with a touch of the power, some with enough to advance him just one small move in the cosmic game. But they always failed him in the end.

Then, there were those who fought against him, seeking to thwart his plans. The Guardians. They sought to preserve precious "Free Will". How free was it, really? Couldn't they see? Hadn't Caine shown them, time and time again, that there was nothing free about it? Mortals were so easily turned from the path of their own choosing any other way which looked easier, or more profitable. There was no Free Will.

Gloria sat stock-still, humming. The deaths at the Fourteenth Precinct had hit her hard. Even Porter was taken aback by the horrific nature, particularly of Captain McElroy's death. Their adversary hadn't been in possession of a disciple this dark and twisted in a very long time. Porter knew that things were all too quickly coming to a head. He only hoped Lieutenant Ferdinand would be ready, would make the right choices. So much more than she could possibly imagine hinged on her.

As he followed Al back toward her apartment, Rob noticed the sudden drop in the number of calls coming over the police scanner. As quickly as it had ignited, the pandemonium in The End seemed to be burning out. Rummaging around in his console, he pulled out his umbilical cord. He realized he hadn't turned on the cell for over twenty four hours. Thumbing the power button, the phone beeped angrily and he saw that he had thirteen missed calls, all of them from none other than Helen, the Barbarian. He would deal with her later, right now, he was onto the biggest story of his career, though he wasn't really certain yet what it was. But he was determined to find out. He started making calls as he wound through the inner city streets toward the detective's apartment. Pulling into the parking lot of the building, Rob was frustrated. None of his sources were answering. They were probably all out burning, looting, and otherwise destroying what was left of The End. Just then, Rob knew he had the title for his piece.

Al jumped out of her car and headed toward the building without even looking to see if Paulpry was following her. She knew he would be. She was still reeling in shock, disgust, and anger from what they had discovered at the precinct. She had never seen anything like it. In all her years at the Fourteenth, counting the time spent there as a child after the death of her mother, she had come to believe sincerely that she had, at least, come close to seeing it all. As she unlocked the door to her apartment, she knew she had not yet even scratched the surface. As she swung the door open and reflexively swept the room with her vision, she heard the heavy breathing and thudding footfalls of the reporter, Paulpry, coming up the stairs behind her.

That was perhaps the strangest and most startling change of all. Who would have thought that she would ever have anything to do with a reporter? Much less, a cat, she thought as she saw the weird little feline sitting on her grandmother's bible on the coffee table playing with a piece of paper. The cat looked up at her, batted the paper off the table, hissed, and vanished into the back of the apartment. Feeling an almost overwhelming urge to pull her weapon and go cat hunting, Al just growled and picked up the piece of paper. It was the Bingo flyer with Frank's cryptic notes in the margin. Frank! She had forgotten all about him. She took out her phone and dialed the hospital number and walked into her bedroom, completely forgetting about the reporter and the cat.

Rob followed the detective into the apartment. This was no great feat as she left the door standing open behind her as she entered, still obviously in shock. Shock was the only explanation Rob could come up with for her leaving the scene they had walked into at the precinct. All of her training and reflexes seemed to just go into hibernation as she turned and fled the Fourteenth. The worst part had been the fear Rob had seen in her eyes. Given his experience with Lieutenant Ferdinand up to this point, fear did not seem like a common emotion for her.

Rob, on the other hand, was quite familiar with fear, and was nearly overcome with it at the moment. Seeking to find something upon which his mind could focus, other than the fear, he saw the bible and flier on the table and Alisha's dream journal on the couch. Suddenly, his reporter brain kicked into gear. He wasn't sure what did it, but the nagging feeling in the back of his skull suddenly reappeared, driving out the thoughts of blood, murder, and fear. Well, maybe not driving them completely out, he had to admit to himself, but shoving them into a dark corner for the time being.

It took forever to get through to anyone at the hospital. No doubt, it was the mayhem in The End that was responsible, so she bit her tongue and curbed her anger while she was repeatedly transferred by the switchboard to one after another extension that no one picked up. The fifth time the phone system reconnected her with the operator, a very pleasant sounding woman who seemed genuinely sympathetic, Al was about to lose the tenuous control she was maintaining on her temper. "I'm so sorry, Miss Ferdinand," the woman said again. "Would you like me to keep trying, or would you prefer to call back later? I don't know what's going on around here, but it seems as though everyone has been called away from their phones."

Al knew full well what was going on. She could easily imagine the bedlam at the hospital as the casualties from the riots, or whatever the hell they were, in The End came rolling, walking, and crawling in. She also knew that the operator knew what was causing the lack of response from the ward. Forcing a smile into her voice, she asked, "Could you just please try the ICU once more? I am really worried about my uncle." The operator sighed a patient sigh, and put her through once again. As the ringing phone buzzed in Al's ear and frustration started to get the upper hand, her thoughts returned to the scene in Captain McElroy's office. "The Case of the Crucified Captain," she thought bitterly.

Just as Al was about to give up, the phone was answered. The nurse who answered it sounded very young and very old at the same time. He voice had a musical quality to it. It wasn't as though she was singing when she spoke, but more that she was about to. "I am terribly sorry about your wait, Lieutenant Ferdinand," the woman said. "Your uncle is stable. He has not yet regained consciousness, but there has been no decline in his condition. He should be fine, but only time will tell. If you have any more questions, please feel free to call back later."

"Thank you, nurse..." Al began.

"You can just call me Gloria," the woman replied, then hung up the phone.

Porter smiled as Gloria hung up the scarred black phone on the diner's counter. "Now, perhaps she can focus on her task," he said, approvingly. The conversation had been hard for Gloria. She had so wanted to give the Keeper more information. Just a hint to steer her on the right track, but she knew that would violate the rules. It was so hard, sometimes, following the rules. As she had this thought, Porter chuckled and nodded his head in agreement. Then, he rose and started out the door just as his radio came to life once more calling in every available officer to the Fourteenth. Caine's distraction had played itself out and the first officers returning to the precinct had discovered the carnage there.

Rob pulled his notes out of his jacket pocket and sat on the couch. He placed the flier, the dream journal, and his notes in a row on the coffee table with the bible and took a minute to look at them as a whole, seeking one of those flashes of inspiration which had so often in the past, led him to the piece of a puzzle which completed the picture for him. All he needed to do was to find the thread which tied the whole mess together and then he could begin unraveling it. He opened the journal, feeling a little like a voyeur, even though Alisha had already let him read it. He decided to skip past the early entries and focus on the ones starting right before everything got weird.

The first entry was just a couple of days before the bar fight when the twenty from the bank job had turned up. Alisha had told him that the drunk victim had his eye plucked out, and, right there in the dream journal, was a head crying tears. Rob double checked the dates, it fit. Rob knew he had to be careful. One of the assignments he had been given on the freaks and frauds beat was a woman who had claimed to be able to solve crimes based on her dreams.

Bonnie Pilcher had been her name. She had wanted Rob's validation in the Times Republican to promote the book she was writing. Like Lieutenant Ferdinand, she had kept a very accurate dream journal which she had let Rob read. Also like the detective, the dates in the journal had pre-dated the events which they supposedly foretold, but something smelled off to Rob. Maybe it was a subconscious reaction on his part to the, at that time, recent Madame Blageur debacle, perhaps it was something in her, but his fraud radar was pinging wildly.

Before leaving, he had made a mark in the corner of the first blank page in the journal. Promising to research her claims, and asking that she call him immediately if she had another prophetic dream, Rob left the one-room apartment and waited.

Three weeks later, he had received an excited call from Ms. Pilcher. She had experienced another flash of insight which had coincidentally foretold the arrest just this morning of a local politician on money laundering charges. Rob told her he would be right over and went to check it out. Leaving the office, someone had asked him why he didn't just conduct the interview telepathically. Rob ignored him.

Bonnie was beside herself with excitement when he arrived. "I didn't know what the dream meant, at first," she gushed. "But when I opened the paper this morning, it all made sense."

"When did you have the dream?" Rob asked.

"I can't really remember," she said. "I'm not very good with dates, but I checked the date with the paper that morning and dated the journal entry, as usual." Rob read the entry, which was written on the page upon which he had made the mark.

"Your certain that this date is accurate?" he asked, baiting the trap.

"Absolutely," she declared. "Isn't it eerie?"

"Very good," he replied. "I don't think you will have any problem selling your book...As fiction." Rob watched as her face fell.

"What do you mean?" She tried to put on an innocent face as she asked him, but he could see the facade crumbling .

"Well, Bonnie," he explained. "This entry was not in the journal when I was here a couple weeks ago. I know this," he said, holding up his hand to stop her protestations, "because I made a mark in the corner of the page." He showed her the mark. "Of course the day after the date on the page, the article came out in the paper that Alderman Finch was being investigated. So, of course, in order to be a prediction, your dream would have had to precede that article, which it does," he finished, again silencing her with a raised hand. "The problem is, this date, which you swear is accurate," she nodded earnestly, "is two days before I came to see you." Bonnie turned redder than Rob thought possible and started sputtering. He simply shook his head, thanked her for an amusing story and encouraged her to read all about it in the paper.

"I'll sue if you print it!" She screamed at him.

"Sue away," he encouraged her. "It will sell even more copies." He had heard nothing more from her. Neither had the police department who she had been hounding for months to let her help investigate their most sensational cases. In fact, she disappeared all together. No doubt, plying her cons elsewhere.

Rob knew that Ferdinand was sincere and convinced, but he also knew that a person suffering from a delusion could and would do anything to make reality fit the fantasy world in which he or she lived. He checked the date on the most recent entry and knew that it was accurate. It was the morning after he had found her in the alley. Without knowing why, Rob decided to trust her and the journal and began digging, comparing his notes with the dates and events of the dreams.

It was when he came to the Bingo game dream that he was stumped. It didn't appear to have anything to do with anything. He picked up the flier Alisha had found on her windshield and stared at it and at Frank's notes. It just didn't make any sense. Suddenly, he noticed a motion out of the corner of his eye. Looking down, he saw the cat sitting on top of the bible, looking intently at him. Glancing back at the flier, a crazy idea came to him.

Al snapped he phone closed and went into the bathroom. She could hear the reporter out in the living room, turning over papers, scribbling notes and muttering to himself, but she didn't have enough room in her brain at the moment to even begin to wonder what he was doing. Now that she knew Frank was, for the moment, at least, out of danger, she needed to process what had happened at the Fourteenth. She felt she needed a shower, too. After making sure the bathroom door was locked and her pistol within easy reach, she stepped into the tub and turned the water on fast and scalding hot.

As she stood with the scorching needles of water beating down on her, she watched the events at the precinct on her internal television. It made no sense. Nothing was making any sense. She knew it all had to do with Caine...and her. That was the first time she had thought of the Bad Man by the name she had dreamed for him. It almost seemed to make him even more real, as if that was possible. Al shuddered despite the hot water. "I'm losing it," she murmured, tears threatening to break through her mental dam.

Rob heard the shower start, "How the hell many showers does this woman take?" he thought to himself. He couldn't believe what he was reading as he began to piece all of the facts together into one sick, twisted story. Even with what he was reading right now, it seemed like some elaborate plot in a thriller novel or movie. Except for the fact that he was right in the middle of it, accompanied by a possibly mentally disturbed homicide detective, chased by a psychotic dream man,...oh, yeah, and a cat, he added, as the feline needled him in the side of his leg with its claws.

"Ouch," he admonished the bedraggled feline as he shooed it off his leg. The cat mumbled something, leapt onto the coffee table, plopped down on top of the bible and proceeded to lick its nether regions. As the reporter went back to his notes, the cat made a strange sound deep in its throat. When he looked up at it, the creature was still sitting with its back legs splayed out, staring at him intently. Rob had gotten leads from some very odd and disreputable sources in his career. From a United States Senator's male prostitute, to an anonymous letter written in burnt umber crayon, to the ill-fated Spike, so, he thought, why not a cat?

He reached out to shoo the cat from the bible. It hissed and jumped to the table, then onto the floor. As the cat leapt to the floor, it sent one of the pieces of paper flying toward Rob. The reporter caught it in his free hand, shook his head, then looked at what he was holding. Again, it was the Bingo flier with the hospitalized sergeant's cryptic notes. Despite the source of this hint, which was currently over in the corner clawing at the drapes, Rob felt that there must be a link among all of the clues, that elusive thread which would tie it all together and make it make some sense.

Bingo and bibles made some sense, anyhow, he thought wryly. Frank was attacked in a church, and Alisha Ferdinand chased someone out of the very same church into that alley and practically into the arms of the Bad Man, Caine. Rob started a flow sheet. At the top, he wrote "Church" and "Bingo" and drew a two-headed arrow between them. Underneath and between them he wrote "Bible". The connection from "Church" to "Bible" was easy. Connecting "Bible" to "Bingo" was another matter, and what about the misplaced and circled numbers on the Bingo card? How did they fit in? He added "G-44" and "G-48" to the chart under ""Bingo" and connected them. His chart struck him as lopsided, but he pressed on, adding "Caine" to the paper and connecting that to "Bible". The spelling was different, but close enough.

Rob then picked up the dream journal and started reading certain passages again. He could feel the thread just tickling his fingertips, but couldn't quite grasp and pull it tight. He was stalled, so, with nothing else to do, he started flipping through the bible.

Rob was not religious, but he had some knowledge. His Aunt Maureen, his dad's sister, had taken him to church every chance she could get. Aunt Maureen considered his mother's visions the work of the devil and felt it was her mission to save young Rob from his influences. So, about once a month, she took him to her church, the Armor of God Open Pentecostal Church. Rob remembered the first time she had dragged him, in his uncomfortable suit and tie, to a service. Afterward, he had asked her why the minister was so mad at them. The man had shouted at them from the pulpit so enthusiastically, that Rob wanted to hide. Couple that with the fact that all the man seemed to be saying was that they were all unsalvageable sinners destined for hell, that it was no wonder that, at the age of six, he was afraid of religion and everything to do with it.

That first sermon had started his fear of religion and religious institutions and, five years later, when Reverend Goodbody (Rob always assumed that was a fake name, but it wasn't) was caught with a hotel room full of prostitutes of both sexes and enough drugs to get the whole congregation nearer to heaven, his mistrust was firmly ensconced.

He was getting no help from randomly flipping the gold-edged, onion skin pages of the old bible, so he decided to start from the beginning. Turning to the listing of the books, he stopped cold. He looked at the flow sheet, then re-read the passage in the dream journal he had just finished and finally grasped the thread and started pulling it tight. He was so intent on reading and scribbling, that he didn't feel the cat jump back up on the couch and snuggle against his leg, or hear Al turn off the shower and eventually come into the living room.

CHAPTER FOURTEEN

Al came out of the bathroom, toweling her hair. The shower had helped some, but she still felt like she was coated in something vile. The images of the carnage at the Fourteenth would not leave her mind's eye. Equally impossible to banish was the confusion over her own actions. Her training told her she should have secured the station house and called for backup, but she had fled. Of course, at the police academy, they had never covered what to do when your nightmares came to life. "So," she wondered silently, "what now?" No sooner had the thought come to her than she felt a little shudder, remembering her father's frequent admonition not to ask that question. He believed that it was no sooner sked or thought than the universe had a perverse habit of answering it. As she walked down the hallway toward the living room, she heard frantic activity.

Rob was sitting on the couch, hunched over the coffee table. Her dream journal, his notes, the Bingo flier, his digital camera, and Grams' bible were spread out all over the table and the couch and he was furiously scribbling on a legal pad. Turning her head to peer at it, she could see some sort of flow chart or diagram. There were words, names, and numeric notations connected by arrows, scribbled out entries, and question marks. None of it made any sense. The damned cat was lying snuggled against his leg purring contentedly in its rickety manner.

He looked up with a haunted, feverish expression in his eyes. "Make some coffee then sit down," he said and returned to his feverish work. Al started to inform him just what he could do with his instructions, but something in his eyes and actions stopped her short. Instead, she walked into the kitchen and, keeping one eye on both the reporter and the cat, made a pot of coffee. Unconsciously stroking the feline between its ears, Paulpry returned to his frantic scribbling and cross-referencing. As she watched him and listened to the combined sounds of the coffee maker, the scribbling and rustling of papers and the impossibly loud purring from the cat, Al got the same sinking feeling she often experienced in her dreams when The Bad Man revealed himself to her. It was as if the world suddenly became shifting sand and was sliding away beneath her feet. She grabbed the edge of the counter and held on waiting for the momentary sensation to pass and wondering if it ever would.

Kevin Morrissey was worried about Lieutenant Alisha Ferdinand. He had been worried about her since their last session. She had been lying to him, he knew it. Early on in their association, he had figured out how to tell when she was lying, but had never let on. It had been of immense value to his treatment of her to let her spin out her transparent fibs. It had led him, on more than one occasion, to the truth behind the lies.

He had checked with the pharmacy and discovered that, though she had been a day or two late occasionally, she had continued to fill the prescription he had written for the sleeping pills. From the way she looked the last time he saw her, he wondered two things. First, how long had it been since she had actually taken one, and then, what had she been doing with them. He sincerely hoped, despite the recent reports about the environmental damage done by prescription meds in the water supply, that she was flushing them. The alternative led down a dark and terrifying path. People only saved sleeping pills for one reason and Alisha desperately wanted The Bad Man to go away... forever. Just as Dr. Morrissey was worrying about his favorite patient (and possibly his favorite person) and what might happen to her his phone rang. Though, professionally and, he thought, personally, Kevin Morrissey scoffed at the notion of premonitions, his heart seemed to freeze and a sick sensation built in the pit of his stomach as he reached to answer the telephone on his desk. He knew, somehow, that the news coming in was bad, very, very, bad.

Detective Mark Cooper stood in the doorway of Captain McElroy's office in shock. In his seventeen years on the force, he had never seen anything like the carnage which had greeted him at the Fourteenth. The insanity of the riots and the bizarre fact that they had spontaneously stopped, all at the same time had been weird enough to last him for awhile. Then, when the desk at the Fourteenth had suddenly stopped responding to calls, he had experienced a very bad feeling, but nothing in his experience, training, or worst nightmare had prepared him for this. The worst thing he had ever seen before this was when that crack head had broken into a house in Fern Valley, the richest development in the county. He was right in assuming that the family was gone for the weekend, but had surprised the maid, a young Filipino girl.

The junkie, high out of his mind, had duct taped her mouth and staked the poor girl to the dining room table, pinning her hands to it with kitchen knives, and tying her legs, spread so widely and violently that one of her hips had dislocated. Cooper had still been in uniform at the time and was the first one on the scene. He had surprised the punk in the process of cutting off the poor girl's panties, intent on raping her. When the crazed punk had turned toward him, knife in hand, Cooper had shot him.

Oddly enough, what he remembered about killing the skinny waste of space had been that the bullet had exited the would-be rapist's back and shattered a very expensive looking vase on the sideboard. At the time, he had thought, "I hope I don't have to pay for that". Weird what the mind does in times of stress and horror.

What he was looking at right now, seemed to have overloaded his coping mechanisms. No stray thoughts or plans of action came into his mind to help him get through and beyond the horror in front of him. He just stood and stared at the crucified captain. He had called in to Main Dispatch downtown when he had found the corporal behind the desk, so help was on the way. Three patrol cars had pulled up moments after, and he had set the uniforms to securing the scene and coordinating a sweep of the grounds. That had been his last constructive act. All capability for conscious thought and action seemed to leave him the moment he had peered through the doorway to the captain's small office. When one of the uniformed officers, a young, sandy-haired rookie whose name tag read R. Pierce, had appeared at the end of the hallway to inform him that the rest of the building was clear, he had stopped him, holding his hand up. He didn't want anyone else seeing what he was looking at right now. Hell, he didn't want to be seeing it himself, but he simply could not stop staring.

What Pierce *had* seen was the look on Detective Cooper's face. It was Pierce who called in and requested the department shrink be sent down here immediately. The expression on the Homicide detective's face had frightened the rookie more than anything he could remember and he found he suddenly had absolutely no desire to see what was inside that office.

The very neatly uniformed cop at the gate of the Fourteenth looked at Dr. Morrissey's ID, then let him into the parking lot. The station looked like a beehive or anthill. There were cops, both uniformed and plain-clothed going in and out, lab techs from CSI in their bright yellow jumpsuits scurrying here and there, and one detective sitting on the bottom step apparently oblivious to everything going on around him. The strangest part of the whole scene, was the lack of noise. Other than footsteps and the background noise of radio chatter, it was absolutely quiet. Kevin Morrissey did not need psychic powers to know something horrible had happened here and that the detective on the steps had seen more than his mind was capable of processing. He also knew somehow, that this was just the beginning. As he calmly approached the almost catatonic detective, Dr. Morrissey was frightened in a way he had never been in his entire life. When he was about six feet away from him, the detective looked up and said in a monotone, "They crucified him," and collapsed, toppling sideways onto the pavement.

Sergeant Porter watched as Dr. Morrissey put his ID away and drove through the gate, parked his car and approached Mark Cooper, sitting on the steps. As always, Porter knew many things. Most of which he could not share with anyone else, except Gloria, who also knew most of the same things. The thing he knew right now, was that this had been Detective Cooper's last day on the force. There was a doorway open to Porter's perceptions which would allow him to know even more, to see the full effect of the horror the detective had experienced on the rest of his life, but he chose to close it without peering into that particular future.

Stan Robertson smiled. Actually, to an outside observer, the disheveled, filthy, stinking heap that once was Sgt. Stan Robertson grinned stupidly, drooling down his front. In his right hand, he held his service revolver, in his left, the oddly shaped bottle containing that wondrous apple liqueur his new boss (why did the word, Master come to mind?) had given him. When he had returned to the church, Caine had been pleased with him. He had performed well, the priest had said. Above and beyond what was expected of him. He had called him a credit to his new position. Deep in the recesses of what was left of Stan's mind, a tiny voice wondered what that position was, exactly, and how long it would last. With a gulp from the bottle, he silenced the voice. He was happy, and experience had taught him that asking questions about his position, whatever it was at any given time, only led to unhappiness.

Caine was pleased. He had to admit that, if he had the capacity for such a useless emotion, he would probably also be a little afraid of his latest disciple. The unfortunate police sergeant had a depth of depravity and a capacity for evil that not even he had ever seen. Even though this was, in its way, a pleasant surprise, he did not like it. He did not care for surprises of any kind. But, he knew that once he had Alisha Ferdinand, once she gave herself to him as she was most certainly going to do, he would never be surprised again. He smiled in anticipation of this too long delayed consummation and somewhere, someone died in unexpected and unimaginable agony. It was not a good thing when Caine smiled.

Gloria felt everything that Caine was feeling. She wished she did not, but she had no choice. She felt the uncertainty and, though Caine denied its existence, the fear about Stan Robertson. She had to admit that these emotions were somewhat satisfying to her. But his anticipatory gloating and that smile... She shuddered as she felt the far-off death the smile caused. True, the victim of Caine's emotions was dying anyway, but to spend one's final moments in such absolute agony, Gloria knew, was the true definition of Hell. She quietly sang herself temporarily out of this existence. Sometimes, she had to go away for a moment in order to carry on. Of course, she was not completely gone. Her link to Porter kept her grounded and available. It was an appropriate name he had chosen for himself this time, she mused. It meant 'Gatekeeper'. As she finished her song and faded, all memory of her vanished as well. She found this troubling in a way that she never had before. If she was completely honest with herself, she would admit that she was saddened by the thought that Rob Paulpry could not remember her. She knew that, when this was all finished, however it turned out, he would have no recollection that she had ever existed, but, all the same, it bothered her in a way that it should not.

Each of the innumerable times that they had come to this plane to thwart his plans, their existence was only the vague shadow of a memory in the deepest recesses of the strongest minds they had encountered. Of course, this had resulted in some unintended consequences, religious beliefs, scientific anomalies, doubt, wars. They had the capacity to make certain that even the remaining traces of memory were obliterated, but that would violate their vow against tampering with free will, so the consequences remained. Just this once she wished not for permission to scour clean the memories, but to let some of them remain.

As Sergeant Porter stood in the gateway to the Fourteenth Precinct parking lot, he, too, was aware of Caine's thoughts and feelings, and the horrible consequences of his emotions. He was also aware of Gloria's awareness of and reaction to those feelings and consequences. It wasn't that the terrible things that happened did not affect him, they just affected him differently than they did Gloria. That was the nature of their partnership. Each of them had a place and their differing reactions to things allowed them to function and keep one another, and so much more, in balance. Gloria's reactions were emotional and personal, his more analytical. Porter was not without sympathy, empathy, and other emotions, but they presented themselves to his mind differently. He saw them as facts and, sometimes, puzzles. He felt the emotions, but was less affected than Gloria. He was a creature of reason and she was one of feelings. Together, they represented the two aspects of the universe. What some called the Yin and Yang, Good and Evil, Masculine and Feminine, Darkness and Light, and so on. Both of these aspects needed to exist in all beings, but rarely were they in perfect balance. Tip the scale too far one way or the other, and you get Caine, as he was calling himself, and his servants, both willing and unwilling, completely aware and oblivious.

Caine and his minions represented the worst of both sides of the equation. Some were so overcome and controlled by their emotions that every feeling became, for them, an unbearable burden which they tried to escape by inflicting horrors upon others. Those on the other end of the spectrum were overcome by logic and reason to the point that they completely sublimated all feelings and emotions. These were the most dangerous ones. They lacked empathy, guilt, or any of the emotions which served to keep the basest carnal desires in check. But they also lacked love, joy, and happiness and were constantly trying to fill that void. That was where the horror began. Lacking emotions themselves, they could not grasp the concept of feelings in others and failed to understand the emotions their actions caused. To them, the feelings others experienced were like foreign languages and they lacked the emotional Rosetta Stone everyone else seemed born with. As strange as it may seem, by eliciting strong emotions in others, they sought understanding within themselves. Though their actions were deplorable, their motivation was at least understandable. If, that is, one could divorce one's own emotions from the analysis. Porter could, Gloria could not. This was as it should be to maintain the all important balance. It was also why Gloria needed to escape periodically. To process it all emotionally, which was much more difficult than processing it intellectually. Porter knew he had the easier path in that respect.

So he let Gloria go, allowing the connection between them to become as tenuous as it was safe for it to be. She needed a momentary rest before facing what was to come. He turned and blocked the reporter trying to slip past him through the gate and smiled to himself over Gloria's assessment of the appropriateness of the name he had chosen for himself. His name had changed many times over the aeons to fit each of the many situations they had faced, but hers always remained the same, Gloria, 'Glory'.

Al stared at the legal pad Rob had handed her. The cat had fled for parts unknown when, at the reporter's beckoning, she had sat down on the couch. He had given her the scribbled flow chart with an expression of satisfaction which seemed to say, "There you are, all wrapped up...Sort of". But she was baffled. None of the arrows, lines, or references made any sense to her at all.

Rob had it all figured out, except that it still didn't really make sense to him. He had handed the detective the flow chart hoping she would shed light on the connections he had drawn to the events and facts of the past weeks. Her absolutely blank look as she stared at his connections dashed his hopes, so he started explaining it all. By the time he had finished, the look on her face almost made him wish he hadn't.

All Al could think about was the warning Grams had given her after her death. About how the Bad Man was real and had been after the female members of the family who had inherited the ability to glimpse the future. How long, she wondered, had he been chasing her ancestors? Rob was saying something, but she couldn't hear him, she waved vaguely in his direction and grunted by way of response. She heard him say something about his cell phone and that he'd be back as soon as he could. Then, she heard the door open and close. She realized that she was alone, which was how she usually preferred it, but this time she felt lonely, and she didn't like it.

CHAPTER FIFTEEN

Rob walked out of the apartment and into the hallway feeling as though he was walking out of a dream or an alternate dimension. Nothing seemed right or normal anymore. Everything he deduced from the dream journal, his notes and pictures, the police reports, everything fit. But none of it made any sense. Alisha Ferdinand had dreamed about Caine?...*Caine*? The fratricidal brother from Genesis? Who had apparently changed the spelling of his name over the past few millennia, and now was alive, real, and killing people, starting riots, and out to get her for some unexplained and nefarious reason? Rob seriously began doubting his sanity, not for the first time, but more seriously than ever before.

Underneath all of the confusion, uncertainty, and fear, Rob's reporter's mind was still working, somehow. He knew he had to call Helen and come up with a good excuse for being incommunicado for the past couple of days, and he knew whatever his reason, short of death, she wouldn't buy it. Maybe, he thought in a whimsical moment, he could tell her he had been out saving the world and would call her after the apocalypse. That thought brought a wry chuckle and momentary smile then, a shudder of fear.

He was also mentally running through his contacts, trying to think of anyone who might be able to shed a small glimmer of light on the situation. After what had happened to Spike, Rob rather doubted anyone would even take his calls, much less give him any information. Passing the doorway to one of the other apartments on Alisha's floor, Rob saw a newspaper lying there and picked it up.

The front page featured a spread on the riots in The End and the murders at the Fourteenth. Staring at the crappy photos and scanning lame text, Rob knew without looking who's byline would be under them. This was definitely Alex Morton's shitty work. The pics of the riots were all taken long after the fact, and the shot of the Fourteenth showed nothing except crime scene tape across the gate and one neatly dressed police sergeant standing guard. Morton hadn't even thought to focus on the cop's face to get some emotion into the shot. His features were blurred beyond recognition as though he had moved just at the shot was taken. Oddly, Rob could read the cop's name tag, "Porter". With all this going on, Rob suddenly realized that he was probably the last thing on Helen, the Barbarian's mind. She had real news happening. He could picture her behind her desk, chewing on a pencil, barking orders and practically salivating over the piss-poor photos. Rob thought, "She should see what's on my camera". Which thought made him realize he'd left his camera in Ferdinand's apartment.

For approximately half a moment, he thought about going back for it, but changed his mind. Later, he would regret the headache that decision had cost him. Right now, he just wanted to get back to his house, shower, change clothes, and figure out what to do next. He was so absorbed in his own short-range plans, he failed to notice the broken passenger side rear window in his car, or the hulking, filthy figure squeezed into the back floorboard of the car. As he slumped over in his seat, consciousness slipping away, he thought, "Wow, you really do see stars!"

Stan Robertson was always amazed at how little effort it took to sap someone into la-la land. Just a flick of the wrist with the right aim and they were out. As he drove the unconscious reporter's car toward the church, all he could think was how pleased his master would be. The word came easily and unbidden now, Stan had completely surrendered all that he was and ever had been to Caine and was happy with his new place in the universe. Happier than he had ever been. But, it had been awhile since he had any of that wonderful elixir. He began to feel a burning desire for the liqueur. Funny, he'd never been a fan of fruity drinks before, but that one... Caine said it was the special very old variety of apple that made it so good. Stan felt clear-headed when he drank it, not fuzzy like with other drinks. It was almost as though it made him smarter, let him see things he couldn't before. He needed some now, he was having a hard time remembering why he was pulling up outside a run-down church in The End with an unconscious reporter beside him. He even got a vague sick feeling deep down in the pit of his stomach, like when he was a kid and had done something wrong, but he hadn't done anything wrong had he?

"No, my son," came the voice in his head, "you are just taking what is rightfully yours, fulfilling your destiny." It was the voice of his master, and he felt comforted and strong as he hoisted the inert body of the newspaper man over his shoulder and climbed the cracked and crooked steps into the church, his new home. Inside, he knew his new father waited. The one who really understood him and was going to reward him for his work.

Caine watched the wretched, filthy, stinking creature which had once been Stan Robertson stumble into the vestibule of the church with Rob Paulpry slung over his shoulder and, again, had the momentary vicious urge to let him see what he had really become, but resisted. He still needed the disreputable creature a little longer and knew that giving him that glimpse would render him mad beyond the point of usefulness. No, it was better to keep his disciple happy for now and sent waves of approval his direction as Stan deposited his limp burden on the filthy, tattered aisle runner and reached, desperately for the bottle of liqueur. Stan Robertson's very last thought before he was wiped completely out of existence would be a vision of what he was and had become. The thought created an almost sexual feeling of anticipation in Caine and he smiled his disastrous smile again, with all its consequences.

Even though Gloria had shut herself away as completely as possible from everyone and everything in order to recompose herself and prepare for what was coming, some things could and did still get through to her. She gasped and came part of the way back the current reality as Rob Paulpry was stunned insensate by Stan Robertson's sap. She was aware enough to sing a soothing song toward the reporter. She knew better than to become so attached to any of the participants in this or any other reality, but there was something in the reporter, a nobility that went far above and beyond what she, or Porter, or anyone else had any right to expect out of any human with all their imperfections and foibles. Of course, like so many, Paulpry had no idea of what lay within him. The normal insecurities, worries, and doubts covered over his deepest self. Life laid these on like many layers of paint, gradually obscuring what was at the core until few were ever required to dig deeply enough within themselves to get to the kernel at the center.

That kernel was the good and pure part of every being. In some, it was very small, but it existed in everyone. Even Caine, as he was calling himself this time, though, over the millennia, his kernel had nearly been ground away by his decision to pursue the path he had chosen. Gloria was probably the only being on any plane of existence who had enough insight to still see the small glimmer that was all that was left of the good within Caine. Even Martha Mae Wilson, standing on the verge of crossing over, where everything becomes clear had not been able to discern its faint glow. But he had surrendered, eroded and buried it for the sake of power. Power wasn't everything, and without responsibility it was nothing, no, she corrected herself, it was worse than nothing. If Caine ever achieved the power he craved, that which was locked deep within Alisha Ferdinand, nothingness would be a blessing.

Al sat and stared at the flow chart. She found she would rather it had remained the meaningless scribbles of a low-life reporter. Once Rob had explained it all to her, shown her the photo of the church, the bible references, and how it all tied together with her dreams and experiences, it made sense...too much sense. But, even though she could see the logic and the connections among all the facts, she still failed to understand it. It was like algebra. Her teacher had tried to explain how to work the problems and why there were letters mixed in with the numbers. She had understood the principles, but had not been able to manipulate the mixed up formulae and make them do what they did for Mr. Reed and the other students. In the end, she had dropped the class and taken Math for Decision-Makers, or "Math for Dummies" as it was called. The difference this time, was that there was no easier class to move to. The Bad Man was apparently here, in the real world, and she had to deal with him.

Grams had warned her that the Bad Man was real, and that he wanted her for some reason, but she still couldn't make herself believe that her personal bogeyman was loose in The End wreaking havoc and trying to lure her into some sort of trap. What could he possibly want from her and the generations of her female relatives with what Grams had always called, "The Gift"? There were other people with the ability to divine glimpses of the future, and do it a lot more clearly than she could, why didn't he just go after them and leave her and the people she loved the hell alone?

She called the Fourteenth. Sergeant Porter answered on the first ring and assured her that she did not need to come in as it was her scheduled day off. She heard the other line ringing in the background and the desk sergeant cut her protestations off to answer it. "Weird," she thought. They should be calling in every breathing member of the force. The End had erupted in the type of riot everyone with any sense had been predicting for decades, and two police officers had been brutally murdered in the station! All hell was breaking loose, and she was to take her day off? Nothing was making sense. She knew that she should go into the precinct and give a statement. She would probably be put on administrative leave and eventually fired for her actions, for leaving the scene and not calling it in. She could use the dreams as an excuse, she supposed. Admit that she hadn't been taking the sleeping pills and show the brass the dream journal. That might get her a license to fly a desk instead of being fired. She'd probably wind up like that sorry drunk, Robertson. Wouldn't that be a fine end to her career, and wouldn't her dad be proud? No, there had to be another way. No one knew that she and Paulpry had been there. As far as the higher ups were concerned, she was still recovering from last night.

Remembering the night before stopped her dead in her mental tracks. Someone had called something in, but what? What information had they been given at the fourteenth? What, she pondered, did they think had happened? Who had filed the report? Everything was spinning like when she had gone on the Tilt-A-Whirl at the carnival as a child. It was her Grams' favorite ride and little Alisha had gone on with her. It was not Al's favorite experience. The cherry sno-cone and hot dog she had just eaten had stained Grams' dress beyond redemption. Of course, Grams had not been angry, she just laughed and signaled the man running the ride to stop it. She could really use Grams right now. She wanted to cuddle up in her old bed with her and tell her everything. Grams wouldn't tell her what to do, she never had, but she'd always had a way of making even the worst situations make at least *some* sense.

Al suddenly felt like she was going to be sick and lay down on the couch. She hadn't intended to doze off, just lay there and wait for Rob to return. Then they'd figure out what to do. She couldn't believe she'd just had that thought. She actually trusted the reporter and felt safer and more confident with him around. Maybe she *was* crazy! She closed her eyes and, just as she faded to an unexpected sleep, barely noted the cat jumping onto the couch and curling up on her chest, purring its too-loud, broken clockworks purr.

Porter smiled. He knew Gloria understood and used sound on a level that no other being in the history of existence ever had or ever would. The thought that the raucous purring of the cat would keep Caine out of Alisha's dreams was a bit ironic given how she had always felt about felines. Of course cats had been used historically as guards of Tibetan monasteries. The monks also understood sound and knew that the purring of their satisfied pets helped them to meditate by blocking out other vibrations. So, Alisha slept. She needed rest for what was to come. Porter wished he could send her reassurance that everything was going to be all right, but there were just too many possible outcomes, too much yet to be decided. Of course, the future was always uncertain, but, sometimes, it hinged on only one or two decisions and events and the possible outcomes were easy to fathom if one knew where to look. But in times like this, every little decision carried possible repercussions well beyond the ability of those involved to comprehend. At this juncture, Stan Robertson's decision to pull the legs off the spider he'd caught crawling along the floor of the church had more meaning than the combined teachings of every religion that had ever existed.

Rob's head was pounding like after a week-long drunk back in the bad old days. He tried to lift his hand and explore the painful swelling behind his left ear, but found his arms would not move. As panic started to set in, the accompanying adrenaline rush sped along the process of returning to awareness and he realized that he was not paralyzed as he had first feared, but that his hands were handcuffed around a post. As his senses began functioning, he smelled dust, smoke from incense and cheap candles and something else. It was an overpowering miasma of all the worst odors the human body can produce and it was getting stronger as he heard someone approaching. Feigning continued unconsciousness, Rob listened to the footsteps as the bearer of the intolerable stench grew closer. The footfalls sounded like something from a horror movie. It was as though the mad doctor's hunchbacked assistant, Igor had gone on a three day bender. The steps were shambling and stumbled around. Rob could tell that whoever was approaching him was a big one, heavy. His captor panted with either exertion or excitement. It was impossible to tell which with his eyes closed, but he was not yet ready or willing to open them. He hoped to gain some more information before his captor knew he was conscious and aware. The headache made it hard to focus and the odor emanating from whoever was approaching him made it hard to breathe. Rob was unsure how long he could continue his charade.

The stinking, shambling creature was right on top of Rob when it stopped. He must be some homeless wacko, Rob reasoned. That would explain the smell, but not why he had been taken hostage. "Still out cold, Master," a whiny male voice slurred. Master?

The groggy reporter felt more than heard the voice which replied. "No, Sergeant, our reporter friend is quite conscious and aware of his surroundings." Rob had no idea how he knew this, but he somehow knew that what he had just heard and felt was the voice of pure evil, the voice of the Bad Man, the voice of Caine and suddenly his determination and self discipline fled him. They were replaced by fear of a magnitude Rob had never known. His eyes snapped open, just in time for the world to go red and sparkly as he was kicked in the stomach.

"We don't like liars and fakers," the nearby voice whined at him. Rob felt something wet land on his face. Opening his eyes again, he found himself looking right into the face of his assailant. The large man was bending over him and drooling. Just as Rob connected this fact with the wetness on his cheek, another drop of fetid spittle landed on his forehead and the brute started laughing. Suddenly, the groggy reporter realized that he recognized his captor, but couldn't place where he had seen him.

"Enough," the other voice resonated. "We need him relatively unharmed...for now. After I have what I require, I will give him to you to do with as you please." Rob suddenly felt as though he was in the middle of a very bad horror flick. Any minute now, he expected a group of black-robed disciples to file in, chanting, and surround him. But that did not happen. What did happen is that his breath returned, his vision cleared and the bulky, odorous being standing over him straightened up, and suddenly Rob knew where he had encountered him before.

The vile creature was wearing a policeman's uniform, or what was left of one. "That explains the handcuffs," Rob thought. He was the surly, drunken desk sergeant Rob had encountered just recently at the Fourteenth Precinct while waiting for Lieutenant Ferdinand. "Well, Sergeant," he said. "Fancy meeting you here. I have to say, I love what you've done with the place, but you've really let yourself go." The filthy, smelly cop turned back toward him, his bleary eyes glaring with pure hatred and malevolent intent. He took a step in Rob's direction and suddenly froze in place.

"Yes, Master," he sniveled, though Rob hadn't heard anything from the shadowy figure which may or may not have been Alisha's nightmare man. This was getting weirder by the minute. Rob looked around as the cop moved away. He saw that he was in the old church where Sergeant McDonnell had been assaulted. Up at the front of the church, he could make out a very large shadowy figure wearing a broad-brimmed hat. Even though every logical part of Rob's mind screamed that it was impossible, he knew that it was him. A few moments before, he would have thought that he was as terrified as it was possible to be, but, with each passing moment and each revelation, he knew his terror was just beginning.

When Al awoke she had that momentary confusion and disorientation which often comes after falling asleep at an odd time. It was dark out, but she didn't know whether it was late night, morning, or evening. The cat was gone, but she could still feel its warmth on her chest so it hadn't been gone long, and the reporter was still gone as well, she realized with a start. Whatever time of day it was, he should have been back hours ago. He was just going for a shower and change of clothes. Suddenly, she was wide awake.

Sitting up too quickly, she looked at the time on the kitchen clock, after her head stopped spinning that is, and saw that it was eight p.m. That meant she had been asleep and Rob had been gone for six hours. She looked around. All of his cryptic notes, the dream journal, bible, and his camera were scattered on and around the coffee table. On her way to the bathroom, she dialed his cell. Though he had promised to have it on, it went directly to voicemail, with a message that his mailbox was full. Al thought it was funny that electronic devices referred to mailboxes and that we still called it dialing when there was no longer a dial to turn.

Returning to the living room, she saw the cat playing with the wrist strap on Rob's camera. Shooing the creature away, she saw that the feline had somehow managed to turn the device on. She picked it up and looked at the screen. It was one of the pics of the front of the church in The End. But, something was different. There were three figures posed on the steps like a family taking a group photo after services. Looking more closely, she felt a fear-induced wave of nausea wash over her. Standing side by side, like siblings were Rob Paulpry and Stan Robertson and, standing behind them with his arms out in a welcoming gesture, was The Bad Man.

CHAPTER SIXTEEN

Gloria returned from her self imposed exile. In a way, it was like waking from a dream. But rather than waking to the peaceful comfort of home, hearth, and bed, she awoke to a nightmare. Everything was building to the inevitable breaking point. Of course, Gloria had known it was coming, it always did. But this time was different. So much more was at stake. The being who was now calling itself Caine had more of a grip than ever before on his intended victim, and she was farther separated from her inner strength. Alisha had worked so hard all her life to develop outer strength to cover her deep seated insecurities, that she had not developed and nurtured the tremendous inner strength which lay at her core. It was her deepest innermost strength she would need in the coming conflict.

"We must let her find it on her own," Porter reminded her. She knew tampering was forbidden, but why should it be if the intent was good? "You know," he reminded her. This was an old argument, older than mortals could even conceive and Gloria knew the answers and their reasons and knew that they were all valid. It did not make it any easier to set on the sidelines and watch. Certainly, they were allowed to give help and clues, but within very strict boundaries.

Gloria had crossed those boundaries once, long ago. She was only helping a good man achieve what he needed to achieve at another time when everything good teetered on the edge of the great abyss. The resulting wars, famines, plagues and destruction were very nearly the end of her. Of course, she could not die, but she almost withdrew permanently to a realm where she would be forever removed from the trials and tribulations of the mortal worlds. Porter (not what he was called then) calmly forced her to face up to her responsibilities in the matter, telling her that she must help restore the world once the chaos she had inadvertently caused had run its course.

Of course, he was right. Not that he was always right, no being is, just as no being is always wrong, even Caine. Once, he had been a being of pure light just like all others that came into existence. But, long ago the thirst for power had overcome him, making him what he was now, irretrievably lost in darkness. Gloria felt he was so deep into the blackness that it would be impossible for him to ever find his way out. Porter held a more hopeful opinion. He actually believed that, should the right incentive come along, Caine could be led back into the light. This was another long standing argument that only immense stretches of time and limitless possibilities could ever resolve. Their arguments were, for the most part, a way of passing the time between the periods when their active guidance was needed, as it was now, perhaps more so than ever before.

Of course there were her feelings toward Rob Paulpry as well. It was not an easy thing for her to define, but there was something more there than should be. It wasn't that beings like she and Porter were without feelings, or even that they were expected to ignore or operate without them. In truth, it was their feelings which allowed them to do what they did. Without them, they would simply not care and if they stopped caring, they would stop helping. Of course, there was their innate sense of duty, but even that was based on feelings, mostly fear. Fear of what would become of the whole of creation should they lose or quit.

"He is special," Porter agreed with her thoughts. It wasn't that he was eavesdropping, or intruding. It was how they communicated best. If she wanted privacy, she had it, but keeping the lines of communication open made their job easier and faster. "More so than he even knows," he continued. "Let us hope that he discovers that fact before it is too late."

Porter remained on guard at the gate into the Fourteenth Precinct parking lot. Inside, the crime scene techs were still poring over the abattoir within the building. Their job was made all the more difficult by the fact that the grisly scene surrounded two of their own. The members of the force were as accustomed as it was possible to be to seeing officers killed in the line of duty. Cops were shot, stabbed, even run over on an all too frequent basis, but this was something else. The wholesale slaughter of two of their own right in the station was unprecedented, even in The End. Of course, Potter knew exactly who was responsible, directly and indirectly and the police would have one of those answers as soon as they reviewed the security camera tapes and ran the fingerprints. Potter knew that this knowledge would not make things better. Discovering that one of their own had perpetrated this horror would be more than many of them could possibly prepare for or process. But this was only the beginning, moving toward an end none of them could even suspect or imagine. The resolution of it all was hanging over the heads of two very different people, more alike than they realized, and even Potter could not see the final outcome. When there were so many possibilities, his vision was limited and clouded. By the time it completely cleared, it was all over, for the good or the bad.

"And we dare not interfere," came Gloria's resignation-tinged voice in his mind, Potter nodded grimly and shooed away a reporter trying to get closer to the crime scene than was allowed. Gloria began singing.

Stan Robertson awoke with a start. He had a song stuck in his head, but the odd thing was it wasn't one he had ever heard. It was a woman's voice singing what sounded like a hymn in some language he couldn't identify. He looked around himself. He was in a dilapidated church and something reeked. He looked down at his right hand and saw his weapon there, in his left was an oddly shaped bottle, then, he remembered. Smiling in anticipation, he drank deeply of the liqueur and it all went away, the song, the momentary fear and the stench which he barely had time to realize was him, before it was borne away in the pleasant haze of the alcohol.

Caine watched this with malicious glee. He had allowed that little glimpse of reality to slip in and savored the momentary confusion and revulsion his disciple had felt before slipping back into his stupor, but in his arrogance, he failed to recognize the voice singing inside the mortal's head. "Soon enough," he promised. He almost relished the thought of allowing Stan Robertson full awareness and the horror that would cause just before it destroyed him as much as the thought of finally possessing Alisha Ferdinand...almost.

Rob peeked carefully out of one slitted eye at his captor. The bulky police sergeant in the filthy remains of his dress blues stirred, looked around as if confused, drank from the strange bottle he was clutching, and faded away. Rob wished fervently he would put the damned gun away. Just the presence of it was enough to give him the willies, add to that the fact that it was unholstered, cocked, and pointed in his general direction, and he could focus on nothing else. He knew he was going to have to get his mind under control and start thinking clearly if he was going to get out of this alive, but it was all so surreal he found it nearly impossible to even take in the situation, much less make any sense of it. It was like trying to wake himself from a nightmare. But this was no dream and there was no waking up.

Al fought hard to keep the panic which threatened to incapacitate her under control. That picture had not been on the camera before. How could it have been? It was a message for her from The Bad Man. He was telling her he had Paulpry and even showing her who had helped him and where they were. Of course, her logical cop mind said, you need to call it in and have backup. But the emotional part of her mind which had dealt with him since she was twelve knew that if she did so, there would be no one and nothing at the church when they arrived and the reporter would be dead. In a weird, twisted moment of fantasy and knowledge of how The Bad Man thought and operated, she felt certain that his death would somehow be pinned on her. No, she had to go it alone, but not unprepared.

Opening her dad's old foot locker, she rummaged around in his old papers and "toys" as he called them. The wooden box which sat at the end of her bed just as it had his as long as she could remember was a tangible history of most of her father's adult life. From his time in the Marine Corps, to his lifetime protecting his city. Sometimes, Al wondered what he thought, seeing the city in which he was raised decline to its current sorry state of existence. She thrust the maudlin thoughts out of her mind and forced herself to focus on the task at hand. Finding what she needed, she double checked everything, weapons, ammunition, and her own resolve. Somehow she knew that what was about to happen was the culmination of generations of strife and battle between the women of her family and the thing that was The Bad Man. She also knew, that, one way or another, it was going to be over, here and now.

Starting her car, her police radio came to life just in time for her to hear the bulletin go out on Stan Robertson, wanted in connection with the murders of Corporal Rick Hartley and Captain John McElroy. The fact that it was another cop made the grisly murders even worse. She had a feeling no one was going to find that puke, Robertson. But she knew where he was, and she was going there right now. Again, her training said call for backup, she told that part of her brain to shut the fuck up. There would be no backup today, this was between her and the creature called Caine.

As Al started her car, Gloria, keeping watch over Rob Paulpry, felt his fear and wished she could do something to assuage it. Instead, she and Porter readied themselves for the coming battle. They did what they could to get innocents out of the way. Even in that act of compassion they were limited, there would still be innocents (and not so innocents, Gloria reminded herself) in harm's way when the conflict reached its climax, but that was the nature of the universe. Overall, there was no reckoning of guilt or innocence when great powers came into conflict. That came later. It all seemed so random at times, even to Gloria who had the ability to look at existence from a wider perspective and see how everything was related to everything and how it all worked to maintain the essential balance. Of course, that did not take into account beings like Caine, who constantly sought to tip the balance in ways which fed their sordid egos. There had been many such creatures over the millennia, but he was definitely the most persistent, which made him the worst.

Eventually, most of those who sought to remake the whole of existence for their own glory and satisfaction saw the error of their ways. The bright spark was rekindled and they moved on beyond the venal desires which had driven them, sometimes for unimaginable spans of time, to conquer, destroy, and recreate. But not Caine. He refused to even acknowledge that the brightness had ever existed within him. He believed that he was separate from all the rest of existence and above its laws, that he actually deserved that which he desired. Gloria thought Alisha's name for him was perhaps more appropriate than any he had ever chosen for himself, he was The Bad Man.

Caine was in a high state of excitement. He felt her approaching of her own free will. In all the time he had been pursuing the women in her family, Caine had never been so close. Alisha Ferdinand's unshakeable belief in him without understanding anything about his nature had given him the access to this plane of existence he had always craved, and her denial of her deeper powers and abilities had allowed him to play on her fears and manipulate her into the position where she would soon give herself willingly to him. The reporter made the perfect bait. He had a core of power, too, but was completely oblivious to it. Trapped by his own fears and weak, quivering flesh, he would be no obstacle when the time came. Caine, momentarily considered just eliminating him. He had done his part, luring Alisha Ferdinand to her fate, keeping the mortal husk that was Rob Paulpry alive served no further purpose. then, he reconsidered. It would be so much more satisfying to have her do it, after she had given herself fully to him. The thought of having the female slowly and tortuously wring every last bit of life essence out of the sniveling lump that was Rob Paulpry was almost unbearably exciting to Caine, and he closed his eyes, savoring the image.

Rob felt something change. It was almost as if some invisible bonds had slipped. He was still handcuffed to the post, but it felt like a shackle which had been clamped around his mind had been loosened, he could think more clearly and a little bit of the paralyzing fear seeped away. Peeking over at the cop, he saw him stir and open his bloodshot eyes and a little of the fear returned.

Stan awoke and looked around. He was confused and angry, neither of which were foreign feelings to him, of course, but they seemed different. He couldn't quite piece together the events which had led up to him being here, in an old church, filthy, hungover, and hurting like hell in every part of his body. Looking around he saw the slumped figure of that reporter, what was his name? Pauper, or something like that, he almost remembered. Somehow, he decided, it must be the reporter's fault. Ever since he had turned up after that whiny little Jew-boy had got what he deserved from the Spic gang, things had gone to shit. Stan couldn't actually remember how, but he knew it was the reporters fault. Looking down, he saw that his weapon was cocked and lying in his lap. Grinning, the cop rose very unsteadily to his feet and headed over to exact a little payback.

Rob saw the hulking form of Stan Robertson stumble to his feet and start toward him with a malicious grin on his face and that huge pistol clutched in his ham-sized fist and the fear returned with full force. Oddly, it wasn't the same as before. There was something missing from the fear, as though the volume had been turned down on it. He found he could still think and even act, and there was something else. He felt a calm, cool core deep within himself he had not found in years, He remembered after his mother had taken her terminal swim to drown her personal demons, he had felt afraid, alone and lost and then, one night, after waking from a dream in which he had acted out his mother's suicide, he had stopped crying and felt that same cool, strong, core. It helped him, somehow, to recover as much as was possible from the death of his mother and move on. He latched onto it now, determined not to let it slip away, no matter what these two lunatics did to him.

Stan saw the fear in the wormy littlie reporter's eyes and drank it in. That fear would be the last thing the newspaperman would feel, but Stan determined that he would do everything he could to magnify it and take it to the breaking point before he released him from it. That scum was responsible for all this, he was convinced of it. He had cost Stan his job, his standing and, he realized with the tiny speck of rational mind he had left, his sanity, and he would pay. He walked unsteadily over to the sniveling sack of shit and planted a kick squarely in the reporter's ribs.

Rob had seen the kick coming and was braced for it, but it still hurt like hell and knocked the breath out of him as he felt the unmistakably crack of one or more broken ribs. He fight to regain his breath as the cop bent down, blowing fetid breath that smelled like something long dead in the summer sun into his face. "It's just beginning," Robertson informed him. "You're gonna pay for what you did to me, you slime bag." He punctuated this last with a vicious kick, which Rob barely managed to keep from landing in his crotch.

"Picking on somebody that's tied up, real brave," Rob managed to gasp out, surprised by his own bravado. Robertson's fist caught him on the side of his head, bouncing his cranium off the pole and Rob, for the second time that day, saw stars, but didn't pass out. Then his tormentor leaned over him, and rob was very afraid and very disgusted. The odor coming off him nearly made him pass out. But, instead of inflicting even more torture, the stinking sergeant reached behind him and unlocked one side of the cuffs.

Before Rob could react to this surprising development, Stan stuck the barrel of his pistol into the still gasping reporter's mouth and said softly, almost sweetly, "Feel braver, now? You're uncuffed, what now?" Before the terrified Rob could even formulate a possible plan of action, there was another change in the room. The cop's eyes grew wide with his own fear, and he looked up toward the front of the church. From that direction, the booming voice rang out, "What do you think you are doing? Were you instructed to inflict tortures?" Stan shook his head, tears streaming down his face. "Do you know what happens to those that disobey me?" Again, Stan shook his head. Suddenly Rob's mind (and somehow, Rob knew Stan's as well) was filled with horrific scenes of the most unimaginable tortures inflicted upon individuals and groups of people, men, women, and children of all shapes sizes and colors. Rob felt physically ill and he saw, to his revulsion, that Stan wet himself in fear.

"Yes, just like when you were a child and your father came in drunk. So weak and afraid, you can do no more than piss yourself!" The taunt hit home, Rob could see. Stan Robertson withdrew again to his corner and took up the oddly shaped bottle and put it to his lips. Rob could see that it was empty and the degraded cop looked up toward his master with a disgustingly pitiful pleading expression on his fat face. "I'll be good, I promise," he whined like a child caught with his hand in the cookie jar. Then, Rob decided he had completely lost his mind. The bottle was suddenly filled with an amber liquid which the cop sucked at greedily, whining and mewling like a nursing infant. As Rob passed out, his brain was filled with the echoing sound of the demented laughter of the dark figure at the front of the church.

CHAPTER SEVENTEEN

Given the nightmarish madness of the rest of the day, "and", Al thought, "I know a thing or two about nightmares...and madness", the police radio in her car was strangely quiet. It was almost like one of her dreams, driving along the dark and deserted streets toward The End with fear permeating every molecule of the air and invading her soul, the radio silent, and the knowledge that something big was about to go down, though she didn't know exactly what. Looking around as she entered the festering microcosm and drove toward the church, she noticed she didn't even see the usual dealers, hookers, and junkies one could count on populating the doorways and corners at any given time of the day or night. It was as if someone had finally gone through and cleared the place out.

Countless politicians and police chiefs had promised to do just that over the years. The result was always the same. A few token raids, a handful of arrests, some cops injured or killed, a lawsuit or two for brutality, then...back to business as usual. The End was, and always would be, The End. I couldn't be politicized or policed away. It was as eternal as the sun, and on some days, like this one, just as hot. But Al couldn't help but wonder where the fuck everybody had gone. She found the lack of life more frightening than anything she had ever experienced. "Gimme a junkie or a crack whore any day," she muttered, more to break the unsettling silence than anything else.

Rounding the corner onto Nodaway (the Land of Nod, according to Rob's rambling dissection of the clues and what he perceived as their biblical references), she found them and immediately wished she hadn't. It looked like the entire population of The End was there. They were sitting in the street, kneeling on the broad, chipped and cracked concrete steps leading up to the church, standing on the decaying retaining wall around the base of the lighted sign which identified it as St. Jude's and offered Bingo on Tuesday night. The thought of Bingo reminded her of more of the reporter's ramblings. The Bingo card on the flier had G-44 and 45 out of place, a fact first noticed by Frank. According to Rob this was a reference to Genesis 4:4 and 4:5, where Cain and Abel brought their offerings to God and Abel was given respect while Cain was shunned. He had gone on to theorize that the marked square, G-48 was a reference to Genesis 4:8, where Cain slew Abel, pointing out that Caine had slain the Abell brothers in the little house on 43rd St. Of course, she had dismissed it all as crazy, but, seeing the sight before her, she was no longer so certain and had to admit to herself, she never really had been.

She got out of the car carefully. Apparently, none of the filthy throng had noticed her arrival, all intently focused as they were on the church. Moving quietly to the rear of the car, she popped the trunk and got out her riot gun and ammo. The junkies, whores, and other dregs of society continued to ignore her. As she carefully closed the trunk of the car and took a deep breath to steady herself, the sound came to her. It was a low, rhythmic chant. It took her a minute to realize where it was coming from. It was emanating from the throng of human refuse littering the street and steps leading up to the dilapidated church. Listening more intently, Alisha's blood ran cold and she nearly fainted in the street. The crowd was chanting a name, over and over again, "Caine...Caine...Caine..."

Inside the church, Caine was ecstatic. He could hear the chant outside and felt her arrive. Soon, he knew, she would be his. He looked over at the once more unconscious figure of the pathetic reporter. He marveled at how someone with her abilities and powers could possibly care about such a wretched, weak, pitiful waste of life. Care enough, in fact to risk her own life. The reporter's mind was a shallow as the baptismal font standing at the front of the church, which would soon be filled with his blood, spilled by the one who, even now, approached with the intent of rescuing the reporter. But, one did not wonder why the animal sought the bait, one simply placed it into the trap and waited, patiently.

Gloria smiled for the first time in a very long time. she was aware of Caine's thoughts, and Caine was aware of this fact. But, because he knew that she and Porter could not directly interfere, he did not bother to block her access to his mind. In fact, he wanted her to see everything from his viewpoint. Wanted her to witness his taking of his bride and final rise to the power he felt he so richly deserved. But there were things he did not know. There was always the danger in arrogance of dismissing one's foes too easily. Caine had failed to delve into the depths of Rob Paulpry's mind and psyche. Had he bothered to do so, he would have seen a wellspring of power which would have frightened even him. Fortunately, in a way, the reporter was, himself, unaware of this inner reserve of psychic power, inherited from his poor, tortured mother. Had he known of it, so would Caine. Gloria only hoped he discovered it before it was too late. She sang a soft song of patience, peace and calm, sending it to the unconscious reporter. Hidden in the melody was a hint, a key which would, at the right moment present itself to him. Gloria could not open his deeper mind for him, but she could point the way. The choice to use it or not, as always, would have to be his.

Rob awoke. It was with the same feeling of disorientation which a death row inmate had once described to him. In his dreams, he had been home, listening to a song on the radio sung by a woman with an unbelievably beautiful voice. Waking, it had taken him a disorienting few moments to reacclimatize himself to the reality of his situation. Oddly, much of the panic he had been experiencing was, if not gone, temporarily shoved into a dark corner of his mind, out of sight. "Welcome back," came the deep voice of his captor, who was suddenly standing right beside him. Rob was certain that he had not been there when he had awakened, but he had not heard him approach. He shook his head to clear it. "You are not hallucinating, Robert Winston Paulpry, I am really here and you really are in my power. But, do not fear, your rescuer approaches and I guarantee she will rescue you, in the only way you pitiful mortals may be rescued. But do not worry, I shall make sure she takes a very, very long time to kill you."

"Alisha," her name came to his lips unbidden.

"Yes, the very one. Before you die, you shall have the pleasure to witness our nuptials." This last statement completely baffled Rob. But before he could ask the hulking figure who called himself Caine what he meant, his tormentor turned toward the doors at the front of the church and whispered reverently, "She has arrived".

The lights in the Koffee Kup Kafe went dark, Sergeant Porter was replaced guarding the gate into the Fourteenth Precinct, and Detective Lieutenant Alisha, "Al" Ferdinand took a step toward the church steps. Her mind was formulating the most effective and conservative use of firepower to clear the steps and save ammunition for whatever awaited her inside the building. She wondered if, in the throes of whatever fervor was causing the bizarre group hysteria, the throng of unwashed...what...worshippers(?) would even notice her approach. She hoped they wouldn't and she could carefully and quietly thread her way through the kneeling and prostrate bodies between her and the doors and slip quietly into the church. They noticed. But instead of blocking her way up the steps, the supplicants parted like Moses' Red Sea, those in the center sitting back and turning to look up at her adoringly as she passed, never stopping their chant, "Caine...Caine...Caine..."

It took all the courage Al possessed to keep putting one foot in front of another, climbing the cracked, worn steps. The reasoning part of her mind insisted that this was what she had wanted since she was twelve years old, a real world confrontation with the Bad Man. The logical part of her conscious insisted that it was impossible that a figure from her nightmares could be on the other side of the massive wooden doors, and the instinctive, primitive part of her brain just wanted to run like she had never run before and put as much distance as possible between herself and Caine.

As she reached the doors, she had the fleeting thought, "What would Nancy Drew do?" She knew the answer, of course. Nancy would stand back and get one or two of her "chums" to storm the church, then claim all the credit. With a pang, Al realized that the only "chum" she could really count on was in a hospital, fighting for his life and the psycho on the other side of these doors was responsible. She realized it was tantamount to suicide to go in without backup. She should have SWAT and every other resource at her disposal surrounding the church. If she put out the call that she had found Stan Robertson, she would be flooded with more help than there were crack whores in The End on a Saturday night. Suddenly, there was someone standing beside and slightly behind her. Two someones in fact, one on either side.

"You must do this yourself," a woman's voice, vaguely familiar, said from her left. Turning, Al saw who it was. Gloria, the waitress from that little dive coffee shop. What the fuck was she doing here? Before Al could even finish formulating the question in her mind, the woman answered. "Very little is as it seems to your limited perceptions in this world," she told her. "You must open your perceptions to the unlimited possibilities in the universe to truly see. Take me, for instance. You see a waitress from a coffee shop, but look a little closer." Without knowing why, exactly, Al did as the dulcet-voiced young woman suggested. Looking more carefully at her, looking beyond the obvious physical form, she did see something else.

"Light," Al murmured, awestruck by the radiance beaming out from within the creature before her. The waitress just nodded.

"We all possess this light," she continued. "It is the essence of life emanating from the universe. It is the pure goodness of the soul, its true nature. Even he has it," she gestured toward the closed church doors. "Over the millennia he has buried it in greed, desire and lust for power, but it is there. I can see it, as could you, if you but look in the right place. With the gifts you possess, you might even be able to make him see it once again, to embrace the light he has shunned for so long. But you must see your own light first. The one you have looked away from for so long." Instinctively, Al knew exactly what she meant. The "gift" she had inherited from the female members of her family going back for who knew how long.

The very thing which had gotten her in this screwed up predicament in the first place. She wished, not for the first time since this had started, that she could talk to Grams. Grams would know what to do.

"You know, too, Lieutenant." It was the other person speaking now. A male voice she recognized right away, Sergeant Porter. turning to the right, she saw him, pressed and polished as always in his uniform. Looking at him as she had Gloria, she saw, if possible an even brighter version of that light. "The answers are all locked within you. You have but to find the key." Al noticed a change in the chant. It was rising now to a fever pitch, as though trying to drown out what she was hearing. "That is exactly his intention," Porter told her. How did he know what she was thinking?

"What are you," she asked them, "angels or something?"

Sergeant Porter, or who or whatever he was, cocked an eyebrow with a slight grin on his face. "Sometimes," he replied enigmatically. "What people call us changes from time to time, and place to place." It was then that Al noticed the haunting similarity in the eyes of the waitress and the cop. Not in color, or shape, or even size, but there was something there. It was the look of someone who has seen too much. A weariness which seemed to look out across centuries, or even longer. She saw pain, doubt, fear, and an unimaginable wellspring of courage and, for lack of a better term, Good.

Turning to look back over the crowd, Al realized that her perception had been opened to them as well. Scanning across the crowd, she saw glimmers of the light, in varying degrees of intensity and shades of color, but always with that core of pure, bright whiteness. She wondered if she would see like this forever?

"You always have, you just weren't aware," Gloria told her. "The gifts you possess have been in large part responsible for your success in your career. Now, with a more conscious awareness, there is no limit to what you can do. You need only to take that awareness..." she stopped at a gesture from Porter.

"I am sorry, Lieutenant," he explained, "but there is only so much information we can give you. The rest, you must discover for yourself."

"But, I don't understand," Al said, becoming more confused by the moment, and unable to stop looking at everyone and everything around her, all bathed in that light.

"Understanding is like light. It's always there, but it doesn't do you any good unless you open your eyes to it," Porter responded.

"Very Zen," Al shot back. "But I don't see how it is going to help me in there." She pointed at the church.

"It's the only thing that can," the waitress replied, almost shouting to be heard over the chant which had risen to rock concert level. The sound was so overpowering, Al found herself tempted to open fire on the crowd just to shut them up.

Instead, she turned and placed her hand on the door handle and said, "Let's do this, then," and realized she was alone once more. Shaking her head as though waking from a dream, she pushed to door open a crack and there was an instantaneous and deafening silence from the mob. She glanced back over her shoulder and saw them all looking expectantly at her, urging her forward with their eyes. Forward into the dark interior of the dilapidated church and whatever nightmare lay within.

CHAPTER EIGHTEEN

Rob heard the sound stop outside. He hadn't actually even been aware of it until it ceased. He realized that the chanting had started softly and had risen to a veritable fever pitch gradually enough that his senses had been numbed by it. "Like boiling a frog," he murmured, remembering one of his father's favorite parables. "If you drop a frog into boiling water," he could hear his dad saying even now, "it will jump out. But if you place it in cool water and gradually raise the temperature, it will stay in the pot and be boiled to death." Rob pondered the story (he really had nothing else he could do right now) and wondered if that was what had happened to The End. The deterioration had happened so gradually that the police, the politicians, and the public had been inured to it. So that, as it became the cesspool it was today, it wasn't so much worse than yesterday...

His reverie was interrupted by a different sound. The soft creaking of old hinges on a door opened very carefully and slowly. His captors heard it, too. The big cop looked up at his boss (master?) and, though Rob could not see his face beneath the wide brim of his hat, he knew that one was smiling (with, unbeknownst to Rob, its usual consequences). He also knew, somehow, that it was Alisha Ferdinand who had opened the door. "Yes, Mr. Paulpry," the shadowy figure at the front of the church said, apparently reading his thoughts. "It is she. Alisha has come to claim her rightful place at my side. Of course, she believes she is coming to rescue you." Here, he chuckled deep in his chest and Rob was suddenly overcome by images of Lieutenant Ferdinand torturing him in ways he never thought he could have imagined, and laughing. The vision was gone as quickly as it had appeared, leaving him shaken. "Oh, she will save you...after a while. But only once she has fulfilled her destiny and become mine." That chuckle again, it sounded, Rob observed, more like the symptom of a lung disease than laughter. The hulking, filthy policeman rose and slipped, surprisingly quietly considering his bulk and condition, into the shadows. Rob took a breath to call out a warning to Alisha. Caine simply looked in his direction and the breath froze in Rob's chest, rendering him unable to utter a sound.

Al paused, allowing her eyes to become accustomed to the dimness inside the building. She remembered the last time she had entered a church before all this. I had been her father's funeral. She had sat in the pew, numb, and just allowed the day to flow past her. Not at all like Grams' funeral. She had been younger and more impetuous then. Grams' sister, Willa, had insisted the event be held in the Catholic church for some bizarre reason. Grams had never set foot in the building, but Great Aunt Willa was adamant. Her dad had complied with her wishes. He said it had been in the interest of family peace, but Al always suspected it was just him avoiding making decisions. The look on the priest's face when little Alisha had dragged the box full of the various religious icons from Grams' room to the front of the church and began placing them around the urn was priceless. He had gotten down on one knee and told her gently, "I don't really think those all belong together like that, honey."

Remembering that someone (probably Aunt Willa) had once made a similar comment to Grams, she replied with the same question and tone, "Why? Are you afraid they might start converting one another?" Her dad had stepped in then and, after a whispered conversation, the icons had remained. They were all still in that same box in her storage unit, she had seen them when she had gone looking for Grams' bible, which now rested heavily in her jacket pocket.

It was the people at the funerals who always intrigued her. Not those sincerely mourning the loss of a loved one, but the others. Casual acquaintances who came, she suspected, just to verify the rumors of the decedent's passing. Especially the "browsers" as Grams had called them. They were the ones who, though they might not know who any of the people who had done so were, carefully read every card on every flower and plant, inspecting them closely, nodding and moving on. Sometimes with a whispered exchange to their spouse or significant other.

A sound broke Al out of her reverie. Someone moving very quietly in the dark recesses of the church. The sound came from her right, but, she realized, that whoever had made it was in a position which prevented his seeing the second doorway into the church. She knew she needed to move now, before the invisible person could get into a position for an ambush. Alisha carefully sidled through the opening and along the back rows of pews, away from the sound of stealthy approach.

Rob saw her slip into the church and along the last row of pews, armed to the teeth, but was still unable to call out to her. He noticed his captor's breathing had quickened and he fidgeted slightly in his seat. Despite his outward facade of confidence, Rob realized the mysterious figure was nervous.

Caine felt his excitement building. At last, that which was rightfully his was within reach and coming closer. Alisha Ferdinand, last in a long line of very talented women whom he had sought and tried, time and again, to possess was voluntarily coming to him. She had been so helpful in bringing him here. Her unwavering belief in his existence beyond her dreams had been the path he had followed to this place. But still, he was nervous. He had sensed them outside. His old enemies. True, they were severely constrained by what they believed was the right and proper way to act, but they had managed to thwart his plans before. But, then, he had never had so much power, so strong a grip on his prey, so much reality. He was certain that it was his time, at last, Caine's Time. Even the name he had chosen and the mythology he had plundered for this battle seemed appropriate. It fit him well. The scorned, fratricidal brother cast out and aside by his deity finally having his day in the Garden. He would raze the Garden, slay the animals and salt the ground before he was finished. All who had ever stood against him would regret their resistance to his will. Especially the two now calling themselves Porter and Gloria. They would suffer the most. The start of their torture would be bearing witness to his marriage to Alisha Ferdinand, the combining of their powers and his ascension to his rightful place in the cosmos...and that was just the beginning.

If there was one thing Caine had learned in his unimaginably long existence, it was how to make suffering linger. His enemies would pay a thousand fold for their resistance to his rule over the aeons. But his attention was brought back to the present before he could imagine and gloat any more, by a sound. A soft footfall at the back of the church. His bride approached.

Stan Robertson also heard the footstep and tensed. Somehow the lieutenant had slipped in without him seeing her, but he knew what his job was and he moved quickly to get to his assigned position. His master's unspoken instructions had been quite specific. Block the doorway. Don't let anyone in, but most importantly, don't let Alisha Ferdinand out. A momentary glimpse of his punishment should he fail in this was enough to make him so afraid that, momentarily, he was too weak to move. The terror-induced lassitude had faded as quickly as it had come and he now scurried toward the doorway. He stumbled when his foot caught a tear in the faded carpet and nearly went down, but he made the outside doors and did as he had been instructed.

Al heard Robertson's misstep behind her and quickly crouched at the end of the nearest pew, pointing her riot gun in the general direction of the sound, waiting. Then she saw him in the small shaft of daylight coming in through the outer door she had left cracked open. Taking a deep breath and letting half of it out as her dad and then her academy firing range instructor had taught her, she waited for a good shot. But the bulky sergeant slipped through the opening into the vestibule. She thought for a moment that he was leaving, but then she saw the sliver of daylight disappear and heard the sound of...a chain(?) and then the "snick" of a large padlock being locked. The sonofabitch had locked the door!

The gloom inside the church was intensified with the shutting off of the little crack of sunlight from the front door and Al's eyes took a moment to adjust. In that moment, she missed her chance at Robertson. As soon as he had locked the exit, he had slipped back into the church and was lost in the darkness. Al let out the rest of her pent up breath and vowed silently that he would pay for the lives he had taken and ruined, and soon. Right now, she reminded herself, she had to get to Rob Paulpry and extricate him from this mess. Especially since it was her fault he was in it in the first place.

Waiting was always the worst and hardest part for Gloria. She knew that should they arrive too soon, it would be as bad or worse than arriving to late, but, still, the waiting wore on her. She sang a more modern tune, one she had recently learned to soothe her jangled nerves, "Moon River". It wasn't one of her normal repertoire, but she liked it. Porter looked at her with a slightly quizzical look, then went back to whatever mental calisthenics he had been doing in preparation. Gloria could no longer read his thought, as he could not hers. They had both closed themselves off to prevent their ancient nemesis from prying and learning too much too soon. This was another necessity that Gloria hated. She felt alone at these times, cut off, as though all of her senses had been stripped from her, rendering her deaf and blind, but even more so.

Porter, on the other hand was glad for the necessary shutting off. He was worried. Rob Paulpry had yet to show much sign of his recognition of his deeper abilities and his part in what was playing out around him and the lieutenant, strong as she seemed, was the weak link. Though her innate abilities far surpassed those of the reporter and Caine, and nearly matched his own, Porter knew that her resolve was the weakest. The creature calling himself Caine had worked on her since she inadvertently let him in at the age of twelve to erode her confidence where he was concerned, manipulating and using her talents against her to plant doubt and worse, fear. Fear was truly, as someone had once said, the mind killer and Alisha Ferdinand's mind needed to be awake, alive, and at its best for what was to come. Porter looked over at Gloria, softly singing and understood her frustration at their limitations. At this moment, he, too, was tempted to intervene. Nothing grand, just a suggestion and a push in the right direction. Rob Paulpry needed his eyes opened before it was too late. But, he reminded himself, that was the slipperiest of slopes, one tiny nudge or suggestion opened the gates to a flood of possibilities and the consequences were unimaginable, especially now.

Kevin Morrissey was exhausted. Helping members of the force deal with the loss of an officer or officers in the line of duty was one of his main responsibilities as Department Psychiatrist, but the circumstances at the Fourteenth Precinct had nearly been more than his training, or his own psyche could handle. Not just the brutal sadistic nature of the slaying of two fine police officers, one a young man just starting his career, and the other a seasoned veteran with years of experience. No, that was bad enough, but the thought that it had been one of their own who had perpetrated the massacre had struck him perhaps even harder than it had the other officers. He could not help but think that he should have caught it, should have seen it coming, should have been able to stop Stan Robertson before he reached this point. He had Robertson's jacket laid out on his desk. Reading through the reports, he could see a pattern plainly evolving. A narcissistic, power hungry sadist from an abusive background. Robertson's record read like a textbook. Of course, the worst of his behavior to date had occurred before Morrissey had taken the job and the man in the position before him had come to it already burned out and no longer able to care enough to connect the dots. But that didn't change the fact that it was his job to see these things and prevent tragedies like this from happening. he chided himself that he had gotten too wrapped up in Alisha Ferdinand to be able to notice anything else.

The thought of Alisha stopped him dead in his mental tracks. Where was she? there had been no sign of her since she had picked up her car at the Fourteenth and driven back into the insanity that had erupted in The End. There had been no report that her body had been found, or that she had called in, it was as though she had finally walked into one of her dreams and vanished from this world. Cautioning himself against being drawn into his patients' delusions, he picked up the telephone receiver and caller her cell. It went straight to voice mail and his panic level rose a few more notches. She had been spending a lot of time with that reporter, what was his name? Paulpry, Rob Paulpry, he remembered. He called the Times Republican and asked to speak to Paulpry. Instead of being transferred to the reporter, the editor, Helen Corydon had come on the line, demanding to know if Kevin knew the whereabouts of her missing reporter. He resisted the urge to point out that if he knew where Paulpry was, he would not be calling him at the newspaper's offices and instead, assured her he would let her know if he located him and hung up. Now, he was really worried. Somewhere, out in The End, there was one homicidal police sergeant, one delusional lieutenant detective, and one missing reporter. There was no way, he feared, that this would end well. Just as he was trying to decide on a course of action, there was a knock on his door and another traumatized policeman was ushered into the room. He would have to worry about Alisha later, this man was here and needed him now. Turning toward his visitor, he said, "And how may I help you Sergeant," he glanced at the officer's name tag, "Porter?"

Gloria knew Porter had to go. She understood that it was crucial that he distract the Psychiatrist and keep him safe and out of the picture, but she hated being alone. It wasn't normally a problem as they were linked so inextricably and had the luxury of direct communication, but cut off as they were at the moment it was frightening. Soon, the final confrontation would happen and they would be there to witness it and play the limited part that they could, but, again, it was the waiting...

Rob was feeling the pressure and stress of waiting as well. Unable to call out and warn Alisha, he felt powerless. More so even than on that night fifteen years ago when he had been confronted by a gun wielding thug. He had been on his way to meet a source, or so he thought. The source had turned out to be a lure in the employ of the thug's boss. He had been told, in no uncertain terms to back off the story. Then, the brute had punched him so hard in the gut, Rob thought something inside him had to be ruptured. As he had been sitting up against the brick wall of the alley, Rob had heard the sound of the hammer being cocked on the pistol, he looked up just as the shot was fired. It had only been the final warning, the bullet slamming into the wall next to his head and sending shards of brick flying and imbedding themselves in the side of is head and face, but it had been sufficient. He not only dropped the story, but his fear of firearms had also been born that night. He wondered, for a moment why he had previously been unable to remember that this incident had started his fear of guns, but the sound of Lieutenant Ferdinand moving broke off his train of thought.

Al slowly and quietly worked her way along the wall of the church. Her eyes had become accustomed to the dim candlelit interior of the building and she could now make out figures. Next to a post was slumped a shape that she assumed was the reporter. Rob sat on the floor with his hands wrapped around the pole behind him, probably handcuffed. At the front of the church was a looming figure that stopped her in her tracks and nearly froze her heart, Caine, The Bad Man himself stood as she watched and beckoned to her. "Come on, Alisha," he said in a voice that sounded like wet gravel, "here is your prize, come and get it." He gestured and Robertson appeared out of the darkness. The sergeant looked like he had been dead for a week in the August heat. He wore rags that might, at one time, have been his uniform. His face in the sickly yellow light from the nearby candle was swollen and puffy, his eyes sunken. He grabbed Rob by the front of his shirt and pulled him roughly to his feet. The reporter appeared to be trying to say something, but couldn't get the words out.

"Let him go, you bastard," Al commanded. "This is between you and me!"

"Truly, it is," Caine agreed. "But I had to have some bait to get you here alone. Don't you want to know why you are here?"

"I know why I am here," she spat back. "To get him safely out and wipe both your and Robertson's sorry asses off the face of the earth." Caine chuckled and Stan Robertson slapped Rob hard, rocking his head so forcefully to the side, Alisha feared his neck might be broken. She breathed a sigh of relief when the reporter righted his head and looked toward her again, still trying to speak.

"I believe your friend has something to tell you," Caine gestured toward his captive and Rob let out an explosive breath.

"Ferdinand, " he croaked. "Get the fuck out of here! It's a trap! They only took me to get you. Go get help." It was the hardest statement Rob Paulpry had ever made. Everything in him wanted to beg for her help the ask to be saved, but at the last moment, he had latched onto something inside himself he hadn't even known was there. There was a glimmer of the brightest white light deep down inside, a glimpse of a greater truth, a vision of something more important even than his life. Rob Paulpry looked into a wellspring of strength and frighteningly clear insight that he didn't know was inside him... and saw the truth.

CHAPTER NINETEEN

Gloria sensed it first. Even cut off as she and Porter were at the moment, certain events could still register on their shared awareness. When Rob Paulpry touched the deep inner light within himself, it created a minor ripple that lightly touched on the senses of those waiting for it. When the ripple reached Porter, he risked a momentary communication with Gloria. It was time.

Kevin Morrissey had found himself doing all the talking to the tall, neatly attired sergeant. Somehow, it seemed all right that the man had come to his office not to unburden himself in the aftermath of the horrendous occurrences of the day, but to see if he could help the psychiatrist in any way, and he did. Kevin felt better. Even his worries about Alisha Ferdinand, still among the missing as far as he knew, were lessened. This, of course was exactly Porter's intention. Whether he had any sense of it or not, Kevin Morrissey had important things to accomplish and a large role to play in the aftermath of the upcoming struggle. That is, if events allowed the world to continue on its present course. There were still so many possibilities, so many wrong turns that could be taken. Even Porter could not yet grasp every thread of possibility linked to this one confrontation.

He left the doctor in a light, dreamless doze. It was what he needed and desired, Porter simply gave him permission to give in to his own needs. He led him to the realization that, in order to help everyone who required his help, he needed to be rested and thinking more clearly. Probably the most important gift he gave him was the gift of self-forgiveness in the case of Sergeant Stan Robertson. Porter saw clearly where hanging onto the guilt would lead Kevin Morrissey and he was too valuable to let that happen. Just as no one saw Porter enter the office, no one saw him leave.

Gloria was waiting for him at the church. They stood outside among the throng of supplicants whose wills Caine had bent to his own wishes. Porter looked at Gloria and she nodded, acknowledging his unspoken warning, "This is where the path leads. No matter how innocent our intentions, we cannot afford to give in to the temptation to meddle with free will". "How is the doctor?" she asked, changing the subject.

"He is resting, when he awakens his path should be a little clearer to him," Porter answered. Gloria looked askance at him. "No meddling, just shining a light into a few dark corners, showing him what was there, and giving him permission to continue on the path he has chosen for himself."

"It's a very fine line we walk at times, is it not?" she asked with a slight smirk.

Inside the church, Al was torn. She had a clear shot at Caine, but she feared Robertson would kill the reporter and Robertson was standing too close to his captive to risk a shot at him. It was a standoff. But she knew from her training and experience that in these situations, someone always blinked and she was damned if it was going to be her.

"We seem to be at an impasse," Caine gloated. "The solution is quite simple," he went on. "You know what you must do, you dreamed it." At that moment, Alisha found herself back in the wedding dream, where she was marrying Caine. Desperate to do something to break out of the nightmare, she raised her riot gun. Caine raised his hand. "But there is more, I can grant you the one thing you have longed for since we first met, when you first came into your own." Alisha paused at this. Seeing her hesitation, the Bad Man continued, "Clarity, Alisha. No more symbolic dreams, half-formed metaphors at best. I will purify your gift. You will be able to see clearly into the future, at your will. No more waiting for dreams and trying to interpret them in time." He spread his arms as though to welcome her into an embrace. "You will have all you have ever wanted. You have only to agree to be mine."

Suddenly, Alisha's resolve returned. Shouting, "I will never belong to you or anyone else, you sick bastard!" she drew a bead on Caine from fewer than twenty feet away. Even though the roar of the shotgun brought her out of one nightmare, it seemed to land her right in another. She saw the Bad Man's long coat billow out behind him, the .00 buckshot shredding the garment and tearing a hole in the plaster wall behind him, but he still stood there, laughing. He should have been cut in half by the charge at that distance, but he was unharmed. Now, Al was really afraid. Thoughts churned inside her like the ocean in a storm. Every nightmare she had had since she was twelve years old swirled in her mind, blending together and wiping out all rational thought. Her police training was useless. They had never covered this at the academy. How did you deal with a bad guy who could not be killed? She saw the light from the others dimming, she could no longer sense it, then she heard a voice, an unbelievably beautiful voice, singing.

Porter and Gloria had felt Caine's assault on Alisha's free will and had known it was time for them to take action. There were things they needed to make clear to her. If she bent to Caine's will now, in her confused state...the consequences were too horrible to even imagine. So Gloria sang. She sang a calming song, one used for centuries to soothe children and the ill and infirm and give them quiet and inner peace.

Rob hadn't noticed the other policeman entering with the waitress from the Koffee Kup Kafe. He was too busy wondering what the hell she was doing here. His mind was still reeling from the fact that he had just watched his captor stand up to a blast from Alisha's riot gun without even flinching. He wondered if he might still be unconscious, if this was some fever dream brought on by the raps he had taken on the head. Rob looked up at Caine, to see if he was still there. He could still smell and feel the bulk of Robertson next to him and could see Alisha and now both of the other two across the church. Caine was looking toward the newcomers. "Ah, Porter," he said, "still carrying on, I see. still guarding the gate?"

The sergeant shrugged, "It is what I choose to do."

"Choose?" roared Caine. "You still believe that there is any such thing as free will? After all I have shown you over the aeons?"

"You know it, too." This from Gloria. She had stopped singing once she had calmed Alisha's senses and soothed her panic. "In fact, free will is the one thing which has thwarted you each and every time. Have you told her yet, or were you hoping to trick her like the others?"

"Told me what?" Al demanded, directing her question to Caine.

"That he cannot bend you to his will," Porter supplied. "Not only is your will too strong for that, but, in order for him to use the gifts you have for his own twisted desires, you must come to him and give yourself freely."

Al continued to look at Caine as she absorbed this information. "Never!" She spat the word like an invective. "You can do anything you want to me you sorry, sick son of a whore, but I will never agree to be yours! I'd rather die!"

"You have been in my control all along. I brought you to me by the simplest of actions. Killing the bank robbers started it all, don't you love the irony of the name? In fact, every step you have made since you were a girl has been me bringing you to this moment." Al started to speak and Caine held up his hand. "Before you answer again, consider, death is not the only other choice." Caine's voice dripped with cold desire and suddenly, she saw herself being tormented in ways she could never have imagined. She was nearly overcome by the horror of the visions, which were more than just visions, more like waking nightmares, complete with tactile sensations and smells. To Al's sensitive nose, the smells were the worst. Burning flesh, blood, the smell of decay, all enveloping her and threatening to suffocate her.

Just as she was about to give in, to offer Caine anything he wanted in return for release, there was a shout. "Hey!" It was Rob Paulpry. "Really, fuckwad, is that the best you can do? Is your imagination really that limited after all the time you've had to perfect your techniques? Those were the same visions you used on me a while ago!" Abruptly, the images vanished, leaving Al feeling overcome and disoriented, like waking from a very realistic dream and not knowing for a moment where you are.

She looked over at Rob, shackled around the post with that sick bastard, cop killer, Stan Robertson still holding onto his jacket, "You could see it, too?"

"Sure, I figured everybody here could," he answered, moving slightly while looking pointedly at her as though trying to convey something. Al got the message. At least she hoped she did. She had to figure out a way to get Robertson away from the reporter if the germ of an idea she was beginning to cultivate in her mental petri dish was going to work, she decided to take a gamble.

"Free will," she stated, looking toward Porter and the waitress, nearly blinded by the return of her ability to see the inner light which shone from them. The girl smiled, and Porter nodded. "So, whatever happens, whatever choice I make, it's all completely up to me?" Al could sense the panic welling up inside Caine. The Bad Man was worried. She pressed her advantage, looking to the hulking star of her worst nightmares, she asked, calmly, "What do you have to offer?" There was a momentary pause, as though Caine was having trouble processing the request. "Well?" she demanded.

"More than you can imagine," he rumbled as he began sending more images to her mind. She could see from his reaction, that the reporter could see them as well. Robertson did not seem to be able to, however. In these scenes, the world was at her feet as she stood next to the Bad Man on a high plateau. Behind them was a massive palace made of gold and below them, throngs of worshippers bearing gifts up to them. The scene shifted, showing her exacting hideous revenge on everyone who had ever wronged her, from the cadet who had grabbed her breast at the academy, to Dr. Morrissey, they all suffered at her hands. She shuddered, not from the images, but from the sudden realization that some deep part of her was enjoying them! She knew it was time to act.

"So, those are my choices, huh?" she asked. "Endless torture or the domination of all existence." Caine crossed his arms and nodded, smiling under the broad brim of his hat. "Then," she went on, "I am afraid, I will have to decline your offers." That rocked him. Caine, obviously had not foreseen this eventuality. Pride, Grams always used to say, truly goeth before a fall. Al put the next part of her plan into play. Raising the riot gun, she placed the muzzle beneath her chin and jacked the slide. "I am the last of my line, Caine. Without me, you will continue to just be a pitiful, lost bogeyman, haunting the dreams of little girls, impotent, ineffectual, and hopeless. You lose, asshole!"

Just as her finger tightened on the trigger, she felt more than heard, the mental command from Caine and Robertson, moving with much more agility than she expected given his bulk and condition, was upon her. He grabbed her wrists, forcing the shotgun upward. When it went off it was pointed harmlessly at the ceiling. The buckshot shattered a light fixture, sending multi-colored shards of glass raining down on the two of them. He wrenched the weapon from her and flung it across the room to clatter down in the darkness beyond the fitful, yellow light of the sputtering candles. Painfully squeezing both of her wrists in his huge hand and keeping her arms stretched overhead, Robertson pressed himself close to her like a lover. Alisha nearly gagged at the stench rising off of him. The filth and unwashed body odor were bad enough, but then he opened his mouth, ugh! He moved in closer and she realized he was trying to kiss her! She spat in his face. He backed off a little, smiling a depraved smile. Reaching his tongue out slowly, he licked the droplet of spittle trailing down his cheek and laughed. "Disarm her," the Bad Man commanded. Robertson shoved her roughly toward the pews, bending her backward over the end of one. Her hands were going numb and the pew felt as though it was going to break her back, but she held onto her mind, fighting off the panic.

He had her pinned, pelvis to pelvis, as he forced her against the pew. With a shudder of disgust, Al realized he was aroused. Robertson ground against her as he ripped the Velcro straps open and removed her vest. He slid his hand downward, roughly fondling her breasts and she saw something in his eyes. It was a slight return of lucidity, a minute exertion of his free will. He pulled the Glock from its holster and threw it away, then his eyes, followed by his hand slid to the strip of flesh showing between her shirt and the top of her pants.

Al had never been shy about using her feminine wiles to coerce a confession or get information from the slimiest of suspects. This was no different she told herself. Fighting down her revulsion, she began moving her hips in time to the filthy cop's gyrations and forced herself to smile wantonly at him. It worked! She saw a little more of the light of personality return. He stopped moving, obviously surprised, then grinned even more broadly.

Suddenly, there was a roar from the front of the church. "She is mine!" Caine was pissed. Again, Al felt the mental wave directed at the putrid sergeant. His eyes widened as though he had just awakened and he staggered back from her as Caine addressed him in a voice she did not recognize. "Stanley, you putrid little worm! Did you really think someone like her would want anything to do with your fat, lazy, stupid ass? Look at yourself! You stink, you look like last week's garbage and you pissed your pants again!"

Turning away, the horror of reality showing on his face, Robertson looked toward the dais, "Daddy," he wailed plaintively in a child's voice. Then he looked around as though seeing his surroundings for the first time, looked at himself with disgust and fell to the floor sobbing. So far, Alisha's plan was working. Now, if she could get to the reporter. She slowly sidled over toward him, hoping against hope that she had truly understood what he had been trying to tell her earlier.

Then, Caine turned his attention to her. "Alisha, my Alisha," he almost cooed. "Aren't you tired of being afraid, feeling powerless, unable to escape the filth and rot that is this city, the nightmares, the frustration and utter pointlessness of your job? Aren't you ready to finally take control of your life?" He left the question hanging for a moment, then, sensing he had her attention, he continued. "Just let me in, Alisha, stop blocking me out of your mind and soul. The secret to stopping the fear is to embrace that which is causing it. It's time to embrace that which you fear, come to me, Alisha." She had him.

Turning to Rob and looking him right in the eyes, she got the biggest shock of the day, nearly losing control of her tightly reined emotions. She saw the brightest light yet, shining out from within him. Brighter even that Porter and Gloria, she couldn't believe it. She could also tell he had no idea it was there. He couldn't see it, she had to show him.

Stan Robertson spiraled ever downward toward the abyss of fear, self loathing and depression that had always been deep at the core of his spirit, always threatening to envelop and destroy him. How had this happened? How had he become the pile of human refuse he could now see. Besides letting him see the world as it really was, Caine had also opened up the memories he had walled off. Everything he had ever done came back to him in a rush. The last few days were the worst. Despite the anger which had driven him for so long, he was sickened by his own behavior. He had become worse than anyone he had ever arrested, a sick, twisted psycho killer. He was finished, he knew that, he couldn't go to prison. A cop in prison didn't stand a chance, especially one like him. Remembering all the beat downs he had administered in the alleys of The End, all the hookers he had forced to do unspeakable things for him, then arrested anyhow, the dealers he had held up, then turned in to Narcotics... The list went on and on. He was done, all right, but he would get his revenge first.

Al spoke, keeping her eyes locked on the reporter's. "He's right, you know," she said. When Rob shook his head in negation, she said, "Look at me, really look at me! You can see it, can't you? the truth, the light..." She saw realization dawn on him, the light became visible. She saw his eyes quickly dart around the room, taking in everyone there and seeing the light within them all.

Rob couldn't believe what he was seeing. One moment he was convinced it was all over, that Alisha Ferdinand was actually going to surrender to the sick creature calling himself Caine, the next, the light. It was shining from within everyone in the room, in varying degrees, except Caine. He was a black hole, no, as Rob looked a little closer, he could just discern the faintest glimmer of a tiny spark within him. He was brought back to reality when Alisha turned away from him and raised her hands, apparently in supplication, saying, "It's time to grasp that which you fear most, Rob."

He was momentarily confused by her words, then he saw what she meant. She had understood what he had tried to tell her earlier. Now, if he could only bring himself to follow her lead. Taking a deep breath as Alisha positioned herself directly in front of him, facing Caine, he brought his arms out, the handcuffs dangling from one wrist where Robertson had unlocked them earlier and did as she instructed.

The pistol had been her dad's backup. The Smith and Wesson .38 Special TP was perfect for the job. There was no hammer to catch on clothing in a tight situation and the five hollow point rounds would stop anything. She felt Rob move and extract the weapon from her waistband. Quickly, she put her hands into her jacket pockets, the right one closing around the cylindrical object she found there. She approached the Bad Man, knowing that whatever happened today, it would finally be over. No more dreams, no more fears, she would finally be free, one way or another.

Stan saw her walking toward the creature he had called "Master" sot so long ago and became enraged. She was responsible for his condition, her, and all the others like her. He knew his life was over, but he was damned if she was going to be rewarded for ruining it! He slowly rose from the floor and started toward her. The reporter wasn't paying any attention to him, he was watching her and she had eyes only for Caine. It was his chance.

"Come to me, Alisha," Caine purred. "It has finally come to pass, the time is now, my time, Caine's Time," he exalted.

"Burn in hell, you twisted bastard," Al shrieked as her right hand came out and her left pulled the pin on the flash bang grenade. She drew back to throw it and there was another wave of psychic command from Caine which froze her, unable to move. Stan continued toward her, Rob didn't know what to do, the light was dimming, his panic overriding his ability to see it. Gloria began to sing.

It was an ancient battle song. A song of hope and triumph, meant to inspire and encourage them. "Shut up, bitch," Caine commanded, sending a resounding psychic slap toward her, knocking her off her feet. "And you," he addressed Al. "You had the chance to have it all, but threw it away like all of your ancestors before you. You stupid, stupid being. How could you?"

"How could I not?" she shot back venomously. There is nothing you could do to me to make me like you. I will kill myself before I give myself to you. You can't hold me like this forever, and the minute you release me we'll see how well you burn!" Stan chose this moment to act, he sprang toward her, opening his arms to tackle the source of his rage and got the last and biggest surprise of his life.

Rob saw the cop launch himself at Al and snapped back to the moment. He stepped between them, raised the funny looking revolver and fired. He was surprised by the loudness of the report and the recoil, but his aim was true. Everything that had been Stan Robertson exploded out of the back of his skull. The bullet had entered right between the surprised cop's eyes. His limp body slid to a stop and Rob turned toward Caine, the weapon leveled.

"Go ahead," Caine sneered. "Shoot me. Doesn't it feel good? Can't you feel the power? Pull the trigger, Rob, feel the rush again. Take another step on the path."

"Don't," Al commanded. "It won't do any good, you can't hurt him with that, I tried already."

"She's right, Mr. Paulpry," Porter supplied. "Shooting him will do nothing." Rob looked over at the two figures, glowing brightly now that his inner vision had returned. Gloria looked shell-shocked, still recovering from Caine's attack.

"There's only one way to end this," Alisha whispered to him. He turned to look at her, and realized what she was asking.

"I can't..."

"Of course you can't," Caine taunted. "You are weak. Like so many of your kind, you know what you want and won't reach out and take it when it is offered to you. Face it, Robert Paulpry, she is mine and you are too cowardly to do the one thing to stop me!"

"Oh, really?" Rob replied, swinging the gun toward Alisha. He felt Caine try to stop him as he had Alisha, but the wave just bounced away, repelled by, he suddenly realized, the strength of his own inner light. He took a deep breath and tightened his grip on the trigger. With a tear running down her face, Al mouthed, thank you, and closed her eyes.

Caine screamed "NO!" as the pistol went off. To Rob it was all in slow motion, he felt the trigger move, saw the oddly shaped hammer rise and fall, and heard the explosion, he just hoped his aim was true.

CHAPTER TWENTY

Suddenly Rob truly understood the meaning of the phrase, "All hell broke loose". His ploy had worked and his aim had been true. The round had hit the grenade in Alisha's hand, sending it flying right at Caine. As the flash bang went off, the bright light and concussion had their intended effect on him, he was blinded, stunned and disoriented. The old, dry wood and fabric of the church caught fire as did Caine's robe. The creature screamed as the flames consumed his garments and they saw him for the first time.

He was, or had once been, a man. His large body was covered in uncountable scars. The flames rose as he screamed in frustration and rage. The fire was now completely out of control, roaring up all around them, Rob looked at the detective and said, "You're welcome."

Suddenly, everything froze and there was quiet. Porter and Gloria walked through the motionless fire and came to them, Gloria held out her hands to Rob, taking his. "It is done," she said.

"Is, is he dead?" Al asked.

"A being like Caine never dies as you know it," Porter informed her. "He is simply gone."

"Where?' Rob wanted to know.

"To another place." Seeing that Rob and Al did not understand the answer, he explained, "There are many realms of existence. Mankind has given them many names: Heaven, Earth, Death, Dreams, Nirvana, Shangri-La, Paradise, Valhalla, Hell...Need I go on? He is among them, as are we all. But most are forced to exist only in one at a time. He and others like him, can, if the circumstances are just right, travel between them."

"What were the circumstances that allowed him to come here?" Al asked.

"Your belief in him. Don't look so stricken," Gloria reassured her. "He fostered and caused it. Because of your powers, he could more easily communicate with you and manipulate your belief. But his power over you ended today. You chose to die rather than join him. Free will wins in the end," she looked at Porter and Al could see a conversation happen between them.

"So," Rob asked, "is he gone for good, now?"

"As I said, he is no longer here. No one or nothing is ever truly gone for good. As for the next logical question, I cannot at this time answer whether he will ever return to this realm of existence, any more than I can say with absolute certainty that you will or will not go to Seattle someday."

"You sound like my Grams," Al told him. Porter smiled in response to this statement.

"Come," Porter instructed and walked them through the motionless flames to the door. "Keep your eyes open," he told both of them and was gone, as was the waitress. With the disappearance of Gloria and Porter, the fire roared back to life and the reporter and detective stumbled out the door to fall right into the arms of the firefighters just rushing up to the building.

CHAPTER TWENTY ONE

Al hated being on desk duty and grumbled loudly about it as another stack of files was deposited by a rather nervous looking rookie. "Oh, quit bitching, Al." It was Frank McDonnell, sitting, still in a wheelchair at the desk directly behind hers. "You're still breathing and the cast comes off in a couple of weeks." She looked down at her right hand, still encased in the cast up to her elbow. She still could not believe that Paulpry had taken that shot! He could have missed and blown her head off. But, he hadn't. Somehow, despite his pathological fear of guns, he had managed to hit the flash bang. The force of the impact, however, had fractured three bones in her hand. Of all the injuries she had suffered in the course of everything, the broken hand was the most inconvenient. Not only had it kept her tied to a desk, being her gun hand, but it had made typing up her report on what happened in The End a royal pain in the ass.

That report, however, had been one of the finest pieces of fiction anyone had ever turned out. Reading over it before she had scrawled what passed for her signature these days across the bottom, she had been quite impressed with herself. She even thought about taking up writing, maybe even inventing the next Nancy Drew.

According to the official report, it was all Stan Robertson, the only body they had found in the ashes, of course. In the report, she had gone in to pull Rob Paulpry out and had shot Robertson in the process. He had knocked over a candle, starting the fire. Rob corroborated her every word without them even talking about it. His big story in the paper had detailed things the same way.

"How about, The Holy Conflagration Mystery?" she shot over her shoulder.

"Conflagration?" Frank snorted in response. Before she could offer a witty rejoinder, her phone rang.

As much as it galled her to admit it, the experience in the church had left her with a weird connection to Rob Paulpry, so she knew immediately who was on the other end of the incoming call, "Purgatory, lowest ring, chief sufferer speaking."

"Chief whiner, you mean," called Frank. "Say hello to the snoop for me."

"Frank says hi," she said.

"Hi to him, too," Rob replied. He was back in Major Crimes with an amazing amount of leeway in chasing down stories. His piece on the riot and fire which had destroyed enough of The End to finally close it down had been picked up by all of the wire services and there was even talk of awards from several sources. "The End of The End," he had called it. His pictures of the riots, the only ones anyone had gotten and more of the fire and the aftermath (thank God, Al had put his camera in her pocket on the way out to the church) had almost been enough to tell the story, but his story, as fictional in many aspects as Al's report had gotten the attention of state and local politicians as well as the media. Changes were coming. There were rumors of a new entertainment district called Eden Park to be built on the ashes of The End. "Hey, he said into the phone, "how about The Nightmare in the Church?" Al relayed the title back over her shoulder to Frank who blew a loud, juicy raspberry in response.

"I guess you heard that," she said into the phone, laughing.

"Good to hear you laugh, Lieutenant," Rob said. "Look, I have to go up to the capitol tomorrow to cover the trial of that guy who fed his neighbor to a wood chipper, so if you run across anything interesting or weird, just call me on my umbilical cord." They bantered for another minute or two then hung up.

"He's not such a bad egg," Frank commented.

"If you like eggs," she answered. Everything had changed since the riot, murders, and fire. Sergeant Porter had been transferred, but his paperwork had mysteriously disappeared, so no one knew where he had gone, or even what his first name was. The Koffee Kup Kafe had closed and a new tenant was in the process of renovating the space, the old Fourteenth Precinct was scheduled to be razed and rebuilt as part of the rejuvenation, as the politicos were calling it, of The End, and Al was sleeping. Dr. Morrissey said it was because she had been through a real life trauma more horrifying than her nightmares and it had put things back into perspective for her subconscious. She had even flushed the bag of sleeping pills. Things had really changed, and were continuing to do so. But, Grams had always said that in order to move forward, life had to change, constantly in small ways, but every now and then in big ways. Alisha smiled at the memory of Grams and couldn't help but wonder what was next?

EPILOGUE
Alisha's Journal
July 13, 2010

I am standing in front of the old Fourteenth Precinct building with Rob Paulpry, like on the day Robertson killed the Captain and that rookie. This time, there are people everywhere, running around like all hell is breaking loose. The reporter looks at me and says, "See, I told you this was coming." I start to ask him what he means, but he just starts walking toward the building, so I follow. Everyone greets him and says how glad they are that he is there, but no one even acknowledges that I am there, too. We go into the Captain's office and Rob sets down behind the desk and says, "All right, let's have everything you know about the case. If you want my help on this one, you need to tell me everything". I panic, realizing that I have no idea what he is talking about, but he just waves his hand dismissively at me and says, "Don't worry, I have everything I need to know right here". He picks up a newspaper and opens it up to...THE COMICS! He points and says, "Yep, just as I thought". I look to where he is pointing and see a Nancy Drew comic strip, only, instead of Nancy and one of her chums, it's me and Paulpry in an abandoned building where there is a meth lab with people running from it yelling that it is going to explode. Then, the newspaper blows up and I am awake.

###

Thank you for reading my book. If you enjoyed it won't you please take a moment and leave me a review at your favorite retailer?

Thanks,

William L. Bowman Jr.

About the Author:

William L. Bowman Jr. is a man who wears many hats. He is a professional magician, black belt martial artist, Physical Therapist Assistant, and a certified locksmith. He has written for Martial Arts Training, Dragon, and The Linking Ring Magazines, and has had poetry and plays published by various publishers.